MEMOIRS OF A COURTESAN

by

ROXANE BEAUFORT

CHIMERA

Memoirs of a Courtesan first published in 2002 by
Chimera Publishing Ltd
PO Box 152
Waterlooville
Hants
PO8 9FS

Printed and bound in Great Britain by
Cox & Wyman Ltd, Reading.

The characters and situations in this book are entirely imaginary and bear no relation to any real person or actual happening.

MEMOIRS OF A COURTESAN

Roxane Beaufort

This novel is fiction – in real life practice safe sex

Horror gave Lucy strength and she wrenched herself free of his grasp. 'How dare you?' she yelled. 'How can you suggest such a thing, and you a man of God?'

'What does it matter to you, *slut?*' he spat, and taking his weapon in hand commenced working the foreskin up and down over his glans. 'You're only a servant who'll end up with child to Lord Ludlow or one of his sons, and then you'll be turned out on the street to fend for yourself and your bastard as best you can. You'll become a whore in the end, so why not start now? You could buy a lot of fripperies with a penny.'

'You disgust me!' she hissed, but could not drag her gaze away from the sight of him masturbating.

Introduction

This is writ by me, Christopher Pembroke, Scribe and Scholar, in the Year of Our Lord Seventeen Eighty-Nine during the Reign of His Most Gracious Majesty, King George III. This taken from jottings and notes that I have barely been able to Scribble down, dictated as they were by She whom I adore, her very Presence in the Room causing all coherent thought to flee from my Head, my Manhood straining erect in my breeches, my blood pounding.

But She has requested that I do it, and I can never refuse Her anything, my Mistress, my Goddess, whose Whip my poor Hinds yearn to feel Scorching the tortured Flesh, and before whom I prostrate myself, at times Spending my Seed over her dainty Shoe and, Whipped sore for this grievous Offence, kneel at her Feet and lick up every trace of my wanton Emission.

And who is this She, this lady of Renown who has thus Honoured me? I am forbidden to use her rightful Title, but shall call her Lucy Browne, once a simple Country maid, but now risen to Dizzy heights of Wealth, Power and Dominance.

'Write it all as I relate it, Kit,' she commands, and sits beside me on the couch, pressing her glorious Breasts against me, and looking at me with those Eyes that ape the colour of the Sky on a Spring day.

'I will, Goddess,' I whisper, feeling the hot blood mount to my cheeks, and such a Spasm in my swollen Cods that I fear my Cock will spurt, willy-nilly.

'*Everything*, mind you. Omit no detail. I want the truth set down so that readers following after shall know the perfidy of man and the suffering I have endured,' she says, and her nimble fingers open the fastening of my Breeks and draw out my inflamed Serpent that nestles in her Hand like a Fledgling returning to its Nest. I fear it is like to Spit, and have scant control over it.

'As you say, Lady,' I gasp and, as she lies there with her Skirts and Petticoats in disarray, displaying milk-white Thighs and that delicious Pudenda with its Fairy floss, so I, poor wretch, am perforce made to Listen and Write, when I am Beguiled by the sight and Rendered near Senseless by the fragrance that Breathes out from her Secret Garden.

How shall I Describe that sweet Aroma? Imagine, if you will, Oceanic breezes wafted by Zephyrs and mingled with Cinnamon and Spices from a Tropical Island, and there you have it. The Exotic, Bewitching scent of my Lady's Cunny.

To remain within my Adored one's sight and Attention, I pretend to be slow in the Execution of her Command, and spend many weeks with her in Literary Composition. Sometimes I reside in her Country house, where we Indulge in Rural Frolics, but more oft in Town, for my Lady shops and Gambles and Attends Soirees and Balls, the Theatre, the Rotunda, rejoicing in the Monies which her wise Counsellors invested on her behalf when she inherited. But I digress. The Tale must be told from the Beginning.

It has quite captivated me. I write of it by Day and Dream of it by Night. Methinks I see it unfolding in my mind's Eye, as if 'twas an Entertainment staged by Actors at The Theatre Royal, Drury Lane. There I see Bawds, Whores, Pimps, Rakes, Debauched Men of the Cloth and Ladies of Ill-Repute tread the boards, and through it all wanders my Lady, an innocent Lass coming to Terms with the Wicked World, robbed of Woman's greatest Prize, her Virginity. Used full Sore she is Chastised, made party to Flagellation, sold like a Common Chattel, but Surviving to tell the Tale.

I admit to being Obsessed by Her and, if I have Embroidered the Narrative somewhat, pray make Allowances for the Fact that I am in Love with the Subject.

Footnote:

On my great-grandmother's death, followed by the division of her property and possessions, I was given a carved wooden box along with its key. It contained a manuscript, tied up with faded pink ribbon. Antiques are my passion, so are old books, essays and journals, so imagine my delight on reading this account of the life of an eighteenth century courtesan. More detailed than Moll Flanders, more intimate even than Fanny Hill, this was a treasure indeed, proving yet again that there's nothing new under the sun and that sex makes the world go round. I felt that I owed it to my ancestor, Kit Pembroke, to bring his work to public notice, but finding the old-fashioned mode of writing tedious and distracting, I took the liberty of transcribing it into modern English and filling in gaps in the story. I then submitted it to my publisher in its present form.

R.B.

Chapter One

The walk to Ludlow Hall was long and the day hot. Lucy Browne paused, pushing back a strand of pale gold hair and wiping the perspiration from her brow. She wanted to cry; tears were stinging behind her eyes and her throat ached. She sniffed, and stiffened her spine resolutely. There was no help for it. She must face the truth. She was just seventeen and now entirely alone in the world. And if she had not been away assisting at a neighbouring farm she, too, might have perished in the smallpox epidemic that decimated the village and robbed her of her parents and siblings.

This was weeks ago, and the kindly farmer's wife, Martha Rankin, had done what she could for Lucy when it was safe to venture home, helping her sell the few possessions bequeathed her and arranging an introduction to Mrs Frisk, the housekeeper of the country mansion owned by Lord and Lady Ludlow. All she could hope for was that she would be employed as a servant there.

Rebellion stirred in her bosom, and she raged at a fate that had taken her kith and kin and left her in such dire straits. Her father, William Browne, had been a proud man, renting land from Lord Ludlow and working diligently. He'd had plans for Lucy, arranging an alliance between his daughter and the son of another yeoman whose land bordered his. Death had put paid to this.

Not that she had wanted to marry the man chosen for her. He had been ten years older, a plain featured, squat individual with cow muck on his boots who had nothing to recommend him to someone like her, with her dreams of fairytale princes and romance. Lucy knew she was pretty, she had glimpsed her heart-shaped face in the river when she went down to beat the linen on the wet stones on washdays, and also witnessed the reaction of the men, young and old, when she passed through the village on her way to market or to attend church on a Sunday.

As for her slim, long-legged body, it was a strangely wonderful thing filled with mysteriously warm feelings around the loins, and her breasts, large and shapely with prominent rose-pink nipples, sent shivers coursing through her whenever she happened to touch them.

Her parents had been sober, God-fearing folk, and though sexual congress had never been discussed, she had been warned to be modest in her bearing and speech, to restrain from unclean acts such as touching herself between the legs, and to never allow a man to take liberties, until such time as she was safely married to him. However, all these half-truths and hints had done nothing but make her more curious and actually prompted her to examine her private parts.

As she walked along the lane leading to the manor, she felt again that melting sensation in her belly and that tingling in the little nubbin she had discovered at the top of her sex lips, a gem which, when rubbed, produced a feeling like no other – a rushing, blinding ecstasy that left her panting and moaning and eager for more. She was tempted to stop, to find a secluded glade somewhere, lift up her skirt, cup her mound and console herself by frigging her bud to bliss.

But she could not, for that would make her late. Much as she loathed the idea of giving up what little independence she had and going into service, the money her father had left her, which accrued by selling his animals and her mother's household goods, had mostly gone to paying debts. She had very little left. It was essential she obtain employment or she would starve. Though Martha was fond of her, she had ten children of her own to feed and another on the way, and could not afford the indulgence of providing for Lucy as well, even though she desperately needed a helping hand around the house.

Lucy eased her stiffly boned, tightly laced bodice and blew down the front of it to cool the deep valley between her breasts. Little beads of perspiration glinted on her skin, which looked touched with honey kissed by the sun, and was, she was always glad to note, free of freckles. Martha had done her best for her, boiling her shirt till it was a snowy white to match the mobcap crowning her wayward curls. Her sturdy boots were polished and the hem of her single petticoat was free of dirt. Her skirt and bodice were of serviceable brown wool and had once been her only outfit, but she had since taken in and altered her late mother's best black dress and added it to her minimal wardrobe.

"'Waste not, want not",' Martha had quoted piously. 'You sew a fine seam, girl. Maybe this will stand you in good stead with the gentry.'

Maybe it would, and considering the possibility, Lucy flew away into those realms of fantasy that had always delighted her. She never really believed she was a farmer's daughter. In fact, her mother had sometimes called her a changeling, a fairy's baby left in exchange for a human one. She was so unlike the rest of the family, blonde and blue-eyed and small-boned and dainty, whereas all her relatives were dark-haired and solidly built. She often entertained the idea she was a foundling left on her family's doorstep, a nobleman's bastard daughter born to a serving wench.

The noonday heat beat down on Lucy's head and her weariness increased. She hitched up her kirtle, climbed over a style, and found herself in the enclosed fields belonging to Lord Ludlow. The manor house was not far now, but even so, she was glad when she saw a cluster of cowsheds and a barn not far ahead. If she could rest in the shade for a few moments, and eat the crusty bread and wedge of cheese she carried wrapped in a cloth, this would strengthen her for the ordeal ahead.

The barn was deserted, and she dared to use the well outside, hauling up the wooden bucket and drinking deeply of the ice-cold water. She splashed her face, droplets of water trickling down her chin and into her cleavage. Then she entered the cool, mauve-shadowed interior of the sweet-smelling building, and climbed the rickety ladder to the loft, where she promptly sank down on a pile of hay. She had not intended to sleep, but within seconds she drifted off…

She was awakened by sounds from below. Disoriented, she imagined for an instant that she was in the bed shared with three of Martha's daughters, and then she remembered. The noises were strange – grunts, gasps, heavy breathing – and she thought at first they were being made by animals. She moved as quietly as she could and peeped over the edge of the loft, and what she saw transfixed her.

A couple occupied the straw beneath her. The man was a burly, tanned young labourer and his companion was a buxom housemaid. Lucy watched with a stab of jealousy as the girl cupped her large bare breasts and her companion sucked at the hard, nut-brown nipples. Their clothing was disordered, her stays fully unlaced and her skirt pulled back over dimpled knees and plump thighs. He was kneeling between them and supporting her rotund hips with his broad, work-roughened hands. His breeches were gaping open and Lucy almost gasped aloud, for she had never seen a mature cock at full stretch before. The only ones she had ever glimpsed had been those of her young brothers, and then rarely. The labourer's erect organ was a revelation. From her overhead position she had an uninterrupted view of the thick, vein-knotted shaft and the bulging, purple head with its twin-lobed, glistening tip

11

dewed by drops of clear liquid. It was a magical weapon, standing up proudly against his hairy belly and pointing towards its unseen admirer.

The woman grabbed the impressive manhood at her disposal and began sliding her hand up and down its smooth length. He arched his back in response, thrusting it into her palm and moaning, 'Oh, Sally... that's it, do it, girl... harder...'

She giggled throatily. 'I'm not bringing you off yet, John Tiller. You got to do something for me first. I wants my little button rubbed.'

'Give us a suck, and then I'll do yours,' he growled, impatiently nudging her cheek with his cock-head and leaving a glistening stripe of wetness across her skin.

'Oh, you are a one!' she exclaimed, and then her fleshy pink tongue darted out and played around the cleft in his helmet, dipping into it and making him jerk involuntarily. She stretched her lips wide and Lucy watched her enclose his mighty tool in the hot, wet depths of her mouth. He pressed closer, until her nose was engulfed in his hairy thatch and his balls jiggled against her chin.

Lucy tingled all over as her hands closed over her breasts, pushing down the neckline and caressing her hardened nipples as she wondered what he would taste like and smell like, and if his juice would resemble the one coating her fingers when she played with herself.

She slid a hand beneath her, wrinkled up her clothing and fingered the delicious divide at her fork. She loved the feel of the crisp hair there, the slippery smoothness of the rosy wings between, the swollen sliver of heated flesh crowning them, and the wetness pooling at the gateway to her virginal passage. Moving stealthily on the loft floor, she anointed her bud and massaged it. She wanted to go slowly but was too excited by the action below her. She managed to stop just as she was about to spill over into bliss, leaving the ultra-sensitive tip and moving her finger to one side. Experience had taught her this was the best way to prolong the pleasure.

'Don't do it no more, Sally love,' John begged huskily. 'I don't want to spend in your mouth. I wants to do it in your juicy puss.'

'But what have you got to do first?' she asked, letting his cock slip from between her lips.

'I'm going to eat your minge,' he said enthusiastically, and hooked her substantial legs over his shoulders to expose the wonders of her cleft, the moist, flushed labia fringed by the luxuriant, curling black foliage covering her mons and lower belly.

Lucy's finger strayed back to her clitoris. It was the first time she had seen another woman's bud. Sally's was red and swollen, standing from the surrounding flesh, the tip like a luscious pink pearl throbbing with life. Lucy longed to touch it, to rub it and hear Sally moaning in response. The smell of arousal was heavy in the air, acting on her senses, and she pressed down firmly on her own nubbin, making it thrum, but still holding off orgasm.

Grinning, John spread Sally's delta even wider, then licked it and buried his tongue in her entrance. As he did so he wetted a finger in her copious essence, rimmed the little puckered mouth of her anal opening, and then inserted his digit to the first knuckle. Lucy's eyes widened and her whole body seemed to be on fire. It had never occurred to her that this dark, forbidden hole might be touched, breached, and enjoyed for anything other than the simple process of elimination.

Sally's eyes closed and strange mewling noises issued from her throat. Her hands supported her breasts and her thumbs rolled around her brown teats. John's tongue was moving faster now, his lips nibbling at the little organ that so much resembled a tiny cock, and she flung her head from side to side in response, her hips straining upwards and pushing her pubis into his face. Though his head now

13

obscured Lucy's view, she guessed by the other girl's increasingly frantic movements that she was approaching her crisis.

Sally's legs gripped her lover's shoulders and a stream of impassioned words flowed from her. 'I've got to have it! Lick me! Suck me! Make me come! Oh yes, *yes*, that's it, Johnny boy, I'm coming... I'm coming... I'm... ah, I'm there, I'm there!'

He raised his head from her pudenda, his lips smeared with her nectar, and smiled down at her as he pinched her nipples. Lucy held her breath as she watched him lower Sally's legs and part them further. The sticky fluid at her entrance glistened invitingly and he positioned his helm against her. Lucy was afraid, and yet filled with awe at how huge his cock was.

Sally cried out as he thrust, driving his weapon deep inside her until his balls slapped her bottom, but the look on her face told Lucy she had not cried out in pain. 'Oh, John... oh lover... push your cock in me harder... harder. Oh yes, it feels so good, so good!'

Lucy was filled with desire and envy. She wanted to feel that great thing inside her, to lose the silly maidenhead she was supposed to prize so highly. She wanted to know what it felt like to have a man plunging and bucking and taking his pleasure of her. She rubbed her clitoris frantically while below her John's movements became more frenzied, Sally encouraging him with groans and a frantic pumping upwards of her generous hips. He was racing towards whatever it was he sought, and Lucy could only assume it was precisely the same sensation she was hell-bent on achieving.

Her sex was hot and wet, her labial lips swollen and open, her nubbin engorged and fit to explode with tension. Never had she been so excited. She imagined John's tongue on her clit, his fingers in both her virgin holes, and then his enormous phallus wresting her innocence from her, ravishing and violating her in her most precious places. She heard him give a savage bark of satisfaction, saw him jerk and look blindly up to where she hid, his expression that of a saint undergoing martyrdom, and she moved her hand faster and faster, stimulating her rock-hard gem, her breaths coming in short gasps as her climax built. Then suddenly she peaked, and rainbow shards of light played behind her closed eyelids as waves of feeling raced from her toes to her cortex. Her climax was overwhelmingly powerful, but she succeeded in restraining her cries.

When she recovered and looked down again, she saw John had relaxed and was slumped across Sally. He stirred and rolled over onto his side, his cock flaccid now and dangling limply from his breeches. He slid an arm beneath Sally's head and she mumbled something sleepily, her legs slack and bent at the knees, her womanly assets on display with his frothy white libation creaming her opening.

Then suddenly she came awake. 'I've got to go,' she said. 'Mrs Frisk will have my guts for garters. She's too handy with the rod, the bitch.' She scrambled up and started adjusting her clothing as John's spunk trickled down her inner thighs.

He got up as well, tucking his cock back into his breeches and fastening them up. Within minutes they were both respectable again, and no one would have guessed they had just been transported with lust. No one except Lucy, that is, who had also taken alarm at the mention of Mrs Frisk, the housekeeper she had an interview with and had completely forgotten about in the heat of the moment.

Mrs Jemima Frisk revelled in her position of power. Climbing to the elevated post of housekeeper had not been easy. Some might say she had clawed her way up, heedless of those she trampled underfoot on the way. The servant

15

hierarchy was strict, and if one wanted to achieve greatness it was necessary to be more than skilled in the rudiments of the stillroom, the laundry and the dairy, and in the management of maidservants. Mrs Frisk had received a smattering of education from the more serious-minded wives of the gentry who were set upon 'good works' and determined to aid the underprivileged village children, which had put her a cut above the rest. She was equipped to keep accounts and present them to the estate manager and to consult on equal terms with the head butler, Mr Thorpe.

A widow, Jemima had buried the man who was willing to help her in every way as long as she kept him as her slave behind closed doors. Her skills on the domestic front were exceeded by her zeal with the whip, and learning that many gentlemen were in need of flagellation in order to achieve a climax, she put this knowledge to good use. She had come from the lowest rank of servants, but managed to wheedle her way into Mr Frisk's affections. He had been Lord Ludlow's valet, and by the time of his demise, Mrs Frisk had met Lady Ludlow and won her confidence. When the former housekeeper died she had been offered the post, and accepted it. Now she sat in her parlour waiting to interview the new girl. She glanced down at her notepad. *Lucy Browne* was written in her neat, copperplate hand, and she had added, *Recommended by Martha Rankin. An orphan recently bereaved.* This was how she liked them, without a friend in the world, lost and alone and so easily controlled and manipulated.

Small, quick and dainty, with bird-bright eyes, Mrs Frisk never missed a trick. She was always dressed in black, with a snowy pinafore in front and a little cap set atop her piled up and powdered brown hair. A chatelaine hung from a chain belt at her waist from which dangled keys, folding scissors, a purse and a fruit knife. She also never went anywhere without the whippy cane that was unofficially her badge of office. The maids lived in dread of her turning up unexpectedly, for she moved as quietly as a snake and used that infamous cane to mete out punishment for real or trumped up misdemeanours, either on the spot or, ten times more humiliating, in public.

Now Mrs Frisk rose from her chair as her latest victim trembled before her, her own hand also shaking slightly as it closed round the handle of the cane. 'Well, Sally, and what have you to say for yourself?' she demanded. 'You're late. This can't be tolerated. Where were you and what were you doing?'

'I'm sorry, ma'am,' Sally muttered, blushing scarlet and lowering her eyes.

Mrs Frisk observed, not for the first time, how the girl's firm haunches moved beneath her skirt and how well suited they were for cane, whip or strap. She glanced across at her companions, who sat on either side of the hearth, mugs of ale in their hands. One was a large, stately personage attired in blue livery with brass buttons, a full-skirted jacket, matching breeches and a long waistcoat, with a plain linen cravat tied precisely beneath his heavy jowls. His face was red as a turkey cock's, and he wore a grey periwig curled at the sides and drawn into a cue at the nape of his beefy neck. White hose and shiny black shoes with cut-steel buckles completed his uniform.

Opposite him sat a vicar in a long black cassock and dog collar. He was as thin, spindly and self-effacing as the other man was corpulent and overbearing. His face was lined and his white bagwig seemed too large for his skull.

'I think this wicked wench is lying,' Mrs Frisk commented, slowly pacing round the unfortunate Sally. 'What do you say, sirs? Does she merit a beating? Mr Thorpe?'

'Well, bless my soul,' the head butler replied, peering at Sally with small eyes set in deep folds of flesh. 'She looks primed for the rod. If it were one of the footmen I'd not hesitate, dear lady. I'd make him jump and squeal, so I would.'

Mrs Frisk turned to the vicar. 'And you, your reverence? Do you take her for a sinner who needs chastising?'

The churchman squirmed and crossed his legs as if attempting to keep his genitals in order. 'If you say so, Mrs Frisk,' he mumbled. 'I'm sure you have much more experience in such matters than I.'

'True, it's my unfortunate lot to be in charge of this younger generation who think of naught but pleasure and idleness.' She ran the cane through her fingers and scrutinised Sally closely. 'Answer me, girl,' she snapped, 'and tell me the truth. Have you been fornicating? Who is your partner in these lecherous goings-on? Confess to me, to Mr Thorpe and to the Reverend Jollian.'

'I ain't done nothing wrong,' the girl insisted quietly.

'We'll see about that. Take off your skirt.'

'But, ma'am, I can't,' Sally protested, glancing over at the men.

'What's this, modesty all of a sudden? Too late for that, I imagine.' Mrs Frisk enforced her command with a blow across Sally's ample rump she knew stung even through the layers of cloth.

'Oh, have mercy, madam!' Sally begged, and dropped her skirt and petticoat to the floor, leaving only her stay-bodice and a short chemise covering her.

'Arms above your head,' Mrs Frisk commanded, and lifted the hem of Sally's chemise. The girl was naked beneath it, and her thighs, belly and mons were instantly displayed. The housekeeper thrust a hand roughly between Sally's legs and then held her fingers up triumphantly. 'Look at this,' she cried. 'She's oozing spunk. Someone has ploughed her field very thoroughly, and not more than an hour since, the dirty trollop.'

Both Thorpe and the vicar rose and pressed closer,

sniffing Mrs Frisk's fingers and bending to inspect Sally's delta for themselves. The butler's breeches were no longer a fashionable fit, but distorted by a huge erection, and even the reverend's loose cassock did not hide the similar disturbance in his prick. Gaining in enthusiasm for their task, they had Sally bend over the table and stretch across it to grasp the far side, so her plump buttocks parted in a spread-legged stance and her deep cleft opened up for better inspection. The amber crack, the puckered anal hole, and the split fig of her labia framed by damp black curls, were now vulnerable to touches and licks and even to penetration by a sturdy cock.

'You see?' Mrs Frisk said loudly, pointing to the excess of moisture seeping from Sally's glistening aperture. 'That's a man's spillage leaking from her cunt. You've been a bad, filthy tart, haven't you, Sally?'

'No, ma'am,' the girl moaned unhappily.

'Liar!' Mrs Frisk brought her strong right arm down with full force across the curve of Sally's opulent buttocks, leaving the scarlet imprint of the rod behind.

Sally yelped and wriggled in protest. 'Oh ma'am, please, I need to use the privy!'

'You should have thought of that before,' Mrs Frisk answered grimly. 'And don't you dare make water on my polished floor, or I'll make you lick up every drop and it'll cost you six more strokes.'

There was a knock on the door.

'Enter!'

A footman promptly ushered in a fair-haired girl who bobbed a curtsy. 'Lucy Browne, if it please you, ma'am.'

'Ah, Lucy,' Mrs Frisk said, tightening her grip on the cane. 'You have arrived at a providential moment. It is my duty to punish this wench for lewd behaviour. You shall watch and learn. This is what happens to errant maidservants under my jurisdiction.' She registered that Lucy was extremely pretty and well worth exploiting before returning to her task. At regular intervals, she administered six more whistling cracks to Sally's buttocks, and the last one proved the poor girl's undoing. Her bladder betrayed her and a golden shower trickled down her legs, splashing on to the floor.

'You wretch,' Mrs Frisk yelled with gusto. 'Dirty, disgusting slut, you've earned yourself six more strokes.'

Sally's squeals became screams as the merciless cane lashed the backs of her thighs, leaving them as red as the rump above them. When the housekeeper had done, the girl lay across the table, sobbing helplessly.

This was the sight that greeted Lucy on entering the housekeeper's domain – Sally being cruelly punished by a hard-faced, flinty-eyed woman in a black silk dress – and she experienced a sickening plunge in her stomach as she wondered what she was letting herself in for. She was further horrified by the expressions contorting the faces of the two gentlemen present. The crude lust expressed by John in the barn had been pure as the driven snow compared to the raw lechery painted on these older, more cynical visages. And one was a churchman by the look of him, which was utterly disgraceful. Yet she could do nothing but stand there and wait for Mrs Frisk to address her.

'You may go, after you've cleaned up your mess,' the housekeeper told Sally coldly. 'However, this time I'll go easy on you and let you use a petticoat instead of your tongue.'

Sally got to her feet and staggered over to where her clothing lay. She then sank to her knees and began mopping the floorboards.

The gentlemen resumed their seats as Mrs Frisk took her place behind the table. She barked out an order and Sally, having completed her task, promptly straightened up and limped from the room. Then the housekeeper's eyes pierced Lucy's like gimlets. 'You want to work for the Ludlows, I gather?'

'Yes, ma'am,' Lucy replied, with a steadiness she was far from feeling.

'Are you a virgin?'

'Yes, ma'am.'

'I want proof, for I'll not employ flirts, harlots and hussies. Is that understood? Martha Rankin shall examine you and report to me.'

'Yes, ma'am,' Lucy said, her chin raised proudly, for she was outraged by the woman's crude words and hectoring tone.

Mrs Frisk's eyes narrowed and her mouth set. 'Don't play the high and mighty with me, you saucy minx,' she warned, her hand closing around the ever-present cane. 'If I employ you, you'll do exactly as I say at all times. Is this understood?'

'Yes, ma'am,' Lucy muttered, but assumed a meeker pose with her eyes cast down.

'What do you think, Mr Thorpe?' The housekeeper deferred to him, and they exchanged a look that Lucy did not understand but which she did not like at all.

'I think she'll do mighty well, dear lady,' he rumbled from deep in his obese belly, and Lucy could not fail to notice the swelling inside his tight breeches.

'And you, Reverend Jollian,' Mrs Frisk asked him, 'do you feel she has the potential to make a faithful servant?'

The vicar seemed ill at ease, his eyes darting over Lucy as his red-knuckled, bony hands rubbed together slowly. 'She seems a fine young lass, a very fine young lass, indeed,' he answered in the singsong voice adopted by those accustomed to addressing congregations from a pulpit. 'And the poor child has suffered a great loss, a very great loss, during the sickness that struck our village. We must go out of our way to care for her, comfort her and pray for her.'

'Amen,' Mrs Frisk and Mr Thorpe agreed in unison.

Lucy was uncomfortably certain that these Christian ethics they gave lip service to screened a very different agenda. She had the distinct impression of dark dealings and matters the likes of which she could not even begin to comprehend, and which frightened but also strangely excited her.

'So, girl, when can you start?' Mrs Frisk asked her crisply.

'At once, ma'am, though I'll need to go to the Rankin farm and collect my belongings.' Lucy was scared and yet elated. She had gotten the position she so desperately needed. 'I don't own much,' she added.

'Be here at dawn tomorrow, or rather at the coaching inn. I intend to send you to the town house.'

'The what, ma'am?'

'The Ludlow mansion in London, it's understaffed and I shall be coming up myself for the autumn season. Meanwhile, present yourself at the gates with a note for my assistant. Your fare on the mail-coach will be paid.'

'But I've never journeyed far on my own,' Lucy protested, her courage fading.

'You won't be on your own, child,' the Reverend Jollian assured her. 'I am travelling to the capitol myself on the very same vehicle and will look after you.'

Lucy wondered why this news did not assuage her anxiety, yet there was little she could do but accept his company and be grateful for it. Mrs Frisk then informed her that all she had to do after letting Martha test her hymen was be at *The Flying Goose* by six o'clock the following morning. The reverend would pick her up at Martha's house and purchase her seat on the coach. He would also give her a covering letter explaining her presence to Mrs Frisk's second-in-command at Templebar House in the famed and glorious capital of England. The king and queen lived there, as did their lords and ladies, and the streets were paved with gold, or so it was said.

Chapter Two

Lucy stood clutching her wicker basket by its leather straps. It contained everything she owned, and was all she had left to remind her of her former life, apart from the clothes she wore on her back and the few coins in the drawstring purse attached to her waistband.

The courtyard of *The Flying Goose* was noisy and bustling with activity, full of the comings and goings of travellers. She had only visited Newford once before, the nearest market town to Cheselton, the village where she was born. Several years ago she had gone there with her father to sell produce. The town had seemed huge to her then, and still did. She stared open-mouthed at the timbered shops and dwelling places, the narrow cobbled streets and wide central market square where the inn was situated. Overawed, she found it impossible to picture the size, breadth and scope of her destination, London; it was beyond imagining.

Once Mrs Frisk had received the token that proved Lucy's maidenhead was intact, plans had proceeded swiftly. It had been an embarrassing and rather painful procedure, with Martha inserting a finger into Lucy's virgin niche and rupturing the hymen, but only slightly. The privilege of complete penetration was to be reserved for Lucy's future husband, whoever he might be. However, it was necessary to make her bleed a bit so the stain could mar the white cloth applied to her vulva. This accomplished, Martha wrapped up the linen and sent her eldest son galloping to Ludlow Hall with this symbol of Lucy's purity. Of course this test, usually carried out on a bride's wedding morn, was wide open to cheating, but

Martha Rankin was a midwife, and respected as one of the most trustworthy women in the area. So Mrs Frisk accepted that Lucy was as yet unsullied and worthy of entering the Ludlow establishments.

Martha wept when the vicar's gig arrived at the farm and Lucy and her luggage were installed within it. 'Be a good girl,' she advised tearfully. 'I shall miss you.'

'And I shall miss you,' Lucy called out as the piebald horse trotted away, bearing her and the Reverend Jollian to Newford and the mail-coach. The last ties with home were severed and she was entirely alone save for the clergyman, whom she did not feel easy with. He was too eager to touch her, although she knew he was only trying to be helpful. She kept reminding herself he was a vicar and that she was safe with him, but she did not quite believe it.

'Come along, my child, we must take our places in the coach,' he urged, seizing her arm in his clammy fingers and leading her towards the large, London-bound carriage containing not only letters and parcels but some half-dozen passengers and their luggage.

Lucy noticed that the guard seated by the coachman was armed with a musket, as were two more men, riding pillion at the back. Though the roads were safer now, highwaymen were still a menace and she shivered wondering what it would be like to be held up at pistol point, robbed of her purse and perhaps of her virginity, too. It was said that some of the 'gentlemen of the road' were handsome and dashing and fancied pretty young women like her.

'Bring my bag, Jonas,' the reverend instructed crisply, and the young groom heaved a leather holdall on to the top of the solidly built vehicle that was slung between large leather straps and harnessed to a team of powerful horses. The carriage stood alongside two others, one bound for Bristol and the other for Manchester.

Jonas smiled roguishly at Lucy. 'Shall I take your basket, too, miss?' he asked in his countrified drawl.

'No, thank you,' she said, hanging on to it for dear life. No one was going to separate her from her belongings.

'Then stow it under the seat,' Jollian advised. 'It'll be in the way otherwise.' He leaned closer, his rank breath fanning her cheek as he asked, 'Have you visited the privy? I suggest you do so before we depart. It will be miles till we change horses at the next inn, and we don't want a repeat of the shameful episode when Sally couldn't hold her water, do we?'

'I'm all right, sir.' She blushed furiously, upset by the memory of Sally's white bottom criss-crossed by hot red stripes, and by the fact that the vicar had made no move to stop this exceedingly harsh punishment.

'Oh, I know that, my girl.' He chuckled.

Ignoring this odd pleasantry, she mounted the iron step the guard had lowered and climbed into the coach's musty depths.

She and Jollian were the last to board. He sat on one side of her, and a large, overdressed woman caged her in on the other. Opposite them sat two youths and a sulky-looking girl.

'My sons, Simon and Rufus, and my daughter, Clementine.' The woman introduced her brood. 'I'm Mrs Clough, and we've been on the road two days already, returning to London from our residence in Bath.' Her voice was strident, and her small eyes darted over Lucy while she smiled archly at the vicar. 'I'm so thankful you're to be our travelling companion for the rest of the way, your reverence. One never knows what uncultured people it may be one's misfortune to cross when using public transport.'

'You have your own carriage, madam?' he asked politely, smirking across at Clementine.

'Naturally,' Mrs Clough answered, fanning herself

enthusiastically, the considerable draft swaying the feathers in her elaborate hat. 'But my husband has need of it, so he said to me, "Dora, my love, avail yourself of the stagecoach. I shall join you in London post haste".'

'How very considerate of him.'

'Yes, indeed, he is a true gentleman.' Mrs Clough's eyes bored into Lucy as she added, 'Is this your daughter, sir?'

'Nay, I have no children. The Reverend Jollian at your service, madam.' He pressed a mite closer to Lucy so she could feel his skinny thigh against hers. 'This is a young person of modest station, an orphan, no less, who is journeying to take up employment at Templebar House, the town residence of Lord and Lady Ludlow. I have church business in the city and offered to chaperone her.'

'I see,' Mrs Clough said with a disparaging sniff. 'So she's a servant. It's hardly fitting for her to be travelling with gentlefolk, is it? Keep her under your eye, sir. Servants are a crafty lot, as I know to my cost. Not to be trusted as far as one can throw them. How charitable of you to bother with her.'

'It is my duty, as the vicar of St John's in my Lord Ludlow's village,' Jollian pointed out with suitable humility.

Lucy listened to this discourse in silence. They were discussing her as if she was a beast of burden with no feelings or opinions. She huddled inside her hooded cloak, her calves against her basket, her eyes lowered. Every time she glanced up, it was to see the garishly attired sons of the unpleasant Mrs Clough staring at her. They obviously thought themselves dandies with their tricorne hats cocked on their heads, their long hair drawn back into ponytails, their jackets fitting closely, their tight breeches tucked into the tops of Hessian boots. It was apparent by their attitude that they considered servant girls like her fair game. However, they were not wearing swords, the mark of a true gentleman, which meant their father was probably just a tradesman.

As for the simpering, whey-faced Clementine, she was around Lucy's age and gaudily dressed, displaying a swelling bosom, her hair curled so tightly into rings it must have been in curlpapers all night. On her dainty feet she wore tight satin pumps with Louis heels poking out from beneath her hoop skirts. A plainer outfit would have been much more suitable for a long journey, but she was attired as if for a soirée at Bath's fashionable *Pump Room*. Even Lucy, who knew nothing about fashion, instinctively sensed that the whole Clough family had no taste at all, and realised she was in for a long and tiresome journey.

The coachman flicked his whip, the horses leaned into the straps, and the carriage rumbled beneath the inn's archway. Somehow, Lucy was not quite sure how, she found herself moved so Jollian sat next to Mrs Clough. He was now between her and the snobbish woman, and Lucy wished with all her heart that she could be free of the feel of his body and the smell emanating from his musty black suit. His wig, too, carried the taint of grease and too heavy an application of powder. He was altogether an unsavoury person. Nevertheless, Mrs Clough was all over him, producing a small bottle from her reticule and inviting him to take a nip of gin.

Simon and Rufus passed the time showing off for Lucy's benefit. They talked loudly of their exploits in town, boasted of their amatory conquests, their phenomenal luck at cards, and about the money they had won at cockfights and horseracing. Yet invariably their conversation reverted to dirty talk about women, until even their doting mother told them to desist, murmuring something about such words not being suitable for Clementine's delicate ears.

Lucy, watching the girl's hot eyes and lecherous smile, guessed she was hardly the innocent creature her mother liked to think she was. No doubt Simon and Rufus had already permitted the raffish companions they knocked about with to seduce their sister. They had probably done it on a bet. Lucy began to detest them. She closed her eyes and pretended to be asleep, but they kept on touching her feet with theirs attempting to gain her attention.

The countryside rolled past the windows – villages, hamlets, small towns and windmills turning lazily on the horizon, the verdant hillsides dotted with woolly sheep. Lucy dozed, lulled by the swaying of the coach over the bumpy roads. She awakened when it slowed down, thinking they must have reached the first stop along the way, another inn that kept fresh horses which could be exchanged for the weary, foam-flecked team.

'Are we there?' she asked the vicar sleepily.

'No, my dear, this is a stop to stretch one's legs and answer nature's call.' His speech was blurred and his step unsteady as he alighted from the coach and extended a hand to help Mrs Clough down.

'About time, too,' the ginger-headed Simon exclaimed. 'Egad, I swear my eyeballs are floating! Out of the way, reverend, there's no stopping a man when he needs to take a piss. Ain't that so, wench?' He tried to include Lucy in the conversation.

She ignored him and, while the rest of the passengers flexed their cramped limbs or made off in various directions in search of privacy, she breathed deeply of the wild flowers scenting the day, enjoying the pale sunshine and the sight of blue sky adrift with fluffy clouds.

'All right, lass?' enquired the driver, a monarch of the highway on whose reliability and skill the speed of the vehicle and safety of the passengers depended. He was a stout figure that inspired respect.

'Yes, sir, thank you,' she replied, and though he resembled him but little, he somehow reminded her of her father.

'Call me Toby, if you like. Now, get yourself rested and comfortable,' he advised, his thick legs placed foursquare on the ground as he produced a large pie from an inner pocket of his triple-capped greatcoat. 'We'll not be stopping again till we reach Westmarsh, and there we'll put up for the night, going on to London in the morning.'

Lucy was hungry. She found a tree stump, perched herself on it, and undid the pasty Martha had provided for her. There was a stone jar of water, too, drawn fresh from the well just as the sun was rising. It was tepid now, but no matter. It tasted like the finest wine to her as she watched the loutish Clough sons vanish into the woods, no doubt intent on terrorising harmless forest wildlife.

After she had eaten, Lucy decided that she, too, would walk amidst the groves to enjoy the tranquillity, and find a secluded spot in which to prepare herself for the next long haul.

She completed her ablutions by dipping her fingers in the ice-cold brook trickling over shiny black pebbles. High in an oak tree, a wood dove declaimed its wistful love song and the peace of the scene permeated her being. She prayed for the souls of her parents and for those of her brothers and sisters, and then wept for them. Afterwards, wiping her cheeks with the back of her hand, she became aware of a bird screeching a warning. The bushes behind her rustled, and she turned around sharply.

Jollian emerged, his presence casting a shadow over the woodlands and the silver water, and there was a queer look on his face that struck terror in her heart. He had overindulged in Mrs Clough's gin and this had apparently loosened the lustful devils within him.

'Lucy,' he muttered, a long string of saliva hanging from his slack bottom lip. 'Pretty, winsome Lucy, you'll be kind to me, won't you? A man gets lonely, needs a bit of female company. Look what I've got for you.' His hand went down to his crotch. The flap was unbuttoned, and as it fell open she saw what she at first took to be the end of a brown scarf. Then she realised her mistake and the colour rushed to her cheeks. He was sporting an erection, and almost hopping before her in his eagerness like some poisonous toad.

'Fasten up, sir,' she cried, leaping to her feet. 'Remember who you are, a priest of the parish, a man to be trusted and respected, a man who cares for his flock.'

'I care only for you, sweetheart,' he declared, grabbing her hand and covering it with slobbering kisses before pushing it down to where his cock reared. 'Rub it for me. Go on, do it hard and I'll give you a bright, shining penny.'

Horror gave Lucy strength and she wrenched herself free of his grasp. 'How dare you?' she yelled. 'How can you suggest such a thing, and you a man of God?'

'What does it matter to you, *slut?*' he spat, and taking his weapon in hand commenced working the foreskin up and down over his glans. 'You're only a servant who'll end up with child to Lord Ludlow or one of his sons, and then you'll be turned out on the street to fend for yourself and your bastard as best you can. You'll become a whore in the end, so why not start now? You could buy a lot of fripperies with a penny.'

'You disgust me!' she hissed, but could not drag her gaze away from the sight of him masturbating. It was fascinating to see how his prick slid through his palm coated with juice, either ringed by that circle of flesh protecting the head or red and straining when left bare.

He laughed and faced her full on, working his tool relentlessly. Then he grimaced and his eyes rolled up, showing the whites. Jets of spunk spurted from him, spattering her skirt. She jumped back, but was too late to avoid his tribute. Furious, she took out a handkerchief and rubbed frantically at the wet spots. That was all she needed, to arrive in London with male stains on her clothing, stains that would have dried white by then, shouting aloud what had made them.

She readjusted her cloak, tossed up her head, and marched back the way she had come, yelling over her shoulder, 'Call yourself a churchman? God must be hard up for helpers if He enlists the aid of a vile wretch like you!'

'Something wrong, lass?' asked the coach-driver, giving her a searching glance.

It was on the tip of her tongue to tell him of the vicar's despicable assault, but he appeared not far behind her, already in conversation with Mrs Clough, all urbane smiles and attentiveness as if it would never have occurred to him to expose himself to Lucy and proposition her. No one would believe her if she accused him. She was a female, and therefore of little consequence. She was also merely a servant.

'Thank you, Mr Tranter,' she said after a moment, 'but there's nothing wrong.' She gave him a smile and climbed back into the carriage, where she sat brooding in silence on the vile duplicity of disgusting old churchmen.

It was already dark when the coach rumbled into the yard of *The White Boar*, in Westmarsh, and made its first official stop. Lucy stepped out, stiff and yawning. The moon hung on its side in the star-flecked sky and dogs barked as the landlord welcomed this last arrival of the day. He ushered them inside, Lucy walking in Jollian's wake, who in turn followed behind Mrs Clough and her objectionable progeny.

'I want a fire lit in my bedchamber,' demanded Mrs Clough, entering the taproom like a galleon under full sail.

'Certainly, madam.' The landlord bowed low. 'At once, madam.'

'And a fire in ours as well,' echoed Simon and Rufus, looking down their noses at the locals, who afforded them a cursory glance before returning to their drinking and shuffle-board.

'I want a fire, too,' Clementine piped up, aping her mother's attempts to play the grand lady.

'You're sharing with me,' Mrs Clough stated firmly. 'One never knows what ruffians creep about at night. You might well be raped if you're left alone.'

'I assure you, this is a most respectable tavern,' the host put in hurriedly. 'We pride ourselves on our reputation for excellent food, clean linen and well-aired beds.'

'Are you listening to what the man is saying, mama?' Clementine asked pettishly. 'There's no need for you to stand guard over me. I'm not a baby, you know.'

'That's what bothers me,' her mother replied heavily. 'No further arguments, the matter is settled.' Then she beamed at Jollian. 'Will you join us for supper in the parlour, your reverence?'

'Thank you kindly,' he said, and Mrs Clough slipped her plump hand through his arm.

Lucy, ignored by all, wondered if Jollian would have more luck with the overbearing woman than he'd had with her, but then decided sadly that it was probably only young women who made him hard. She was hungry and uncertain about where she was to spend the night, which forced her to speak to him. 'What about me?' she asked frostily. 'Where shall I have supper and sleep?'

'Ah yes… unfortunately, I don't think the money Mrs Frisk magnanimously paid out for your travelling expenses included a room.'

'Then what am I to do, sir?' Lucy could not prevent a note of petulance creeping into her voice. 'I'm very tired and very hungry.'

'Come in with us,' whispered Simon, and insinuated an arm round her waist from behind. He ground his pelvis against her buttocks, deliberately making her aware of his thickening cock. 'My brother and I will keep you warm. Virgin meat, are you?' His voice shook with excitement.

'Is it possible?'

Under cover of her long skirt, Lucy stamped down hard on his toes. He leapt back with a grunt, releasing her.

'This is your maid, madam?' queried the landlord. 'She might occupy a truckle-bed in your room, perhaps?'

'Certainly not, she's nothing to do with me,' Mrs Clough declared haughtily.

'She is my responsibility,' Jollian put in. 'I'm escorting her to London on behalf of Lord Ludlow's housekeeper. She is to take up a post at Templebar House.'

'In that case, sir, I suggest she pass the night by the fire in the parlour,' the landlord suggested. 'I can supply her with a blanket and she'll not be disturbed. This is somewhat irregular, though. Most gentlefolk travelling with their servants make provision for them, even if it's only sharing a room with others of a like ilk. And where, may I ask, is she to eat?'

'Not at our table, and that's for sure,' retorted Mrs Clough.

'Come to the kitchen, girl.' The landlord cast a friendly eye on the downcast Lucy. 'My wife will feed you there.'

With her basket gripped tightly to her, Lucy followed him, her nose instantly responding to the mouth-watering smells coming from the back of the inn. The kitchen was like a warm womb, reminding her poignantly of the one where her mother had reigned supreme, and her friend Martha's kitchen had also been the heart of the farmhouse.

The landlord shouted as they entered, 'Annie, my dear, here's a poor wench who's not been provided for by those who consider themselves to be her superiors. I've said she can sleep on the settle in the parlour, but she's in need of a meal.'

Annie turned from the open, blackened fireplace where she was using a wooden ladle to stir a big cooking pot hanging from a crane suspended on a hook over the flames. A side of beef revolved on a spit, the juices dripping into a pan set beneath it. A boy, nearly engulfed in a sacking apron, was sliding a paddle under loaves of hot, crusty bread, taking them from the baking oven. Coals glowed at the base of it and heat blasted out as from a furnace. Scullions were busy at the long central table, which was overhung by saucepans and cauldrons, their task to peel and chop vegetables while a further team washed up at the stone sink and replaced platters on the dresser. Lucy immediately felt at home.

'Sit down, deary,' Annie said, her arms akimbo, knuckles planted on her ample hips. 'Now then, tell me all about it while I serve you up a helping of my best soup.'

Lucy could feel tears forming in her eyes as she told Annie about her recent bereavement and what had happened to her since, barring the incident with Jollian. She was still unconvinced she would be believed. She wanted to trust this plump, apple-cheeked woman who nodded sympathetically and set a steaming bowl in front of her along with a plate of homemade bread and a mug of beer, but she did not dare risk it. Then hunger overcame her and she did not stop eating until every crumb was gone, the bread used to sop up the remnants of the delectable game pottage. Apple pie came next, served with dollops of clotted cream.

Full to the brim, the beer making her feel sleepy, Lucy wished she could stay here forever, but then the landlord came in and said, 'The parlour's empty, my dear, and you're bone weary.'

'Where are the rest of my party?' she asked, rising reluctantly.

'Gone to bed, and I've got rid of the taproom crowd and locked the door. Time for us all to sleep, I think. What say you, wife?'

'We're nearly done here. Goodnight, Lucy Browne.' Annie handed her a blanket and a goose-down pillow.

'Come back in the morning and I'll see that you have breakfast.'

In the parlour, the fire was smouldering and the oak-settle drawn close to the inglenook. The seat was sparsely padded, but Lucy was too tired to fret. She wrapped her cloak round her, and then the blanket, tucked the pillow beneath her head and was asleep in seconds.

She dreamed, or it seemed she dreamed, that she was tightly bound and could not move a muscle. Hands were roaming all over her, touching her in intimate places, but she could not see who it was, as if her eyes were blindfolded. She wanted to scream but there was something pressing against her mouth, something hot and hard and wet. It was like a steel bar... but no, this was more pliable and the surface was warm, not cold...

She rose from the enveloping folds of sleep and came to herself in the parlour. Memory returned, and she found herself trapped in her cloak. Arms were also holding her tightly and hands were clamped round her head. She could not breathe because someone was kneeling astride her and driving a thick tool into her mouth. She gagged, threshing wildly, but she could not free herself from the man as he pushed in harder, until her nose was buried in the musky-smelling reddish hair coating his groin. He rocked backwards and forwards, his cock sliding deeper between her lips until the glans butted the back of her throat.

'Be quick,' a voice hissed. 'I want my turn.'

'Shut up, and be damned to you,' growled Simon Clough. 'I'll do as I please.'

Fired by horror, she struggled even harder, and showing no mercy, bit down hard on the length of swollen flesh gagging her.

Simon yelped and slapped her. Stars lit the darkness behind her closed eyelids. The taste of him was in her mouth, rancid and strong, and she was aware of Rufus tugging at the blanket and pushing up her skirt and of his hands groping between her legs. His brother, concerned only with his own satisfaction, was thrusting faster and harder against her face, sitting on her chest so his weight pinned her down. Then Rufus began licking her quim, but it gave her no pleasure though she had often longed for someone to do that to her. He was hurting her delicate membranes, tormenting her sensitive nubbin, vandalising her virgin orifice. Then Simon gave a sharp bark and shuddered violently as hot spurts of semen filled her mouth and flowed down her throat.

Coughing and sputtering, she managed to shove him off her, and before Rufus had time to force her knees open, she slithered from the settle to the floor. She spat, ridding herself of Simon's secretions.

'Whore!' Rufus hissed, giving her a disdainful kick in the ribs. 'Bitch! Dirty little trull! Don't tell me you weren't gasping for it.'

'Of course she was,' Simon said. 'Look at her, the scruffy, draggle-tailed tart.'

'It's all right for you, you came off, but I'm still hard.' Rufus angrily pulled off his belt and whacked her with it mercilessly as though it was her fault.

She crouched beneath his blows, still sick to her stomach from the taste of spunk and shocked to the core by what had happened. 'Stop!' she cried. 'I'll tell your mother!'

'Tell away,' Simon sneered. 'Do you think for a moment she'll listen to anything you have to say?'

'Come on, hold her for me to have a go,' urged Rufus, flinging aside the belt as he took hold of his tumescent tool and rubbed it vigorously.

Lucy moved before they could grab her again, snatched up her basket and cloak, and ran from the parlour with the two brothers in hot pursuit. She managed to get to the back door and escape out into the yard. The stables were before her, a lantern glowing in one window. She dashed through the big double doors, and found herself in the warm, sweet-smelling interior where horses fidgeted in the stalls, their iron-shod hooves ringing on the flagstones.

'Help!' she screamed, hearing the brothers running in behind her. 'Someone help me!'

'What's going on?' answered a deep voice from the rear of the building. 'Who's that upsetting my nags at this hour of the night?'

Toby Tranter's shadow, huge and menacing, fell over the Cloughs as they rushed in, colliding with each other as they pulled up short at the sight of him. They glanced at the blunderbuss in his powerful hand, and backed off.

'It's nothing,' Simon replied brazenly. 'We're but jesting with the lass, that's all. It's a fine night, not conducive to sleep.'

'I suggest you go back to the inn, good sirs, and leave Lucy alone,' Tranter advised sternly. 'I'll see she comes to no harm.'

The brothers turned and left obediently.

'Thank you for that, Mr Tranter,' Lucy murmured, dragging her cloak around her and longing for a mug of clear fresh water to wash away the taint of Simon's juices.

'Were those young tykes annoying you? You'll be safe here with me.' He guided her to the tack-room where visiting coachmen ate and slept, a comfortable place with deep chairs, beds made up on hay bales, and a stove that glowed promisingly with mulled wine warming on the round iron top. A trestle table with benches at each side was well provisioned, and Toby was the only one awake; the guards were dead to the world.

He indicated she should occupy a bale covered with a horse blanket, and she sank down on top of it gratefully, though painfully aware of the welts left by Rufus's belt, and aware, too, of the shameful excitement the whole dreadful episode had inexplicably awakened deep inside her. This business of congress between the sexes was all so strange and new it terrified her, but she wanted to learn more. The things she had experienced over the past two days had been a revelation. They had caused mayhem in her loins and unrest in her soul. It was as if, like Eve, she had eaten an apple from the Tree of Knowledge and the paradise of innocence was lost to her forever.

She glanced across at Toby, who was seated in a chair, his boots propped up on a stool near the stove. He appeared to be not exactly asleep but meditating deeply, a clay pipe clenched between his teeth. It was comforting to have that big, burly driver with his gun close at hand keeping watch over her. She would have liked his strong arms round her, but she was frightened he might misinterpret the signals if she asked him to hold her. The last thing she wanted right now was another man trying to make her do things to his cock.

Chapter Three

'It's high time you varied the entertainment, Maggie, I'm quite weary of Tahitian love feasts and the whipping of recalcitrant concubines,' Lord Hallagon drawled, 'and even slave auctions fill me with unmitigated boredom.' He launched this complaint into the receptive, if cynical, ear of Mrs Margaret Main, the notorious owner of the most fashionable and decadent bagnio in town.

'And what about my bathhouse with its hot tubs and skilled masseurs of both sexes?' she enquired, lounging beside him on a low divan in her boudoir. Her impressive bosom was exposed, and her flimsy skirts yanked high to reveal white silk stockings with gold clocks ornamenting the outer sides, buckled garters spangled with diamante particles fastened just above her dimpled knees. Her alabaster thighs gleamed, wantonly parted, her milk-white fork denuded of hair, a fascinating nook where tiny hoops pierced the rosy lips, each set with a sparkling gem. Her clitoris stood out proudly, large and well formed, as fine an organ as Tarquin had ever seen, and he was a connoisseur of fine pussy.

Maggie's apartment was a sumptuous retreat, rich in tapestries and filled with immodest statues of couples in the throes of ecstasy. There were also numerous erotic paintings featuring dainty shepherdesses disporting themselves in green meadows, crooks discarded, their bodices lowered and their skirts upraised over firm bottoms impaled on the rigid cocks of virile rustic swains. Incense spiced the air, wafting from bronze dragons' snarling mouths, and harpsichord music tinkled from an alcove, each plucked note crisp and clear, resonating round the room and vibrating sensually on the eardrums.

'The *Hammam* is delightful,' Tarquin agreed, 'but even it wanes after a while.' His lips curved up in a sardonic smile and his handsome face took on a beautifully demonic cast. 'You know very well I hanker after novelty.' He could have been foreign with his dark, deep-set eyes and incredibly long, curling lashes, but he was English through and through. Born to high estate, well bred, well educated and inordinately wealthy, Lord Hallagon despised women and Maggie's sort in particular, but he could never resist their lure. A voluptuary as well as a philosopher who had studied at Cambridge University and at various other seats of learning abroad, he had made it his lifework to root out every lustful quirk buried within him and to indulge it to the full. At twenty-eight, he had probably more sexual experience than most people achieved in four score years and ten.

Thirty years old, in her prime and beautiful, Maggie knew all there was to know about human desires. When the mood took her, she sometimes serviced favoured customers herself, and there was no whore in London more accomplished than she. Tarquin knew this to be so, having fornicated with a large number of them and been the recipient of Maggie's skilled ministrations as well. Like him, she appreciated the paradox of pain and pleasure, and relished whips, chains and bondage, humiliation, submission and domination. Simple straightforward copulation was never enough for either of them.

'Have I shown you my latest acquisition?' she asked in the low, mellifluous voice she reserved for these occasions, restraining the screech she used when upbraiding one of her girls, or a client who made the grave mistake of attempting to pay less than he had promised.

'No, madam, and what might that be? A Creole, perhaps, from the Americas, with skin like chocolate, smooth as silk and smelling of saffron?' Tarquin tested his reaction to this possibility, and was disappointed to find that her question roused little curiosity in his restless brain, not to mention in his groin. He had come here seeking relief, looking for something to titillate his jaded appetite. Women were easy to come by, as were young men, and he enjoyed them both. He was free to masturbate, to bury his cock in a variety of orifices, to sate his lust where he willed, yet there was something missing, and he was not sure what it was, which irked him.

He had risen late and, surrounded by an army of footmen under the command of his valet, a Welshman called Powys, he had washed, been shaved by his barber, and donned a new outfit cut in the latest mode. It was his intention to show it off at *White's Club*, where much coffee was drunk and play ran high. A Member of Parliament had recently lost ten thousand pounds at a cast of hazard. Tarquin gambled, but always kept his wits about him. For a gentleman in his position who had no need to soil his hands with work, he was remarkably shrewd when it came to dealing with his accountants, bankers and estate managers. No one was going to rob him of a farthing through chicanery or clever sleights of hand.

His snuff-coloured, fine woollen jacket fitted him without a flaw, snug around his broad shoulders. It had wide lapels and opened down the front casually, displaying a waistcoat of the same material also partially buttoned. Lace frothed from his loosely tied cravat and at the slit cuffs of the jacket's narrow sleeves, and his buckskin breeches were skin-tight, moulding his thighs and the hollows of his flanks, his neat arse and the substantial bulge at his crotch. They were closed at the knee and met the tops of highly polished riding boots. His hat rested on a chair close by, not a three cornered one but a low-crowned, wide-brimmed felt hat of informal shape and of sporting origin, which was now very much *à la mode*. The other club members would be impressed when he strolled in, but then no one there was likely to risk gainsaying him. Quarrels at the gaming tables often led to duels and his sword was ready to leap out of its scabbard on the least provocation. There was no other remedy for insults than a duel, and it was sometimes fought on the spot. Tarquin was renowned for being invincible with the rapier, and also a crack shot if it came to pistols. He might read Rousseau and Voltaire and talk politics at length, discussing the pros and cons of the troubles in the American colonies and the unrest in France, but he was, first and foremost, a deadly opponent.

'Well, my lord, don't you want to see my new toy?'

He felt Maggie's fingers weaving themselves through his raven hair. White powered wigs were going out of fashion and were ridiculed by the dandies. Tarquin had never worn one, preferring his own long and luxuriant locks, which he tied back with a velvet ribbon or, as now, allowed to tumble freely over his shoulders. Her touch was exciting, her supple fingers massaging his scalp, his neck, and then penetrating the cravat and caressing his chest, combing through his dark mat of hair and tweaking his wine-red nipples. At once his cock twitched and started to swell. He caught her wrist and removed her hand, bringing it to rest on the erection tenting his breeches.

'Very well,' he said. 'Fetch this object, but it better be good.' He sent her off with a sharp slap to her bottom. Her dress was thin, one of those new, high-cut floating creations with a wide sash around the waist. He approved of these latest designs from Paris. They were tantalising, revealing women's bodies so much more readily than the boned bodices and vast panniers of yore. Rounded breasts, pert nipples, slender limbs, plump buttocks, and even the shadowy outline of a pubic wedge, could be glimpsed through the gossamer fabrics. It was now the vogue for ladies to look as if they were fresh from the country in dresses suitable for a stroll around one of London's squares or across a father or a husband's estate. The old order huffed and puffed about the immodesty of such garments, but it was freedom unconfined for the modern girl and a boon if, like Maggie, one ran a whorehouse.

She smiled at Tarquin over her shoulder as she strolled over to an armoire. She opened the doors, and took out a brown Malacca cane made from the long, thin stem of a rattan.

Tarquin shrugged his shoulders. 'Is that it? Ye gods, Maggie, it's nothing new, I've wielded many a one when bringing unruly slaves to order.'

'I know that, my lord, haven't I helped you on occasions? But this one is exceptionally strong and pliable. My supplier assures me it will prove immensely satisfactory and give years of wear. Some snap so easily, a nuisance when one is in full swing, so to speak.' As she talked, she swished the weapon through the air so its sinister song hummed between them.

Despite his doubts, Tarquin's skin crept and his fingers tingled with the urge to hold that instrument of chastisement. He knew what it would feel like – like an extension of his arm, of his body, his sex and his personality meting out punishment, bringing agony and burning desire to his victims...

'Give it to me,' he commanded, getting to his feet, tall and distinguished and towering over Maggie.

She handed him the weapon, moving well out of his range, her silks slipping off her sloping shoulders as she moved and completely baring her breasts.

A spasm of lust lurched through Tarquin's genitals when he saw the apprehension in her eyes and the way her areolas crimped and her teats stood out. He flicked the cane, listening to its whistle and feeling its response. She was right. It was better than any other he had used before.

'You want to test it, perhaps?' she asked breathlessly.

He could smell her arousal, and shared in it as he plunged

his free hand into her fork and felt the heat throbbing there, his fingers slippery with her dew. There was more to this than the simple trial of a new implement. He was aware of a bond between them, a shared wickedness in which they both revelled. Not for nothing was he called a depraved sensualist, his wild orgies in the caves beneath his mansion, Greyfriars, looked upon askance by respectable folk. But there were others all too eager to join him, and not only loose-living young bucks sought membership. King George III, well meaning but weak and not too bright, ruled England through ministers, many of whom were corrupt and diabolically clever profligates and debauchees. Some of these could not wait to enter Greyfriars' unholy portals, and it was all grist to Tarquin's mill since one could never have too many friends in high places.

Maggie gyrated her crotch against his fingers and then pulled away, clapping her hands. Immediately, three men entered the room. One was a strapping black male with a shaven, tattooed head, and the other two were fair-skinned blue-eyed youths with light brown hair. The black man was stripped to the waist, his oiled body gleaming, his waist girded by a wide leather belt holding up a pair of transparent Turkish style pantaloons slit at the front. His gargantuan weapon protruded from the opening, twelve inches of thick dark flesh, the foreskin removed and leaving the bulging plum-coloured head bare.

'Come here, Jamal,' Maggie ordered, and gripped his cock, sliding her palm up and down it, her fingers and thumb unable to meet round its girth.

He grimaced and rocked his hips to aid her frottage. She slapped his balls hard, turning his pleasure into discomfort.

'Ah, mistress,' he grunted, 'I'm sorry.'

'You will be, if you do that again,' she snapped, squeezing his testicles. 'Now then, bring in the girl.'

While she waited, Maggie turned her attention to the two youths. They stood with their eyes lowered staring down at the Persian carpet. They wore nothing but studded collars and leather straps crossing their chests that fastened to a belt, from which were attached further bonds circling their masculine equipment. This device cradled their balls and lifted their cocks high. Their nipples were pierced with rings and linked by chains, and their attitude was one of complete subservence.

Tarquin paced slowly around them and traced the tip of the cane over the V formed by their shoulders tapering down to supple waists. He then trailed the cane lower, tapping their perfectly formed buttocks and insinuating it into the deep creases between them.

'Bend over,' he said crisply, 'hands clasping your ankles.'

The cane dipped into the area exposed as the young men took up the required position, pursed anal mouths and dangling cods fully displayed and vulnerable. The cane slid over their already swollen cocks, enchanting Tarquin with the view. He never could make up his mind which excited him most, the sight of a female's labial lips with the sharply defined slit containing her secrets, or the arsehole of a man and the way his balls moved like ripe fruit in a hairy net beneath the length and hardness of his phallus. His own appendage was chafing uncomfortably against his silk undergarment, damp and hot and acutely sensitive. He was obsessed with the need to drive it into an orifice and rid himself of his spunk. Any aperture would do, be it mouth or pussy or rectum, even the channel formed by two breasts pressed together, or a tunnel made of fingers.

The vision of those raised hindquarters made the cane come alive. He could not resist lifting it high, and whacking it down across both proffered buttocks in quick succession.

Both young men yelped in unison as livid welts sprang into being across their tight bottom cheeks.

Tarquin was so exhilarated that he very nearly spent himself in his breeches, but he controlled himself. The game was afoot, he was in his element and determined to make it last.

Jamal came through the door again dragging a lissom woman by a chain fastened to manacles around her wrists. She was semi-nude, wearing only a fragile silk chemise that barely reached her *mons veneris*, her straight dark hair falling around her face and partially concealing her breasts. Tears coursed down her cheeks and she hung back reluctantly, but Jamal jerked her forward. She sank to her knees before Tarquin, and Jamal put a heavy bare foot on her neck, forcing her to lie flat on the floor.

'Ah, Lady Cordelia Wareham,' Tarquin said slowly, an ironic gleam in his eye. He knew her very well, and knew also that the two youths were viscounts, the eldest sons of earls; he had met them all socially. These indulged scions of noble houses moved, like himself, in court circles, but sought their pleasures in odd places, not the least of which was *Maggie's Temple of Joy*, where no questions were asked as long as one paid up.

'I'm a slave-slut wanting only to do your bidding,' Cordelia said softly, daring to glance up at him.

If this was the role she had decided to play that night, he was more than happy to oblige her. Maybe he would use a multi-strapped deerskin flogger on her thighs and pussy once he had given the cane a thorough test. She would be fully aroused by then and willing to perform any act, no matter how degrading. She had been coming here longer than Tarquin, seeking relief from her daily life, in which she was the bossy, organising wife of a dithering, half-witted baron who adored her. She ruled the roost and her servants trembled before her. Word had it she ate men alive and loved every minute of it, and then she turned tail on herself and did penance in Maggie's torture rooms.

Tarquin could not be bothered to pursue her motives further, however. She was going to be chastised severely, and then he would bugger her until she screamed for mercy. 'Lick my boots,' he commanded.

Cordelia cooed softly and slithered up to support herself on her forearms. Without using her hands, she lowered her mouth to Tarquin's instep and extended her tongue, sweeping the tip over the smooth leather.

He nodded to Maggie, who gestured to Jamal. In an instant, the latter had drawn back the crimson brocade curtains at the far end of the room to reveal an X-shaped wooden structure. The two young men hauled Cordelia to her feet, and frog-marched her over to where Jamal stood, his arms folded over his mighty chest, his biceps bulging. He seized her, stripped off her diaphanous chemise, and pushed her against the whipping post, pressing her face against it. Her grabbed each of her wrists, forced her arms up and out, and snapped manacles around them attached to chains fastened to ringbolts. Tugging on them to insure they were secure, he kicked her feet apart and tethered her ankles to the lower struts. She was now spread-eagled and entirely helpless. Her slender white back, her doll-like waist and her plump buttocks were all exposed along with the fuzz-fringed purse of her sex, tempting Tarquin to tickle it with the cane.

'Jamal, the clamps,' he ordered, and the slave master presented him with an open, velvet-lined box housing several pairs of wicked-looking devices. He took up a pair and examined the alligator teeth and the screws for tightening. They were made by a silversmith and had rings attached to the ends for the purpose of hanging jewels or small weights from them.

He strode over to Cordelia, his feet making no sound on the thick carpet, and snapped a clamp onto the fleshiest part of her right labia. She moaned as he adjusted the screw, but he ignored her protests as he subjected her left labia to the same abuse. Her pink wings turned red, swelling around the teeth, nevertheless, he added a little lead weight to each, obscenely elongating her sex lips.

'Oh, that hurts,' she cried. 'That hurts!'

'Be quiet or I'll use a ball-gag on you,' he threatened, and running a hand over her silky skin felt her shudder with longing at his touch. Few women could resist him, and he found their adoration tedious at times. One had even attempted suicide when, weary of her histrionics, he snubbed her in public. Cordelia could also easily become a nuisance. He preferred his relationship with Maggie; both of them were horrified by commitment.

The owner of the establishment was watching the proceedings with a feline smile while also amusing herself by tormenting the viscounts, tugging at the straps that held their testes and making sure their cocks were in a permanent state of erection. She rubbed them, toyed with them, dipped the tip of her little finger into their weeping tips and massaged the pre-cum around their glans and down their straining stems.

Tarquin took off his jacket and waistcoat and rolled his shirtsleeves above his elbows. The candlelight glinted on the fine ebony hair dusting his forearms. No longer bored, he congratulated himself on his strength and fitness, the result of a tough regime of fencing, wrestling and boxing. He kept Cordelia in suspense, watching her body settle into its restraints. He moved the cane over her exposed sex and watched her quiver, grinding her pubis against empty air as if already seeking orgasm. His cock jerked and he ached to release it, but knew that by keeping it under control the force of the sensations would increase once he finally let it go. He ran a hand down her spine, caressed the sweet valley between her buttocks, and then stepped back. She moaned her distress and he smiled grimly as he brought the cane viciously down across her bottom. She screamed and twisted her hips desperately, but she was going nowhere. The weights hung lower, stretching her labia even more cruelly as she writhed in agony.

He followed through, the rod beating the insides of her thighs and the under-hang of her buttocks, attacking her tortured vulva and laying several blows on hard where her bottom crack parted and her alluring anus beckoned. Her copious juices glistened, wetting pubic hair and membranes and giving the lie to her anguished protestations. Welts resembling crimson roses with long stems bloomed on her skin, contrasting with her pale colouring. They fascinated Tarquin, and he used his ingenuity and skill to vary his strokes, never landing a blow on the same place twice, precise in the distance he maintained between those fiery lines. Then he laid down the cane and picked up the flogger.

He abruptly removed the clamps from her labia, and she screamed in misery as the blood surged back into her pinched flesh. He laid the deerskin softly against her, letting it caress her throbbing pussy, and her cries changed to mewing sounds much like those of a female cat in heat. He could see the spasms building in her sex, and then the mood of the flogger changed as he snapped his wrist and its tails struck her relentlessly, each one carrying its own sting. She trembled, and her journey towards bliss became a part of him, too. His cock pulsed as he alternated her punishment with blows from the cane and the flogger. Then he threw both aside and slipped a hand between her thighs, cupping her mound and rolling his thumb over her swollen clitoris. She heaved her hips up against him as far as her manacles would permit, and he felt her orgasm rip through her.

'Ah, Tarquin,' she gasped, 'my lord and my master!'

He opened his breeches and his phallus leapt out, slick

with pre-cum. Wetting her arsehole with her own slippery juices, he held his cock to the puckered aperture, and then propelled it into the tight passage with a neat thrust of his hips. For an instant her sphincter fought back, denying him entrance, and then her muscles relaxed and sucked him deep into her dark depths. Just for a moment he felt a twinge of superstitious fear, as he always did when taking this forbidden pathway, and then pleasure overcame him as she began shunting backwards and forwards. He churned and beat at her interior, unable to contain his moans of delight as he reached the quintessence of ecstasy and scalding semen jetted from him into her clinging fundament.

He gripped the wood of the cross, his legs trembling as his penis slipped from her, his creamy tribute trickling down her thighs. He unchained her, and she collapsed into his arms. He held her with a feeling amounting to distaste, and then handed her over to Jamal.

'She's too willing,' he said to Maggie over the supper table later, a civilised meal served in her private dining room. The food was superlative and there were footmen in attendance, stalwart, upright fellows in plush coats with flashy gold brocade wearing white wigs clubbed at the neck. Each footman had been handpicked by Maggie for his height, breadth of shoulder, the shape of his calves – displayed in pastel silk stockings – and the largeness of his cock outlined by tight-fitting satin breeches. Sometimes she made them serve at table without nether garments, liking to finger their naked tackle as they solemnly collected used dishes and brought in the next course. She found it amusing to try and crack their carefully expressionless faces.

'Who is too willing, Lady Cordelia?' she queried, tearing at a chicken wing with her teeth, her tongue licking over the meat with as much enjoyment as if she was giving fellatio. 'I thought she protested very well.'

'These great ladies with their alley cat morals,' Tarquin grumbled, fastidiously dipping his digits into a crystal fingerbowl filled with rosewater, 'simply do not present a challenge. I want a girl who hates me and fights me. This will make the conquest all the sweeter.'

'A virgin, my lord?' Maggie lifted her crystal wineglass to her lips and studied him over the rim, which glittered richly in the candlelight. 'A rare commodity, unless you're prepared to settle for a very young chit, and that isn't your bent, is it?'

'Most definitely not,' he said, frowning. 'I want a fully developed beauty, a defiant, rebellious wench it will be worth my trouble to subdue. Find me such a one and I'll make it worth your while. And don't think to cheat me. I know the tricks you whoremongers play to convince the unwary that the girl on offer has an intact maidenhead.'

Maggie left her chair and dropped to her knees beside him. 'Would I do that to you, my lord?' Her artful fingers removed his cock from his buckskins.

'If you thought you could get away with it,' he grunted, as he watched her red mouth cover his helm, her oval fingernails shining as she moved them over his tool with ease, and swiftly sucked him to completion.

'Trust me, Lord Tarquin,' she said after swallowing his tribute, 'I will find you what you want.' She resumed her seat and used a damask table napkin to wipe the residue of his pleasure from her lips.

'Just do it, and then we'll see about trust,' he answered caustically, nodding to a footman to refill his glass.

Lucy woke with a start when someone poked her.

'We're here, girl,' the Reverend Jollian informed her in his nasal voice.

'In London?' she cried, excitement waking her up completely.

'Yes, London, you ignoramus,' snapped Mrs Clough.

Lucy felt for her basket. It was still there. Simon and Rufus were already preparing to alight, and did not even glance her way. Thankfully, they had left her alone since last night knowing Toby Tranter was keeping a watchful eye on her.

The coaching inn was larger, grander and busier even than the one in Newford. The courtyard was extensive and enclosed by a three-story building.

'Go and find a hackney carriage,' Mrs Clough ordered her sons from where she stood surrounded by luggage. 'Will you share one with us, vicar?'

'That's most kind of you, I'm heading for Charing Cross,' he accepted the offer, and then addressed Lucy. 'Templebar House is a goodly walk from here, but you should find it without too much difficulty. I've written down directions for you.'

Simon returned with a hired cab and the Cloughs piled inside, their baggage strapped on top. There was obviously no room for Lucy, and she could not wait to get away from them all anyway. She gazed longingly at Toby, who was stretching his great frame and talking with other coachmen while his horses were led away by stable-hands, to their reward of full nosebags and a well earned rest. She wanted to ask him if he could help her find her destination. It was all very well the reverend giving her written instructions, but she could not read. She took a step forward, but just then Toby disappeared into the taproom and she was too shy to follow him in.

At a loss as to how to proceed, Lucy became aware that she was attracting attention as a lone woman in a crowded tavern yard. She pulled her hood over her blonde hair, hefted up her basket, which was by no means light, and walked towards the large archway leading out onto the crowded streets of the city wondering if she could also hire a coach to take her to her destination.

The road was narrow, overshadowed by the houses looming on either side. The steaming piles of horse manure made it difficult to traverse, and the pavements were not wide enough to protect the pedestrian from being spattered with mud as carriages, brewer's drays, tradesman's carts and coal wagons rumbled by. Creaking signs swung overhead, some painted with symbols to indicate bookshops, butchers, clothiers or cobblers, while others hanging above tavern doors boasted pictures of blue boars, unicorns, sheaves of barley and golden crowns. Housewives hurried along, baskets over their arms. Liveried servants ran errands for their employers. Apprentices lurked outside shops, grabbing the arms of passers-by and attempting to drag them into their masters' emporiums. Hucksters occupied street corners, trays around their necks offering cheap trinkets. Porters staggered along with loads on their backs. There were beggars and cripples, ballad singers, ragged waifs and sober merchants on their way to centres of business.

The raucous noise deafened Lucy's ears on every side. The foul odours rising from primitive drains sickened her nostrils. Outside the city the day had been sunny, but here the sky was grey, darkened by smoke from factories and tanneries. This, then, was the famous London, dirty and colourful, frightening and exciting.

She walked along, her eyes round, drinking in the sights and trying to keep out the bad smells while relishing the appetising odours drifting out of pie shops and bakeries. She wondered if she dared spend a few pennies, it having been a long time since breakfast, but decided to wait to be fed when she reached Lord Ludlow's mansion. Trying to avoid being noticed, she kept her eyes down, but even so people seemed to be staring at her. She darted a glance round, and a cheeky apprentice who caught her eye deliberately placed himself in her path.

'Can I help you, love?' he asked in a patois she was

soon to recognise as pure cockney. He was unattractive, with spiky hair and ears that stuck out framing a crop of pimples and crooked teeth.

Lucy could feel a blush rising to her cheeks, but she succeeded in holding his impudent gaze. 'I'm lost,' she confessed. 'I need to find Templebar House. Can you tell me which way to go?'

'I might,' the lad replied. 'What'll you give me if I do?'

She noticed that several other apprentices were watching them, grinning inanely and making obscene gestures. 'I have nothing to offer you,' she said coldly. She was already weary of men and their obsession with putting females at a disadvantage.

'Sure you have,' he persisted, winking at his colleagues. 'What about a kiss?'

'Stand aside, fellow,' she commanded. 'I have no kisses for the likes of you.'

'Hoity-toity,' he mocked her, and moved closer. Then he whipped aside his apron and she realised his breeches were undone when she saw his small, pinkish cock sticking out of the gap. 'You can do more than that,' he teased. 'Give this a suck and I just might put you on the right road.'

His mates sniggered and circled her, but kept a wary eye on the shops they were supposed to be guarding.

'Get out of my way!' she hissed, and using her basket as a battering-ram charged through the lads, taking to her heels and putting as much distance between them and herself as possible.

Now she was thoroughly lost, having left the main thoroughfare and dived into a side alley. It was dark and smelly with an open sewer running down its centre. She dropped her basket and leaned against a slimy wall, gasping for breath, a stitch clawing at her side. Perspiration beaded her face and her hair had come tumbling down as she ran. She pushed back the hood of her cloak, needing to feel cool air on her skin even if it *was* dank and smelled awful.

It was then she saw movement as two women emerged from the gloom and sidled towards her. One was young, her pale face starred with bright dabs of rouge on either cheek. She was so painfully thin her gaudy dress hung off her as though she was nothing but a skeleton beneath it, and Lucy cringed away from her, for her bony chest was covered in suppurating sores. The other, older woman was also attired in ragged clothing that had once been fine, her hair dyed a vivid red, her bosom bare, the mottled skin heavily layered with chalk-white powder. The fumes of strong alcohol formed a nauseous aura around her.

'What's this?' she asked in a slurred, guttural voice, edging closer to Lucy. 'A fine ladybird, ain't she, Dolly?'

'She's on our patch,' snarled her young companion, bedraggled feathers drooping from her enormous hat, her lank, greasy hair falling in limp ringlets beneath the brim. She clenched her hands into fists beneath torn lace mittens and sashayed up to Lucy. 'You trying to poach, bitch? We walk this territory. The punters what come here looking for a poke are ours. Get it? Now sling your hook!'

'I'm sorry,' Lucy said, taking another step back. 'I don't know what you're talking about. I'm lost, trying to find Templebar House. That's where I'm going to work as a maid. I've only just arrived from the country. Can you show me the way?'

'Listen to her, Peg,' Dolly sneered. 'So you don't know where you are? Is that so, you saucy little cow?'

'Looks like she's a liar, don't it?' Peg remarked, baring crooked teeth in an ugly smile. 'That's what they all say, ain't it, the tarts who want to walk this alley? But they've no business here. This is our pitch. Our regulars know where to find us, sixpenny whores what give satisfaction, we do.'

'And we knows how to deal with them what try to

muscle in, don't we?' Dolly declared, and tugging at the strings fastening Lucy's cloak ripped it from her shoulders. 'I'll have this for starters.'

'Don't, please!' Lucy begged, and began tussling with her even though she felt revolted by any contact with the diseased body. 'That's all I've got! I'm not rich and I've told you the truth. Won't you help me find my way?'

Dolly fetched her a backhanded blow that set her ears ringing. '*Help* you? You got to be joking. No one comes down here save Peg and me. Ain't that right, Peg?'

'You never said a truer word,' the blowsy slattern declared, and made a grab for Lucy's basket.

Lucy thumped her hard.

Dolly grabbed a handful of her hair, tugging on it violently while Lucy kicked and screamed. She felt her fist connect with Peg's nose, and savage satisfaction welled up inside her as she heard the bone crack. Next she clawed Dolly's face, but was felled by a vicious left hook delivered by a creature who scarcely looked strong enough to walk. She was knocked to the ground, and Peg, blood bubbling from her nose, straddled her chest.

Dolly snatched Lucy's purse and tossed it to Peg, who caught it expertly. Next she lifted Lucy's skirt and stared lewdly at her naked belly and fair bush. Meanwhile Peg clamped her beefy hands round Lucy's ankles, splaying them and holding her steady while her friend subjected those clean, unmarred genitals to a close scrutiny.

Lucy lay stunned, and then shuddered when she felt Dolly's dirty fingers running over her pussy and flicking her clitoris.

'Oh look at this, little Miss Prissy is wet and her nubbin's standing up for fine weather. She ain't as innocent as she makes out.' Then both women abruptly left her, bleeding and dazed and robbed of all her worldly possessions.

Terror of the whores forced Lucy on. She dashed from the alley and headed for the main streets. Her head was throbbing, the scratches inflicted by Dolly stinging, her scalp burning with pain from where they had pulled on her hair. She was cold, already missing her cloak, and to make matters worse her bodice was torn and her skirt had a long rip in it. She hardly looked better than the hideous harridans from whom she had just escaped.

Then the full implications of her desperate plight started to penetrate her confusion.

She had no clothing, no money and, worst of all, the scrap of paper containing the address of Templebar House had vanished as well.

She darted across the road without looking where she was going, and became lost in a maze of wheels. A powerful equine head appeared above her, a monster with blazing eyes and a frothing mouth. Its teammate galloped beside it tossing its mane, and half blinded by glittering harness, she heard the trampling of mighty iron shod hooves and the squealing of brakes. Then something struck her a violent blow and she was flung beneath the carriage.

The coach juddered to a halt, and Lucy was aware of the driver leaping down and a woman stepping out with a soft rustle of skirts. Then it was all too much for her and a merciful darkness swept her away.

Chapter Four

Lucy was still feeling groggy as she peered through her lashes. Her head throbbed and her body ached, but her curiosity was equally strong as she wondered where on earth she was… there was a soft mattress below her, and clean linen sheets and feather pillows and the scent of potpourri in the air. She was not dead and in heaven, but she was somewhere close to it.

Lying motionless on her back, she discerned a fine room in which a middle-aged gentleman stood before the marble fireplace. He was stocky but of a dignified appearance, his legs spread as he rocked on his heels, his hands clasped lightly at the small of his back just above his coattails, which had flap pockets and wide cuffs. His waistcoat was embroidered with flowers and fruit. His ruffles and his formal wig, his black silk breeches, stockings and buckled shoes, all suggested a person of quality. A silver-headed cane was propped by the mantelpiece, and an open leather bag sat on a low table displaying strange objects she assumed to be medical paraphernalia.

He glanced across at the canopied bed where she lay, and then down at the woman seated on the couch. 'She's recovering nicely,' he stated in the cultured, confident accent Lucy associated with aristocrats. 'No bones broken, just a bump on the pate. What are you going to do with her?'

'First I will ascertain if she belongs to anyone and, if she does not, then I shall keep her, Dr Blake,' the woman replied in dulcet tones, her back to Lucy. All the patient could see were white shoulders and a mane of russet hair swept up from a graceful neck.

'You make her sound like a stray dog,' he replied, the lines on either side of his mouth deepening in disapproval.

'You know me better than that, doctor. Shall you call in and see her tomorrow? You will of course be paid as you always are at the end of the month for services rendered to my girls. Add this one to my account, and good day to you, sir.'

He bowed over her hand, but there was a stiffness about him that suggested he was not entirely happy with the situation. Either he did not approve of the lady or she had offended him in some way. He picked up his hat, his cane and his bag, and then the door closed behind him. Immediately another door opened, admitting a woman Lucy vaguely recognised as the one who had tended her when she was lifted from the muddy street and placed inside the coach that ran into her.

'The doctor says she is almost recovered, Letitia,' the woman rose from the couch as she addressed the newcomer, smiling in Lucy's direction. 'This is intriguing, my dear. Who is she and where does she hail from? Is she a maiden, or a trollop whose love-hole has been enjoyed by many a lusty fellow?'

'Her hymen is intact,' Letitia replied. 'I took the liberty of examining her while she was senseless.'

Lucy opened her eyes all the way, stirred slightly and pressed a hand to her forehead. 'Oh, where am I?' she murmured faintly.

At once Letitia approached her. 'You're safe, my child,' she said soothingly, 'and recovering. Unfortunately, you ran under the wheels of my carriage, but you were not badly injured. I brought you here and have been nursing you for two days. I'm Mrs Letitia Evelyn and this is my employer, Mrs Margaret Main.'

Mrs Main swept towards Lucy. She was a regal looking person, a proud, cool beauty in a black taffeta gown sparkling with sequins and beadwork. Her necklace looked costly, the skin of her shoulders and half-naked breasts was smooth and fair, and her hands were heavy with rings. She exuded the kind of confidence Lucy envied, a poise born of experience ad wisdom. 'What is your name?' she asked Lucy, and her level tone was reassuring yet stern.

'Lucy Browne, if it please you, ma'am.'

'You have a country accent. What are you doing in London?'

'I came here to fill a position as a maidservant, but my money was stolen along with the address of the house where I was to work. Oh ma'am, can you please help me find Templebar House? It's owned by Lord and Lady Ludlow. They paid for my seat on the mail-coach and will be expecting me. I'm their new servant.'

The two women exchanged a glance, and then Mrs Main said, 'I've never heard of it, but I can make enquiries. Meanwhile, you can stay here. You will address me as mistress, and on occasion as Maggie, depending on the circumstances.'

'I have no money,' Lucy repeated, close to tears. 'I can't pay for lodgings.'

'Don't worry.' Maggie patted her hand. Then her hazel eyes became thoughtful as she almost absentmindedly caressed Lucy's breasts where they swelled against the loosely tied ribbons of her nightdress. 'Tell me, have you a family who might be concerned as to your whereabouts?'

'No, ma'am,' Lucy gasped, shocked by the wave of desire that obliterated both her mental apprehension and her body's discomforts. 'I'm an orphan. There's no one cares about me.'

'Fate guided you to me,' Maggie answered, nodding sagely. 'I shall undertake your education and prepare you for a better role than that of a servant.'

'That's so kind of you,' she breathed, overwhelmed.

'But why are you doing this?'

'Shall we say that I am of a philanthropic nature?' Amusement gleamed in those astute light eyes beneath a hedge of thick, dark lashes. 'I have several young women like yourself living under my roof.'

'Is it a school?' Lucy asked earnestly. 'A place of learning? I've always longed to be able to read and write and find out about history.'

'You could call this an academy, I suppose.' Maggie played with Lucy's curls, and then lifted the quilt off her to study the lines of her slim body outlined by the linen nightgown. 'An academy of life,' she added, her hand straying to Lucy's mound and remaining there as her fingers caressed the sensitive point at the top of her cleft through the thin material covering it.

'Shall I meet the other girls?' Lucy asked with breathless eagerness.

'Of course you will meet them, and the sooner the better.' Maggie reached for a hand bell on the bedside table. 'Are you feeling well enough to rise and take a bath?'

'Um, yes, I think so.'

Maggie rang the bell briskly and almost immediately a maidservant arrived, a comely creature whose full skirt was covered in front by a small lace-edged apron. She was big bosomed and wasp-waisted, and these attributes were exaggerated by an extremely tight crimson satin bodice and a padded bum-roll. As she walked her skirt parted, giving a glimpse of stockings, plump thighs and a pronounced pudenda in front, while in back when she turned around her generous rump quivered invitingly. Lucy was flabbergasted to see that the twin globes of the girl's bottom cheeks were deeply scored as if by a rod or a whip, and yet her furry mons glistened with dew, betraying her sexual arousal. Her mouth was a rosebud and her hair was twisted in fat ringlets, each one tied at the base with a pert bow.

She tottered over to Maggie on her high heels and knelt at her feet. 'What is your will, mistress?' she asked humbly, even while peering at Lucy with avid interest.

'Where is Jocelyn?' Maggie demanded, her eyes flashing angrily as she bent over to administer a sharp slap on the maid's backside.

'I don't know, mistress,' the girl whimpered. 'I've not seen her today.'

'Fetch her at once, Babette, or it will be you strapped to the whipping block later,' Maggie warned, watching Lucy's reaction. 'It's so hard to find staff these days. I believe in the old adage "spare the rod and spoil the child". Don't you, Lucy?'

'Whatever you say, ma'am,' she replied, as thoroughly confused as she had been when Mrs Frisk chastised Sally.

'Come, come, you must have some opinion,' Maggie chided her.

'I've not had much experience,' she admitted.

'How old are you, Lucy?'

'Seventeen.'

'And a virgin?'

'Yes, ma'am'

'So you've never seen a man's organ?'

'Ah well… yes, I have…' A blush crept over her neck and face.

'Oh?' Maggie said sharply. 'And how did this happen?'

'Men won't leave me alone!' she blurted. 'There was the vicar, he'd offered to chaperone me to London, but at the first opportunity he was rubbing himself in front of me, then inviting me to do it for him. Then there were two brothers, passengers in the mail-coach. One pushed his thing into my mouth. And there were a gang of apprentices in the street outside the inn where the coach stopped, and one of them exposed himself to me. That's why I ran away full tilt, and was attacked and robbed, and after that I was so bewildered that I collided with your carriage.'

Maggie and Letitia both laughed heartily.

'Oh, my dear girl, you've a mighty lot to learn,' Maggie said when she had recovered her composure.

'But the Reverend Jollian was a churchman.' Lucy was still indignant about this.

'They're usually the most perverted,' Maggie informed her. 'Never trust a prelate with your money or your daughter, or even your young son, for that matter.'

'You've never said a truer word,' agreed a handsome young woman from the doorway. 'So you're awake, are you?' She approached the bed and stared down at Lucy with a curious expression on her face, in which mockery and pity vied for dominance.

'She is, my pet, and what an innocent,' Maggie said, draping an arm around the newcomer's shoulders. 'I want you to befriend her, Jocelyn. She needs bathing and dressing and training in our ways. Later, she can meet some of the girls.'

'You mean me to prepare her for the entertainment?' Jocelyn asked. She was a sprightly brunette with sparkling grey eyes and a trim figure plainly dressed in eggshell-blue, but the material of her dress was flimsy enough that her lithe torso and long legs could be discerned through it. Her breasts were enclosed by the low, square neckline, and the bodice had elbow-length sleeves with a closely corseted waist, a demure effect contradicted by the sharp points of her nipples raising the bouffant gauzy kerchief worn to give an impression of modesty.

'Not exactly,' Maggie replied, her brows lifting significantly. 'She is a virgin, and as such must be protected. I'm relying on you to safeguard her virtue until the time comes when we find the right gentleman for her.'

'What are you saying?' Lucy cried, alarmed by the words and actions of these unusual women, the likes of which she had never met before.

Maggie chucked her under the chin and looked deep into her eyes as she spoke. 'Every unattached girl in London needs a gentleman to set her up in keeping, Lucy. I might even be able to find you a husband. But until such time as either of these circumstances arise, you must remain pure.'

'I thought I was to be schooled in reading, writing and arithmetic,' Lucy reminded her, refusing to back down under that steady stare, 'with perhaps needlework and housekeeping skills included. And if this isn't the case, then I'd be grateful if you could tell me how to set about finding Templebar House.'

'Hush, hush, not so fast.' Maggie placed her scented fingertips across Lucy's lips. 'Did I say anything about you not being schooled? I'm but looking to your future. We entertain extensively and, in the fullness of time, you'll be meeting gentlemen guests.'

'There are a number expected tonight,' Jocelyn put in.

'You mean the students from the college across the road, don't you?' Maggie asked, her crimson mouth curled up in amusement. 'Well, she may be introduced to them, but she must be accompanied by one of us at all times. Do you understand?'

'Yes, mistress,' Jocelyn answered, as solemnly as a magistrate.

'Try to get up, Lucy,' Letitia urged, and placed an arm at Lucy's disposal. Feeling slightly dizzy, Lucy leaned against her for support.

'Where's that idle jade, Babette?' Maggie asked angrily.

'I'm here, mistress, I'm here!' The girl staggered back into the room beneath the weight of two wooden buckets filled with water. A footman followed her into the chamber similarly laden, and they both set the pails down near the fire. Then Babette disappeared into an adjacent dressing room and returned dragging a hipbath. It only took a matter of minutes for this to be set up on the hearthrug and filled with water, both hot and cold. Then Letitia swished it around with her hand, pronounced it to be satisfactory.

'In you get,' Letitia told Lucy, and she and Jocelyn began undressing her.

Maggie sat on the side of the bed, one long shapely leg crossed over the other and a cup of hot chocolate in her hand, wisps of steam rising from the delicate porcelain. A strapping young manservant had delivered the beverage on a silver tray. To Lucy's amazement, Maggie had run her hand over the cock-finger resting against his inner thigh, and then jiggled his balls in the well-tailored breeches that formed part of his smart livery.

The youth's brief appearance in the room had alarmed Lucy. She wanted desperately to be left alone to bathe, for she was unaccustomed to being stared at by strangers, her female secrets on full view. When her nightgown had been removed she stood with her knees together, one arm covering her breasts, her other hand spread over her mound.

'Don't be shy,' Maggie said. 'Though such modesty is a charming attribute, you have no need to fear anything from us.'

'I know that, ma'am,' Lucy murmured, 'it's just that I'm not used to being naked, or to bathing, for that matter. It wasn't considered necessary, or even healthy, where I come from. "Too much bathing weakens you", my mother used to say.'

'So did mine.' Maggie smiled wistfully. 'But that was long ago and far away. I didn't always live like this, you know. Like you, I'm no stranger to hardship.'

'Is that why you go out of your way to help young girls?'

'You ask too many questions, my dear.' Letitia held out a hand, which Lucy took. 'Now, in the tub with you.'

A knock at the door sent Lucy hurrying into the water,

crouching down with her knees drawn up beneath her chin as she tried to hide her naked body beneath the floating soapsuds. Her nipples were concealed, but not the upper curve of her breasts or her bare shoulders. The footman had returned with more buckets from the kitchen, solemn and straight-faced and showing no surprise whatsoever at finding a young lady in the bath.

When he had gone, Maggie said, 'I could not avoid seeing the marks of a beating on your buttocks, Lucy.' She plumped up the pillows on the bed behind her and relaxed against them, stretching her legs before her and crossing her feet at the ankles. 'New welts by the look of them, too, laid on by a belt, I'll wager. When did this happen?'

'The night before I reached London,' Lucy replied slowly, her head bowed as Letitia soaped a big yellow sponge and applied it to her hair, shoulders and back. 'Rufus Clough, one of the brothers I told you about, did it to me, and you're right, he used his belt.'

'You didn't get pleasure from your whipping?' Maggie asked, her hands cupping her breasts almost absently.

'No, ma'am!'

'Is this the truth? Didn't the lashes burn through your flesh and arouse your sex? Wasn't your humiliation tempered with the longing to impale yourself on his cock?'

Lucy's head hung lower so her dripping hair veiled her face. The woman's assessment of the event was uncanny. How could she possibly know the dark desires concealed in her heart? 'No, ma'am,' she whispered while Jocelyn lathered her palms and started smoothing them over her breasts and belly.

'Speak up, girl,' Maggie demanded.

'I said *no* ma'am,' Lucy repeated, suddenly bristling with annoyance. The woman was beautiful and had sheltered her in her hour of need, but this did not give her the right to order her about like this.

'Stand up and spread your legs,' Maggie said brusquely. 'I want to see your pussy.'

Lucy half rose from the water, and then recovered herself enough to snap, 'And what if I don't want you to see it? Am I to have no privacy here?'

'Defiant, are you?' Maggie's features hardened. 'We'll see about that. I expect obedience at all times. Do you understand?'

Lucy stepped from the bath and Maggie pounced on her, snatching at the towel she had grabbed to shield herself. It fell to the floor and, at the same time, Maggie's palm connected with her buttocks in a resounding slap that brought tear's to Lucy's eyes. She hopped to one side but could not avoid a second spanking blow.

'Oh, ma'am, don't, please!' she sobbed. 'What have I done to deserve this?'

'Nothing as yet, apart from giving me lip,' Maggie answered with ice-cold detachment. 'You need to be disciplined. You're a pretty piece and I will carry out my part of the bargain.'

'I don't recall making one.' Unable to cover her nakedness, Lucy flaunted it, standing upright with her head raised proudly as she resisted the temptation to rub her sore posterior.

'Not in so many words, perhaps, but the bargain is I will shelter you, and all I ask in return is that you follow my rules and take my advice when it comes to choosing a suitor.'

There was nothing sinister about this request, and Lucy really had no alternative but to agree with it. She was still feeling shaky, and her confrontation with her strong willed hostess had tired her. She was glad to sit on the dressing table stool while Letitia and Jocelyn fussed over her, drying her hair and brushing out the curly blonde tresses.

Maggie shrugged her fringed cashmere shawl about her, and drifted towards the door. 'I leave her to you,' she said, her hand on the latch. 'I shall expect her to be presentable by seven o'clock. She is to be dressed as befits a blameless virgin.'

When Maggie reached her own room, she stood for a moment collecting her thoughts. She had lied when she denied knowledge of Lord Ludlow and his townhouse. He was one of her regular customers, with a weakness for being wrapped in bandages until he looked like one of those Egyptian mummies she had seen at an exhibition of curios. Bound, blindfolded and gagged, with only his male member bared, he got his jollies by being bullied and then masturbated by one of her oldest, most dominating ladies.

She could hardly believe her incredible luck. At almost the same moment Tarquin had expressed his desire for a girl who would challenge his mastery, the Fates had delivered Lucy to her. He would be delighted with her, though suave enough to let no flicker of emotion show on his lean, saturnine face. Maggie would go up in his estimation, and though she never permitted herself to fall in love any more, having done so before and suffered the penalty, she harboured feelings for him that were better left undeclared. Besides which he would pay handsomely for a virgin, especially one as spirited and lovely as Lucy.

However, such a priceless commodity as a maidenhead was easily lost, so she decided to contact him without delay.

Seated at her escritoire, Maggie spread out a sheet of paper and chewed the end of her feather pen wondering how best to word her letter. Then she dipped the quill into the glass inkwell and wrote, *Lord Tarquin Hallagon, White's Club, St James Street, London.*

Here she paused for a moment wondering if she would not have done better to send the missive to Greyfriars. Then, after further consideration, she decided he was more likely to receive it sooner in that fashionable watering hole, and continued writing, the quill scratching across the parchment in harmony with the gentle sound of an ember collapsing into crumbling grey ash in the ornate fireplace. Humming beneath her breath, she read what she had set down, experiencing the usual warm glow at the sight of her elegant script.

She had been a guttersnipe once with no learning, no skills, and no prospects except that of whoring until she died of a horrible disease. It had either been selling her body or thieving and winding up dangling from the gallows. But now, as a result of hard work and careful use of her native wit – coupled with her willingness to take part in the most excessive and debauched areas of sexual activity – she owned a substantial residence in a respectable part of town, a secluded mansion surrounded by a large garden only a stone's throw from Hyde Park. Her splendid home had many bedrooms, a withdrawing room and a parlour, a large kitchen located in the basement and staff quarters in the attics. There was a reception area large enough to provide the venue for a ball, if required, to say nothing of punishment rooms in the cellars equipped with racks and pillories, whipping posts and chains and a cupboard full of paddles, canes, birches and riding crops. She pandered to all tastes, including those who preferred to roger young men, though male prostitutes and transvestites had their own brothels, known as *Molly Houses*, in another part of town. Though many madams were not so fussy, she drew the line at selling children and compromised by sometimes dressing up a few of her smallest ladies as schoolgirls.

Maggie kept an extensive wardrobe where the costumes included those of exotic Eastern concubines, pious nuns and demure housewives, dainty milkmaids and leather-clad, strident hussies expert at flagellation. Some of the rooms of her house were decorated to provide settings for any amount of fantasies, including a mock chapel for those who desired to seduce a holy woman. And then there was her own private apartment, consisting of a bedchamber and boudoir, where the most beautiful draperies and furnishings had been squirreled away. Her deprived childhood had made her greedy and she was determined never to go without again.

She folded the letter, wrote Tarquin's name on the back of it, and sealed the missive with a blob of red wax melted in the candle's flame. Deciding who should deliver it for her, she mentally ran through a list of possible candidates. Then her eyes narrowed and she smiled like a cat about to help itself to the cream.

She snuffed out the candle and ran lightly from the room, making for the backstairs connecting her wing of the house with the tradesman's entrance, the yard and the stable block. The letter held in one hand, she raised her skirt high to keep the hem out of the muck and entered the largest outbuilding, which housed her carriage horses and several vehicles. She blinked in the gloom. A single ray of light, grainy with dust, slanted through one of the windows, evoking bright sparks from the brass adorning polished harnesses hanging from hooks on the stone walls. Above her head, attained by a flight of rickety steps, was lodging for the grooms.

'Madam,' said a tall young man, his blue eyes lighting up at the sight of her.

Desire uncoiled like a spring in Maggie's womb. 'I have an errand for you, Barry,' she said softly, tucking the letter into his pocket. 'Deliver it to *White's Club*. Hand it to the porter there, and say it is for Lord Hallagon.'

He clicked his heels and stood to attention. 'Certainly, madam.'

He was a new groom who would soon be driving one of her grand carriages if he played his cards right. Her heart beat faster in her breast. There was no doubt about it; Barry was certainly worth bothering with. She liked the manner in which his beige breeches and tight boots fitted his long legs, and she saw that the promising bulge at the apex of his thighs was growing larger beneath her appraisal. Days ago, when he had first applied for a job, she had made a note of his firm, well-moulded arse.

He returned her stare, flushing to the roots of his toffee-coloured hair. He was bold enough with maidservants and shop girls, no doubt, but in awe of her. She was the boss, the woman who paid his wages, and he was afraid of offending her and losing his position.

She moved closer, unable to resist idling her fingers over the side of his face, feeling the rasp of stubble and permitting them to linger on his full lips. He stood like a statue as she insinuated her little finger between his lips. She felt his tongue circling it tentatively and wondered if he knew how to pleasure a woman by going down on her and nibbling her clitoris.

She withdrew her finger and he backed off a trifle. 'Don't worry,' she murmured, and linked her arms round his neck where his hair was plaited in a pigtail. 'How would you like to become a house servant? I'm sure I can find a vacancy.'

'Thank you, madam, but I want to work my way up to becoming a stagecoach man,' he answered enthusiastically. 'They're kings of the road.'

'I see, but you'll find working inside the house has its compensations,' she whispered and, taking his hand, placed it flat on her warm mound through her skirt.

He grunted in surprise, but unable to resist, he pushed the pad of his broad middle finger in deeper, penetrating her silk-veiled pussy. She moved sensually, rubbing herself on his digit, and he thrust in response, pressing his pelvis to hers with smooth motions. She could feel his hardness, a long bulge in his breeches, touching her groin with each stroke. The blood was singing in her veins, her nubbin tingled and her pussy yearned to be plugged by his cock. His eyes were glazed with lust and his rough hands grabbed at her breasts, pushing her bodice down to expose the alabaster flesh. He lifted her from her feet, lowering his head, and the touch of his lips on her nipple dragged a cry of pleasure from her, the sweet sensation echoing in her most intimate parts.

She fumbled with the placket of his breeches. It opened, and he was naked beneath it. His fuzz-coated lower belly felt hot and sweaty as she slipped her hand inside and took out his tool. It was so long and thick that she could not circle its girth with one hand. He groaned, and she experienced that thrill of power that always possessed her when she was in charge of a man's penis.

The stable was deserted. The only sound was the restless fidgeting of iron shod hooves and a gentle snorting as the fine, glossy coated beasts breathed in their stalls.

'Where is everyone?' she asked.

'In the nearest hostelry,' he replied hoarsely, and she saw the glint in his eyes in the semi-darkness as he looked down at his cock cradled in her hand.

'Just the horses and us,' she murmured. 'I can remember riding bareback and bringing myself off against the beast's bony spine helped by the rocking motion.'

'I can do better than that, ma'am,' he whispered, his voice increasingly husky with desire. 'You can see how horny I am. I'd love to be your mount and feel your tits bumping against my back and your juicy cunt rubbing against my arse.' He turned her around abruptly so her back was pressed against a hard wooden partition. A horse neighed behind it and tossed its head, expecting a feed bucket. The smell of hay was sweet and arousing, taking Maggie back in time to early exploits in similar surroundings.

'Shut up, Corsair,' Barry growled, and the animal quietened. His mouth sank over Maggie's thirstily and his hands hitched her skirt above her waist. He found her cleft, parted her sex lips, and his thumb landed unerringly

72

on her clit, rubbing it furiously.

She climaxed almost at once, erupting violently and crying out her pleasure.

He let her finish before lifting and impaling her on his swollen cock. She slid down over it, taking it all the way inside, her legs wrapping possessively around his hips as she did so. She flung her arms up and gripped the wooden beam above them, bracing herself against his violent pummelling as he slid her swiftly up and down the full length of his shaft, grunting with exertion and ecstasy. She clung to the beam and clasped him fiercely with her thighs, rising and falling, pumping and grinding against him, aware of the power gathering in his loins ready to explode in a white stream deep inside her.

A final convulsion shook him and his erection jerked, filling her with a hot blast of semen. He heaved against her, and then his spent weapon slipped out of her and she lowered her legs to the cobbles, his emission trickling down her thighs. It was like being a two-penny tart again giving some punter a knee-trembler against an alley wall. She liked the idea; it made her feel dirty and debased. It was fun to indulge herself like this now and then, knowing very well that she was rich.

Barry stood there looking sheepish as he tucked his penis away and did up his breeches.

Maggie let him stew for a moment, then when her dress was decently in place reached up on tiptoe to plant a kiss on his lips. 'Go straight to *White's* at once,' she told him firmly. 'Do you hear me? Deliver the letter. If you fail me, you'll find that my anger is as swift and fierce as my lust, and much more painful.'

'I feel like a princess,' Lucy said, her cheeks pink with excitement as she hesitated at the top of the wide staircase leading down into the ornate hall, illuminated by three chandeliers hanging from the elaborate plasterwork ceiling.

Each one must have held a hundred candles, at least; she had never seen so much artificial light. The dazzling rings of brightness hurt her eyes and threatened to bring back her headache as she peered down at the soft-footed lackeys bearing trays of drinks, their faces bland and disdainful surrounded by opulent decor. There was a great deal of crimson velvet and gilding, and she was convinced the king's palace could not be more luxurious.

'You *look* like a princess,' Letitia agreed, proud of her handiwork. 'A far cry from the poor creature I rescued from the streets.'

'She's cleaned up well, I'll grant you,' Joyce remarked from Lucy's other side. 'Get rid of that West Country twang, give her a few lessons in dancing and deportment, fashion and small talk, and no one will be any the wiser.'

Lucy caught a glimpse of herself in one of the several large Venetian mirrors hanging on the gallery walls. She was dressed entirely in white, in a loose-fitting cotton muslin dress that swirled around her ankles, her small waist emphasised by a satin sash fastened with a large bow at the back. The gown's neckline was oval, the sleeves short and puffy, and made her look younger than her years, as did her loosely arranged blonde curls. She wore flat-heeled black kid pumps crisscrossed with ribbons, which added to the overall impression of innocence and immaturity.

'Come along, my dear,' Letitia urged, and led her by the hand down the stairs into the black-and-white tiled hall, which boasted marble pillars, alcoves containing naked Greek statues or spiky tropical plants, and glorious stained-glass windows. Dance music emerged from the saloon as people drifted from room to room, laughter and conversation mingling with the sound of lutes and harpsichords.

Letitia took her around, introducing her to this person and that, and Lucy could not help noticing that while several of the women were as sedately gowned as duchesses, others leaned over the railing of the upper landing wearing nothing but corsets and frilly chemises, their legs exposed in silk stockings and their nipples bright with carmine. It was also strange to see a mother superior amongst the guests wearing the traditional black habit and white wimple, and shepherding three schoolgirls in matching uniforms who seemed overbold as they flirted with male guests, actually encouraging them to touch them.

Lucy felt herself becoming the centre of much interest, but then Maggie appeared and took charge of her. 'My goddaughter,' she explained, leading Lucy by the hand and easily warding off impertinent questions and amorous advances with this explanation. 'She is not to be confused with the rest.'

Lucy was bemused by the rococo furniture, the hand painted wallpaper with its oriental motifs, the bevy of gorgeous women and the plethora of good-looking men mingling with older gentleman who were mostly overweight and unattractive. 'I thought you said there would be students here tonight,' she reminded Maggie.

'Oh, there are, and they're all in the parlour playing blind man's buff.'

'Can I join in?' Lucy asked, feeling oddly out of place and wanting to fit in somehow.

'Can she, mistress?' enquired Joyce, with a smile.

'She may watch, that is all,' Maggie answered sternly, and swished the crop she carried against the side of her purple taffeta skirt in silent warning.

'There's a gentleman here to see you, madam,' announced a footman.

'Is it he whom I expect?' she asked, touching the whip to her lips thoughtfully.

'Yes, madam.'

'Then I shall leave you for a while, Lucy. Make sure you carry out your instructions to the letter, Joyce, and don't be careless. You are in charge, Letitia.'

The side room was dimly lit and cosy. It had once been a library, judging by the amount of books in glass-fronted cases lining the walls. Young people of both sexes circled a girl who groped about in the centre, her arms outstretched, her eyes covered by a black scarf. She was naked to the waist, and the rest of the players were also in various stages of undress. They pretended to be frightened of her blind search, ducking and weaving away from her, but she finally caught a wiry youth with long dark hair and shrieked in triumph, 'I've got you!' as she pulled off the blindfold. 'You must pay a forfeit,' she declared, 'and then it's your turn!'

All he had on were his breeches, and now he unbuckled his belt and dropped them, bending over to free his feet.

Lucy did not know where to look, her cheeks burning as her eyes were irresistibly drawn to his dark thatch and pronounced genitals. The situation was obviously exciting him, for his cock was as stiff as a lance, and several girls gathered round him to caress it, giggling happily.

'Naughty ones!' Letitia exclaimed, pretending to be shocked. 'What are you doing?'

The girls giggled even harder as the young man grinned.

'Oh, come on, Letitia,' a fellow with a swarthy face and dark hair said coaxingly, 'you know what we get up to in here. We pay extra for it, don't we?' He slipped an arm around her waist and pulled her close to plant kisses on her ample bosom, and then silence her protests with his lips.

More than ever, Lucy did not know where to look.

One girl lay on the floor now, a man between her upraised thighs, his cock buried deep inside her. Another girl was seated astride a youth's lap, his weapon thrust up into her belly as his hands tweaked her nipples.

The girl who had been blindfolded leapt upon the fellow she had caught, bearing him down on a daybed and sitting on his face, enveloping him in her scented avenue.

Letitia shook off the dark young man. 'Well, my dear,' she addressed Lucy, 'what do you think of it all?'

'To tell the truth, ma'am, I don't know *what* to think.' Everywhere she looked there were couples engaged in the most intimate acts. 'Does this happen frequently? What about our lessons?'

'Aren't these the most important of all, lessons in love?' Jocelyn asked tenderly, her arm snaking around Lucy's waist. 'Or perhaps you prefer the embraces of your own kind?'

'I don't know what you mean,' Lucy gasped.

Jocelyn laughed. 'I really believe you don't. But come, Maggie wants you taken up to her room.'

Chapter Five

Lucy had thought the downstairs rooms were the height of magnificence, but she was rendered speechless by her first sight of Maggie's private quarters. It seemed incredible, downright cruel and unfair, that there were some who lived in such luxury while others inhabited the squalor she had experienced, albeit briefly, in the London streets. Where had Maggie acquired her wealth? Had she inherited it or married into it? There seemed no evidence of a husband anywhere about, so perhaps she was widow.

'You like this?' murmured Letitia, her breath tickling Lucy's ear. 'You've never seen anywhere more opulent, have you? A far cry from the cowsheds and pigsties of home, eh?' She was as proud as if the rooms belonged to her.

Lucy nodded, gazing down at the carpet's arabesques and stylised flowers. Then Jocelyn took her by the hand, led her through the boudoir to the sleeping chamber beyond, and across to the bed. The headboard was inlaid with silver and had a domed tester like an Arabian tent, the corners surmounted by plumes plucked from an ostrich's tail. The coverlet was a pristine spread of white fox fur, the sheets and pillowcases embroidered in slippery gold silk.

'Take off your clothes and lie down,' Jocelyn ordered gently.

'But I can't,' Lucy protested. 'I don't want to, and it's all too grand, and she'll be angry if I crumple her bed.'

'Silly goose, we're following Maggie's instructions.' She smacked Lucy's bottom with such surprising strength that the sting of the blow penetrated her skirt. 'Now strip.'

Lucy was tired of enduring the slaps the women of this household thought they could administer any time they wanted to, and the scene in the library had shaken her to the very marrow. 'I want to go to my room,' she said coldly, taking a determined step towards the door. 'I'm not fully recovered. The way you speak to me isn't nice, and the behaviour of the girls who live here is downright vulgar. I'll trouble you no further, and take my leave of you in the morning. I'm sure there must be some friendly soul who will advise me how to reach Templebar House.'

'Leaving us? How sad.' Jocelyn's smile was so sweet that Lucy's resolution wavered. 'We shall miss you. Shan't we, Letitia?'

'You are not going anywhere, Lucy, not until the mistress says you may,' Letitia said briskly. 'On the bed with her, Jocelyn.'

Before she knew what was happening, Lucy found herself sprawled across the furs, her face buried in the scented pillows, cushions stuffed under her belly raising her hips high. Then Letitia looped thick silk cords round her wrists and ankles, and tethered her to the bedposts as Jocelyn folded her skirt back over her waist and lifted her short chemise. Cool air on her warm skin and exposed sex told Lucy the lower half of her body was now naked, apart from her white stockings and black kid pumps. The fur beneath her thighs felt seductively soft, nothing like the patchwork quilts her mother had made by begging scraps of material from friends and staying up till all hours sewing, straining her eyes in the feeble light of a tallow-dip. Nevertheless, she longed to be home again away from the tainted atmosphere of this fine house, and away from these painted harpies who pretended to be kind and affectionate but who obviously had hidden motives. It was like a dream, not a nightmare exactly, it was too luxurious for that, but she still hoped to wake up in her narrow bed under the thatched roof of her father's farmhouse.

'You must learn not to be impertinent to those who have your welfare at heart,' Letitia reprimanded her mildly, 'and who are willing to teach you the lesson of submission.'

Without warning, pain shot through Lucy as a hand landed with merciless force across her exposed bottom. She bucked against the cords holding her down. 'Damn you!' she swore. 'You can't do this to me! I'm not your servant or a slave! I thought I was a guest here!'

'It's for your own good.' Letitia delivered another blow, harder than the first and followed by two more of equal force.

'Oh please, stop!' Lucy begged, writhing against the bed. Then she felt fingers kneading her stinging buttocks and dipping into the valley between them. They were busy fingers, their soft tips darting over her arsehole and going lower to delve into her moist delta before flickering up to her clitoris. This flirtation with the heartland of her pleasure made her moan with reluctant pleasure, and even though she did her best to suppress it, a sweetly unbearable ache began in her sex.

Jocelyn leaned over her, wormed her hands beneath her breasts, and lightly squeezed them, toying with her nipples.

'Oh yes, that's so good,' Lucy whispered, relaxing. 'I'm sorry. Untie me, please, I *want* to learn, I really do.' The pain of the spanking had dimmed to a pleasant warmth spreading through her buttocks and down into her thighs and lower belly. Her labia felt wet, her clitoris deliciously swollen.

'We can untie you now that you've had a little taste of chastisement,' Letitia said, and slipped the cords off Lucy's wrists.

She sat up, and the glittering bed enfolded her like some exotic flower as Letitia and Jocelyn began removing their garments piece by piece, their movements slow and sensuous. Lucy was shocked to see the stigmata of punishment on the hinds of both women. Here was a strange school indeed, where even the teachers were caned.

'This is the first lesson,' Jocelyn said, 'how to disrobe alluringly. It's something of an art.' She leaned over so her pert breasts popped out above the frilled edge of her waist-clinching corset. Pretending to be unaware of Lucy, she pinched each of her taut brown nipples, and then hooked a finger into the front lacing, freeing it until the garment unfolded and she was able to whip it off. Her gown already lay over a chair along with her petticoat. Now, with seemingly careless abandon, she removed her chemise, placed a foot on the edge of the bed, and walked her fingers down to her fork, playing with herself before unbuckling her garter belt and slipping off her stockings. Finally, she wetted a digit in her juices and trailed it across her young student's lips.

Lucy was hugely embarrassed. Until that night she had never seen women naked any more than she had seen men without their clothes on. It had not been considered proper; no one in her village had celebrated the pagan rites of the flesh or gloried in it. She could not keep her eyes off the mature Letitia, whose bosom was full and heavy, her waist thick and her hips of equally generous proportions. In contrast, Jocelyn's figure was almost boyish, sharp-hipped and firm-breasted. Letitia's mound was coated in crisp dark hair, but Lucy was astonished to see that Jocelyn's was smooth, without the slightest trace of down.

The young woman laughed at Lucy's surprise, and taking her hand placed it on her shaven pubis.

Lucy found the sensation enchanting. Its stark nudity made its shape more pronounced and the smooth, budlike lips struck her as extremely lovely.

'You like?' Jocelyn asked, leaning on the bedpost and eyeing her seductively. 'I expect Maggie will have you shaved as well. Some men demand it, you see. You want to feel it some more?'

'Yes,' Lucy murmured, even though there were several life-size portraits on the walls in the shadows beyond the candlelight that all seemed to be staring at her, and judging her shocking behaviour.

'Go on, then,' Jocelyn urged, thrusting her pelvis up a little and giving Lucy greater access to her treasures. The strong perfume of honeyed juices rose from her, and Lucy advanced a nervous finger, scarcely daring to brush her hand across the fascinating delta.

'She's not ready yet,' Letitia warned. 'Let's show her what to do.' And suddenly she drew Jocelyn down with her into the silky depths of Maggie's bed.

The two women stroked and caressed each other, touching their breasts and bellies and pubic areas. Their mouths met and they kissed with their eyes open, savouring the taste of wine-flavoured lips as their tongues danced together. Then after a while, Jocelyn smiled over at Lucy. 'Join us,' she urged.

They looked so relaxed and happy that Lucy hoisted her skirt up and crept closer, her nubbin pulsing with need.

'That's better.' Disentangling herself from her lover, Jocelyn sat up and unfastened the sash and the buttons at the back of Lucy's dress preparatory to lifting it up over her head, followed by her chemise. Then she turned back to Letitia and gently fondled her breasts, sucking the stiffened nipples and drawing little moans of delight from her. Their movements were leisurely, and yet though they treated one another like loving friends, they were breathless with passion. Jocelyn spread Letitia's legs and stroked her fissure, using two fingers to hold back the hair-fringed lips, and licked her paramour's clit until she reached the pinnacle of delight, from which she brought her down slowly, soothing the ardent little organ and lying back so Letitia could make love to her in return.

Lucy was enthralled, her reticence swiftly giving way to lust. She had never realised women could gain such joy through intimacy with their own kind. She watched Jocelyn surrender herself to pleasure, the delicate sap of her sex smelling like pinewood floating on seawater. Then Letitia dipped her fingers into a pot of fragrant oil on the nightstand and massaged Jocelyn's body, working upwards from her feet to her shoulders. She knelt over her and her fingers worked on her calves, her knees and her thighs teasingly, then moved up to caress her nipples, her ribs and her navel before finally making their way down to her cloven inlet.

Losing control, hardly aware of what she was doing, Lucy grabbed at her crotch, spread wide her legs and frigged her little nubbin wildly. She was very wet, her heart thundering and her excitement mounting, as she kept pace with Jocelyn's approaching crisis. The older, more experienced woman reached her apogee first, shuddering and gasping as she trapped Letitia's hand between her thighs.

'Ah yes, I want it, too,' Lucy cried, her finger moving frantically over her clitoris. 'I want to come...'

'No!' a man's voice commanded, and she stopped dead on the point of climax, her hand cupping her pulsating pussy, her head lifted to stare at the apparition that had manifested with such startling speed from a sliding panel in the wall. She scrambled off the bed as he strode across the room towards her, towering over her. She looked up into a pair of dark brown eyes in which she read desire, and a frightening, age-old knowledge. She suffered an impression of arrogance and power staring up at an angular face with a strong nose and sensual lips framed by hair the colour of jet. Everyone else seemed to vanish as she

83

felt herself lifted and suspended by an invisible force, every nerve in her body screaming the warning that she did not want to know this man.

'Make obeisance, girl,' said Maggie, who had followed close on his heels. 'This is Lord Tarquin Hallagon.'

Lucy dropped into a deep curtsey, though it was hard to be graceful when she was trying to hide her nakedness with her hands, all the time wondering how much he had seen. She dared to glance up at him again, and at once Maggie rapped her smartly on the head with her knuckles.

'No one has given you permission to move, girl.'

Lucy studied Tarquin's elegant boots as he reached down and placed an aristocratic finger beneath her chin, lifting it so she could not avoid his eyes.

'So, you are Lucy Browne,' he drawled, and she knew she was lost forever. Suddenly, she knew that whatever happened in the future, this man would always own a part of her soul.

'Yes, sir…'

He took her hand and helped her rise. She felt the clasp of his fingers and his thumbnail tickling her palm. No one had ever done that to her before and it gave her goose bumps and made her pussy juices flow. His clothes were superb – a jacket of sombre black velvet, a waistcoat scintillating with silver thread, a black cravat, a black fall of lace at his cuffs, and the tightest of black breeches that clung as if moulded to his lean flanks and accentuated the shape of his penis curled beneath them.

'She's delightful, Maggie,' he remarked, releasing Lucy's hand and producing a snuffbox from an inner pocket of his cravat. He gathered up a pinch, balanced the brown powder at the base of his thumb, and gracefully applied it to his left nostril, and then his right.

'I'm glad you're pleased,' Maggie said, gazing at him alertly and affectionately.

'Ecstatic, struck dumb,' he elaborated, his voice laden

with sarcasm. He flicked out a lace-edged kerchief and dabbed delicately at his nose, then nodded towards Letitia and Jocelyn, who were kneeling on either side of him. 'You gave a pretty display of Sapphic love, most uplifting. I very nearly spent in Maggie's throat as I watched through the spy holes, but I decided to keep it for later. I had a fine view, peering through the eyes of that painting over there,' he gestured laconically, 'the one of a deceased justice of the peace, though you'd never guess his exalted position as he chose to be painted wearing his mother's ball gown.'

'We were about to introduce her to lesbian ways, my lord,' Letitia informed him, and Lucy was astonished to see how much respect she accorded him.

A frown drew his black brows together and his eyes flashed fire. 'As well for you that you did not!' he thundered. 'Maggie says she's a virgin and I shall be the first person to bring on her crisis. Not only her cunny and arsehole will be stretched by me, but her bud shall experience untold delights when I lick and finger it.'

'Oh, so you've decided to buy her, have you?' Maggie asked acerbically.

'I may,' his eyes penetrated hers as his lips curved up in an ironic smile, 'if the price is right.'

Lucy could endure no more. 'This is monstrous!' she cried. 'I am not a chattel to be bought and sold!'

One of Tarquin's brows arched and he raised the gold lorgnette dangling round his neck on a black ribbon. He lifted it to his eyes and quizzed her through it, his movements languid. 'Did I say you could speak?' Without waiting for her reply, he dropped the eyeglasses and went on matter-of-factly. 'That is precisely what you are, a piece of property, at the present time owned by Mrs Main but soon to belong to whomsoever offers her the most money for you.'

'No!' Lucy stormed, stamping her foot, her naked

breasts bouncing. 'I shall go to the magistrate and tell him all about you, and about you, Mrs Main! I see you for what you really are now. You're nothing but a bawd and a brothel keeper! You should be flung into gaol!'

'Ungrateful bitch!' Maggie shrieked, and launched herself on Lucy, but Tarquin grabbed his hostess, pulled her up short and administered a flat, open-handed smack to her *derrière*. 'Leave her to me,' he said crisply.

Maggie jerked herself free of him. 'She isn't yours yet,' she snapped.

'As good as, damn it.'

'We've not struck a deal yet.'

'All right, how much do you want for her?'

'Fifty guineas.'

'Daylight robbery,' he snarled.

'Take it or leave it,' she retorted. 'I shan't be short of punters. Every man wants a virgin, a tight little unused cunny that won't give him a dose of the pox.'

Lucy almost admired her. It took a lot of spirit to argue with such a man. He was so self-assured and certain of his God-given right to ride roughshod over everyone that his mere aura made her shiver with trepidation. Yet at the same time, she had never felt more alive in his presence as the focus of his attention.

'Forty,' he growled, and Lucy was amazed at the sums being bandied about for her. Back home a farmhand could not expect to earn that much during the whole of his working life.

'Forty-five, and she's yours.' Maggie stood her ground without flinching.

'Done,' he said, and they shook hands. 'Will you take an IOU? You can collect the money tomorrow.'

Maggie pressed close to him, a sensual woman but also a vixen believing in nothing and no one. 'You don't touch the girl until the money is in my hands,' she stated in honeyed tones, and kissed him as punctuation.

'You have my word as a gentleman,' he said icily.

'That's why I hesitate. Gentleman, indeed! They're the very worst of liars. "Who sups with the devil needs a long spoon", my lord.'

'I want to test her myself first,' he insisted haughtily.

'I can assure you her maidenhead is intact. Letitia examined her.'

'And that is supposed to reassure me?' His sarcasm was scathing. 'You can't fool me, Maggie. String her up so I may find out for myself and, if I'm satisfied, you'll get your money.'

'Money before you finger her,' Maggie repeated stubbornly. 'If she doesn't come up to scratch, then I'll give you a refund.'

He swore, but thrust a hand into his coat pocket. Out came a purse that clinked invitingly. He passed it over to Maggie, who sat down at her desk and poured out a stream of gold coins. She counted them quickly, and then looked over at him with a bright smile. 'All right,' she said sweetly.

'How did you know I'd carry that amount?' he enquired, flicking an imaginary speck of snuff from his lapel.

'A calculated guess, my lord. I figured that once you clapped eyes on Lucy you wouldn't be able to resist or wait until tomorrow to possess her. I was right, wasn't I?'

'Aren't you always, you witch?' Leaning over her, he took her hand in his and raised it to his lips reverentially.

'I've been in the business long enough to know men's failings and weaknesses,' she explained, but her voice was husky and her eyes glowed as she gazed up at him.

Lucy had had enough. These despicable persons were discussing her as if she was a heifer brought to market. 'And what about me?' she asked belligerently. 'Don't I have a say in it? I don't *want* to belong to his lordship. I don't *want* to be owned by anyone, man or woman. I want the freedom to go where I wish and with whomever I choose.'

Maggie stood up and walked over to her, her skirts rustling, a slender, beribboned cane grasped in one hand. It was not only a fashion accessory, like her fan, but had another, more sinister purpose. The ferule trailed up Lucy's leg and stopped when it reached her fork. She stood transfixed as it burrowed into her cleft, parting the moist lips and rubbing their folds to tease her clitoris free from its fleshy cowl. Then Maggie withdrew it and held it up for all to see.

'You may protest all you like, Lucy, but your body betrays you. My cane is soaked with love juice where it touched your cunt. You owe me, and the debt must be repaid. I took you in off the streets, nursed you, had a doctor attend you, and supplied you with a bed, a nightgown and a party dress. I fed you, as well. The bill for all this would be extensive, but I'll settle for Lord Tarquin's forty guineas and consider I'm being over generous with you.'

'You had this planned all along, didn't you?' Lucy cried, pointing an accusative finger at her mercenary hostess. 'As soon as you found out I was a virgin, you thought of ways to make money out of me. All right, I'll become your maidservant and pay off my debt even if it takes me a lifetime to do so, but I'll not whore for you, not ever!'

'Oh fie, what a temper,' Tarquin scoffed. 'I admire such spirit, but you'll find you can't say nay to me, wench.'

'Can't I? We'll see about that!' But even as she began another fiery tirade, Lucy found herself unable to concentrate under his penetrating regard. She faltered, and fell silent. A damning moment passed, and in the room's sudden quiet she was sure they could all hear the thudding of her heart.

'I don't need another servant,' Maggie said smoothly.

'Do what you will, my lord, to satisfy yourself I spoke the truth when I vowed she was unspoilt.'

He moved with the speed of a striking cobra. Seizing Lucy's wrist, he pulled her against the heat and muscular hardness of him. She struggled, but when his free hand cupped one of her breasts and began moving over every inch of her exposed body, something strange happened inside her. The will to resist him dissolved. The jacket rubbing against her nipples was of the finest weave, the lace at his chest chaffed her, but it was an expensive titillation, reeking of class and position. He was a true gentleman, and she had always dreamed of such a man. If he declared his love for her, then it would be different, but to be sold to him was unendurable. So when he bent his head to kiss her, she jerked away from him and spat in his face.

Tarquin let her go, his smile deadly. He grabbed a handful of her hair, and wiped away her spittle with it. 'A spiteful little kitten,' he said mockingly, 'but you will endure my examination, and you will enjoy it. I dare you to look into my eyes and deny the longings that wrack you, Lucy, the lust that is screaming out to be fulfilled, the need to be mastered. You can't lie to me, can you, my dear?'

'I hate you!' she hissed.

He threw his head back and laughed. 'Bravo, that's excellent! It adds to my pleasure. There's little amusement to be gained in rogering a willing wench. Fight away. Kick and scratch and claw me like a wildcat. The end result will be the same.' He nodded to Maggie. 'Time for a little correction, I think.'

'Indeed, sir, she's a fiery wench.'

Lucy glared at him as he lowered himself onto an armless brocade chair, but in a flash Maggie grabbed her and shoved her down across his lap. Too surprised to do other than splutter, she was acutely conscious of his hand on her backside, of the scent of his body, of the nap of his breeches and of his hidden cock pressing into her side. 'What are you going to do?' she gasped. 'Let me go at once, sir!'

'Do? I am going to spank you for being such a troublesome jilt,' he replied, his voice husky. But he made her wait, prolonging her anxious anticipation. 'You're a dirty slut, aren't you? You like this. You're very, very wet, but you must learn I'll not tolerate your lechery, Lucy. You must keep it all for me, unless I give you leave to do otherwise, and you must acknowledge me as your master.'

'Never!' she cried, and felt a sudden draught as he raised his hand and brought it down smartly on her bottom. She yelped, more from shock than from pain. He slapped her again, harder this time, and she threshed across his thighs, trying to escape. He increased the force of his blows, and the heat of her welt-covered posterior became almost unbearably intense. He stopped for a moment, laying a cool palm on her reddened skin, and then resumed spanking her with such energy that she bucked frantically against him trying to fling herself to the floor.

'Oh no you don't,' he growled, and his free hand pinioned her round the neck as his blows rained down on her burning buttocks. 'You seem to be one of those stubborn, spirited girls who need to receive a lot of punishment,' he muttered. 'But I'll break you, young lady, never fear.'

She screamed and squirmed and begged him to stop. She bounced up and down against his rock-hard knees, each assault on her fiery flesh accompanied by a resounding clap that echoed around the room. Then the burning sensation began mysteriously communicating with her clitoris, and she ground down against his thighs seeking friction on her rampant little button even as her action dumbfounded her.

'Say it,' he commanded. 'Call me master.'

'I won't,' she shouted, and started crying she was so

confused by all the contradictory feelings raging inside her.

Tarquin stopped spanking her and shoved her off his lap. She hit the carpet with a dull thud and hugged herself, sobbing. He stood up.

'She needs more persuasion,' Maggie concluded. 'Bring her.'

Letitia and Jocelyn each took hold of one of Lucy's arms, hauled her to her feet, and dragged her, protesting and struggling, into the boudoir.

There was something different about it, and then she realised the crimson drapes she had noticed before had been drawn apart to reveal a low stage on which stood a strange and frightening object shaped like a cross, and her heart missed a beat as she saw it had ringbolts screwed into it.

With strength born of desperation, Lucy wrested free of the two women and sprinted towards the outer door, but a whistling crack gave her scant warning as the long lash of a bullwhip wrapped itself around her body and wrestled her to the floor. It stung and paralysed her, leaving a long pink stripe against her skin. The whip was wielded by Tarquin, and she struggled to her knees as he tugged on it, dragging her across the floor towards him, the hide lassoed around her. Planting his feet firmly apart he struck a pose, his upper lip curling in contempt.

'Ah no, my dear, I've not finished with you yet.' The plaited handle of the whip was wound around his hand, and he gave it a jerk. It snapped away from her as if with a life of its own and quivered into a coil at his feet.

The boudoir took on a fearsome aspect. Lucy could see implements hanging on hooks near the stage or standing in large Chinese vases. He must have snatched the whip from one of them without a second thought and used it to prevent her escape. He was as ruthless as he was handsome and she was repelled but also fascinated by him. Her body shivered and her spirit quaked as she remembered the sinister hissing sound that preceded the kiss of the whip searing her flesh. And as she was hung on the crosspiece, metal cuffs on her wrists, manacles on her ankles and a wooden spreader bar between her knees, somewhere in the midst of her humiliation she became aware of a small, still space like the eye of a storm inside her where she found herself accepting, even welcoming, his domination.

'Doesn't she look pretty, my lord,' Maggie crooned, pacing round her slowly. 'I knew from the start that she'd adorn my whipping post. For so rural a chit, she has a certain natural elegance and grace. With training in speech and deportment, we could pass her off as a duchess.'

'And wouldn't that be amusing?' he replied, examining implements and selecting a wooden paddle covered in black leather. 'I've a mind to do just that. What a jest to introduce her to royalty at a gala held at Buckingham Palace. I'm certain I could get away with it. Who should I say she is…? I know, Lady Lucinda, the daughter of the Duke of Sheerwater.' He struck the paddle against his palm.

Lucy cringed, though it was nowhere near her bottom, and gasped when he stroked it over her thighs. Then, with an agile flick of his wrist, he brought it down more forcefully. It was less painful than Rufus's belt, but hurt more than being spanked even though she sensed he was holding back.

He let fly another blow, aiming at her belly just above the sharp line of her pubic triangle, and she whimpered in anguish, sagging in her chains as the paddle made a slapping sound every time it hit her flesh, moving gradually up her body so that not even her breasts were spared. She had sworn to herself that she would not cry or beg for mercy, but her good intentions abandoned her as he paddled her with steady, inexorable determination.

'Please, oh please, my lord, stop!' she howled. 'That's

enough!'

He stood back and tossed the paddle to the waiting Letitia. 'I trust you are now willing to call me your master, Lucy?'

She could hardly draw breath, but she managed to pant, 'Yes!'

'Haven't you forgotten something?'

'Yes... *master*.'

He bent and kissed the crimson marks he had left on her belly. His hair fell forward, brushing across her sore thighs, and as his tongue caressed her, the pain began fading even as the heat remained and transformed into a deep excitement.

He looked up at her. 'My dear, you are an apt pupil,' he said almost kindly. 'Soon you will accept that women are complicated and need to be mastered in order to feel loved. Are you beginning to understand this?'

Lucy wanted to shake her head, but she did not dare. She had thought love was a caring, sharing process, but the dichotomy of the pain she was experiencing coupled with the fiery darts of pleasure from her nipples to her clitoris, were changing her ideas quickly and dramatically.

He stroked the soft brown hair of her mound, the edges of her plump labial wings, and then the dusky avenue between them. His fingers fondled her gently, and then teased the hard nub of her clitoris as she moaned and thrust against his hand. He probed the entrance of her vagina with his thumb, and she flinched.

'You see, my lord,' Maggie said, 'Letitia was right, hers is a virgin portal.'

'It appears to be so, I'll grant you,' he agreed, and rimmed Lucy's anus with a curious finger. 'This one, too. I may have to use butt plugs on her. Her arse will need stretching.' He pressed down hard on her clitoris and waggled the stiff little organ from side to side, smiling up into her stunned eyes. 'Take punishment along with pleasure, girl. You can't begin to imagine the delights I can show you. I'll lead you down dark pathways of lust, and it's what you want. Isn't it, darling? You want me to bring you off with my fingers.'

'Oh yes, but it's not right,' she moaned, anguished and ashamed.

He laughed deep in his chest. 'You've been brought up in the country among God-fearing peasants. You've been taught you can't expect to enjoy yourself without paying the price. You believe God's counterpart is Satan, and that if you enjoy the sins of the flesh you'll end up in hell. This is nonsense, my dear. Why did this so-called God give us lustful feelings if he did not expect us to act on them?'

'You blaspheme, sir,' she cried, desperately fighting her wicked desire to climax.

'Rubbish,' he murmured, and sealed her mouth with his.

She answered his kiss passionately, intoxicated with need, pushing down on his hand with her hips and wantonly encouraging his exploration. She was close to her culmination, her nubbin throbbing with approaching bliss. Hanging limp from the cross, she totally surrendered herself to Tarquin's experienced seduction. She was straining to reach her peak, but he kept her suspended on it for long moments, displaying his power over her. Then with a final hard caress, he shoved her over the edge into an orgasm so intense she blacked out for an instant.

She came back from a star-filled space expecting him to consummate the act. He did not. He unlocked the cuffs and leg irons, and caught her in his arms as she fell. He steadied her, and she chafed her sore wrists waiting for his next move, anticipating he would take her, wanting him to. She was eager to feel the size and force of the impressive phallus distorting the front of his breeches. Instead he put his hands on her shoulders and pushed her down until she was kneeling before him. Then using a handful of her hair as a reign, he pulled her head towards his crotch and loosened the flap of his breeches.

Lucy drew in a sharp breath as his erection sprang out at her from a nest of black curls. It was swarthy and veined and curved upwards, the foreskin retracted to expose the bulging, twin-lobbed helm and a glistening bead of moisture crowning the tiny slit. She had been disgusted when the vicar showed her his penis and asked her to rub it, but this specimen was impressive, shockingly large and for some reason profoundly exciting. Suddenly she longed to impale herself on it, to ride it and lose the cursed virginity that was causing her so much grief.

'Take it,' he growled. 'Suck it. Make me groan with pleasure.' He shifted his hips so the tip of his prick nudged her lips.

In her imagination Lucy saw Simon's revolting cock, smelt its cheesy odour and felt its length jabbing the back of her throat. She hesitated, but only for a fraction of a second, then she took Tarquin's shaft into her mouth's soft warm cavity.

Sucking him was easier than she had thought it would be. In a high state of arousal, she stroked her hands up and down his pillar, her tongue responding to its satin smoothness. She ran the tip around the ridge of his foreskin, finding a different flavour there, and then burrowed into the little hole at the top. She was a novice, but she followed her instincts and the carnal desire making her clitoris glow and her nipples stiffen.

'God God, it's second nature to her,' he breathed.

Hearing his praise she grew bolder, pushing her other hand below his rampant cock and cupping his balls. This was a new delight and she weighed them, letting her fingers enjoy the texture of the skin, and the line dividing them into a pair of fruits ripe for the plucking. And as she petted them, she did not let up on the regular rhythm of her stroking hands or on the sucking, squeezing motion of her mouth and the busy tickling of her tongue.

Allowing herself a quick glance upwards, she saw that his head was thrown back and his whole body was taut with desire. She rocked on her heels, all her pain forgotten, as she felt a mysterious power surge through her. With dextrous agility she brought him towards his crisis with her hands and her lips, her cheeks hollowed with the effort she made to please him. He could not resist chasing his orgasm, a victim of her mouth and his bodily demands. He thrust and thrust and she nearly gagged as she felt his semen spurt in creamy jets onto the back of her tongue and down her throat. She swallowed it, and went on milking him until he slipped abruptly out of her mouth and spattered her face, her hair and her neck with the last drops of his spunk.

He wiped his cock on his kerchief and adjusted his garments without looking at her. Then he strolled over to Maggie. 'Keep the money,' he said. 'She's a virgin now, but not for long.'

'Don't you intend to enjoy her to the full tonight, sir?' she asked, pouring him a glass of claret.

He took a sip before replying, 'I have plans for her deflowering. You know I like diversity. I'm not some brutish clod who throws himself on a girl and satisfies his base lusts with a few crude thrusts. No, I prefer my meat garnished, and I have a more sophisticated feast for the senses in mind.'

'You want me to keep her here in the meantime and possibly apply dildos to her anus, my lord?'

'I think not. She shall live at Greyfriars and there I will undertake her initiation myself.'

'Where are my clothes?' Lucy blurted. 'If I'm to travel with you, sir, I can't go naked.'

'We threw away the things you were wearing on your arrival,' Maggie informed her with a look of distaste. 'They were only fit for the ragman. Keep the white dress and a shawl. They should suffice until you're taken shopping. Don't you feel better now? You should thank me for providing for your welfare.'

Lucy dressed hurriedly. She had no alternative but to obey. She was afraid and yet also strangely exhilarated. Her head held high, she flung the shawl around her like a royal robe, and ignoring the women she felt had betrayed her, followed the handsome young lord she now belonged to from the room.

Chapter Six

Tarquin viewed his new piece of property with mixed feelings. She was seated silently in his carriage as it bowled through streets of London. Her face was briefly illuminated by the flambeaux the law decreed must be kept burning after dark outside every great house in the Mayfair, Hyde Park and the West End district in a bid to cut down on crime, a forlorn hope at best. No expression crossed her face; she looked like a graven image. He sat opposite her and touched her foot with his now and again, amused by the way she clamped her legs together and shrank back against the green plush upholstery, as if fearing he was about to demand his money's worth and wrest her maidenhead from her without further preamble. He could have done so, of course, there was nothing to prevent him, but this was not his way. As he had already told Maggie, he had other plans for Lucy's deflowering.

The girl intrigued him. She was not quite what he had expected when Maggie first told him about her find. Lucy's mien suggested an infusion of aristocratic blood in her veins somewhere along the line, maybe centuries before when some feudal lord had exerted the *droit du seigneur,* his alleged right to take the place of a village bride's husband on her wedding night. Tarquin's cock stiffened at the thought. How exciting it must have been to have so much power over vassals who had no option but to do your bidding, no matter how much it went against their grain. And it must have done, especially with resentful, hot-blooded bridegrooms forced to give up their new wives.

Lucy was haughty as well as exceptionally beautiful. The way she defied him kept his prick almost painfully erect. He prided himself on his remarkable restraint. He had not sheathed his weapon in her tight, uncharted passage, but used only her mouth. The way she had taken to this task had surprised and pleased him, but it was almost too easy for her. He resolved to be harsher with her, to push her to the limit, compelling her to perform gross indecencies that would make her sob with remorse even as he forced pleasure on her and subjected her to orgasm after orgasm.

He leaned forward, and she jumped. 'Open your legs for me,' he commanded.

'No, sir,' she answered in a quiet but determined voice.

Tarquin liked it; a thrill made his prick pulse deliciously. 'Do as I say,' he insisted. 'Would you disobey your master?'

'That is an unreasonable order,' she countered, and the stubborn set of her chin made him itch to reach Greyfriars and get down to the serious task of disciplining her. His lust was boiling like lava in his balls, but control... control is what he had trained himself to, what he had learned from the most highly skilled exponents of the erotic arts while travelling far and wide seeking them out. He knew holding back would only serve to make the ecstasy of the final capitulation all the more potent, raising mind as well as body to extraordinary heights.

'Open your legs,' he repeated patiently.

'No.'

He sighed as if dealing with a recalcitrant child, pushed up her skirt, and placed a hand firmly on each of her knees to prise them apart. She was trembling, and an answering frisson darted through his palms where they made contact with her flesh that moved up his arms and down his spine into his loins. He dug in his nails and shook her. She gasped, and her thighs went limp beneath his touch. He eased her hips forward a little, and lifted her skirt back further until she was fully exposed. Light flashed through the window glass, enabling him to admire the creamy nakedness between her waist and her stocking tops. Even when the coach interior was dusky again he could still discern her skin tones, darker than the whiteness of her dress but paler than the triangle of fuzz crowning her fork. She sat perfectly still and her hatred was almost tangible to him; he could taste it on his tongue and sniff it in the air, and it delighted him. Forty-five guineas for such a treasure was money well spent.

He combed his fingers through the curls at her groin and, with the practiced ease of a libertine, alighted on her clitoris. She drew in a breath but her torso remained unyielding, even as her sex opened to him like a flower beneath the sun. She was damp there, and this did not suit his purpose. He drew out his kerchief and dabbed her inner lips. After sniffing the linen, he slipped it back in his pocket and teased her bud, pushing back its hood. Then using his left hand he stretched her clit up while the middle digit of his right hand tickled the sensitive, dry head.

He guessed how this would feel, calculating the effect with an expert's knowledge of female arousal. The swelling of the erectile tissue beneath his fingertip told him she would find the caress almost unendurable. He rubbed her clit lightly, and then turned his attention to the shaft and labial wings flanking it.

She spread her legs wider and jerked her pelvis upwards, silently begging him for more.

He returned his attention to the head, hard and dry as a pea.

She squirmed and pressed it forcibly against his tormenting finger. 'Oh yes, sir, yes,' she panted.

He laughed quietly and took his hand away. 'I am your master now. *I* decide whether or not you shall have satisfaction. I could take my will of you and leave you frustrated every time. Think yourself lucky that is not my intention, for it is all some unfortunate women ever get. I took pleasure in seeing you come.'

'Then do it again,' she begged softly, caressing herself frantically.

He gripped her wrists and stopped her, holding both her hands out and away from her body. Her bottom thrashed up and down on the sea as she tried to bring her thighs together so they might press on her tormented clit and bring on her crisis, but he prevented this by thrusting his knee between her legs. 'Later, perhaps,' he vaguely promised. 'If you do precisely what I tell you.'

The coach rocked to a halt.

'We have arrived. Stand up, Lucy.'

Sullenly, she obeyed him, and he took the hem of her muslin dress and tucked it into her sash, lifting it so high that her mound was laid bare. He turned her around and did the same at the back, so her bottom crease was naked for all to see. She tried to shroud herself in her shawl, but he snatched it away.

A groom opened the door of the carriage and unfolded the iron steps.

Tarquin alighted, and then held a hand up for Lucy. Her reluctance to accept his assistance gave him another thrill, and his sense of dominance was more potent than wine. The groom was struggling to remain poker-faced, but the bulge in his white breeches was monumental, and Tarquin smiled to see a stain appearing just where the cock-head rested against the man's belly. The fellow was obviously in distress, and this amused him greatly. He held Lucy firmly, his hand under her elbow, as they stood on the circular gravel drive. He knew she longed to smooth down her skirt and cover herself, but he made her walk up the wide steps leading to Greyfriars's massive portico with all her private parts shamefully exposed. Light streamed from the wide open door and inside stood his personal manservant and valet, Powys, several housemaids and footmen, and a tall half-caste attired in white cotton breeches and a loose-fitting shirt. He was a striking man with thin features, copper-toned skin, smoky grey eyes and ebony hair worn in fancy ringlets.

Tarquin could feel Lucy pulling back, but would have none of this. He propelled her forward, showing her off. She belonged to him and he had the right to treat her as he chose. He could copulate with her in front of them all, fuck her and sodomise her and then permit his underlings and slaves to slake their lust with her as well.

The great hall was well lit and Lucy's nether regions were on full display – the red blotches bequeathed by the paddle, her fair pubic hair and her delectable round buttocks. Tarquin was finding it hard to restrain himself, his cock like a fiery serpent pulsing in his breeches longing to spit. He beckoned to the mulatto and the statuesque, coffee-coloured woman beside him. She was a haughty beauty wearing a white, off-the-shoulder blouse that emphasised the upward tilt of her breasts and jutting nipples, big as cherrystones. Her flounced skirt was of many bright colours, and she wore gold hoop earrings and a scarlet bandanna tied round her kinky black hair.

'Benjamin, this is Lucy,' Tarquin introduced his new prize. 'I want you and Chloe to look after her, train her, and guide her in our ways here at Greyfriars.'

'Yes, master,' they replied in unison. Then the woman turned compassionate brown eyes on Lucy. 'Don't be afeared, *cher*,' she said in a rich, deep-throated drawl, 'we'll take care of you.'

Lucy had never seen a black person close up before, and she was frightened. She had overheard her father and his cronies discussing British policies and trade abroad and heard about the sugar plantations manned by slaves brought across from Africa, a practice shared by Dutch, French, Portuguese and Spanish settlers. According to them, these black-a-moors where savages, headhunters and cannibals, and now she was actually being handed over to two of them.

'I brought them from my plantation, Lucy.' Tarquin flicked Chloe's nipples and made them even harder. 'My family acquired their vast wealth in the Americas.'

'The Americas?' she repeated, aghast. The huge continent beyond the Atlantic seemed as far away as the moon.

'Oh yes,' he assured her, continuing to finger Chloe as she stood before him impassively. 'They settled in Virginia in the middle of the last century, exiled Royalists fleeing for their lives after the defeat of the Cavaliers and the execution of King Charles I. Later, my great-grandfather bought back our estate in Cornwall and this London residence, as well. I came into my inheritance before I was twenty, and my formal schooling over I travelled to Virginia to view my profitable lands. They were all I could have hoped for, and more. I became fascinated by the South and went to New Orleans in Louisiana, which is largely owned by the French. The planters there lead a hedonistic lifestyle very much to my taste. I won *Auriville* from a conceited young jackanapes at the turn of a card, along with a substantial colonial style house, acres of prime land planted with sugar cane, and dozens of slaves to work it. That's how I came to own you, isn't it, my black pearl?' He hiked up Chloe's skirt and bared her long brown legs, crowned by a dense bush of black hair coating her mons.

'Yes, indeed, master.' Her eyes narrowed and her back arched as she pressed her sex against his questing fingers.

Tarquin knew Lucy was watching and guessed that, already aroused again, she was panting with eagerness for his caresses to be lavished on her rather than Chloe. He raised his head and gazed at his new possession. Her face was flushed and her hands clasped to her bosom. Holding her eyes, he continued exploring the swell of Chloe's pubis, and then thrust two of his fingers into the woman's wet pussy. Chloe's excitement matched his own and he was sorely tempted to unfasten his breeches and let his erection drive into her dark mysteries. She was one of his favourite concubines, born on the Caribbean island of Martinique, the stronghold of the African religion known as voodoo. A high priestess, the secrecy of her involvement in the cult appealed to Tarquin, for slaves in Louisiana were forbidden to practice it. This did not stop them, of course. They risked flogging, being branded with the *fleur-de-lis* or being put to death in horrible ways in order to carry out their religious rites, and Tarquin, intrigued by the unashamed sexuality and exoticism of the ceremonies, encouraged and protected them.

He slid his fingers in and out of the shuddering woman as she gasped with pleasure. Bringing a priestess to orgasm made him feel like a god. Then he released her indifferently and she recovered at once, smoothing down her skirt, her face calm.

'I put her in your care,' he spoke sternly. 'Her name is Lucy Browne and she is a virgin. Guard her well, for she is to be penetrated by me first. If you so much as allow a man to put the tip of his cock in her, I'll have you flayed alive.' He turned to the mulatto, adding, 'And should it be you who tries, then you shall be castrated.'

'Yes, master, I understand.' Benjamin bowed low, his long ringlets sweeping the floor. 'No one shall touch her,' he promised.

'Good. Go with them, Lucy, and do exactly as they say.' Tarquin tipped her face up to his. 'Your schooling begins here, and I expect you to be a quick learner. I have so many delights in store for you, my dear.'

Lucy's feet scarcely touched the floor as she was borne along between Benjamin and Chloe. She was aware of other servants staring at her, the men eyeing her lecherously, as the Creole couple guided her across the hall. The panelled walls were hung with torn flags and dusty battle trophies that alternated with large renaissance paintings depicting ancient Greek landscapes. Lucy wanted to linger, but was only permitted a glance at scenes of hermaphrodites locked in sexual embraces, nymphs impaled on the enormous phalli of men with goats' legs and horns, gods mating with swans, and goddesses playing with the pert cocks of pretty, winged cherubs.

She was shocked and embarrassed. Not even at Maggie's house had she seen such blatant examples of lewdness. But she had no time to dwell on her shameful position as she was hustled up the great central staircase, down empty corridors lit by candles in sconces, and through echoing galleries. Finally she was led beneath the carved architrave of double cedar wood doors.

The apartment in which she found herself was beyond her wildest dreams. Her first impression was that everything in the room was scarlet or black, the colours of blood and darkness. The two dramatic colours were used sumptuously on drapes, carpets and furnishings embroidered with gold thread that scintillated in the firelight. The air was thick with perfume from joss sticks burning in brass chafing dishes moulded to resemble coiled snakes, and fresh flowers breathed out a pungent aroma, huge white blossoms with large petals and flaming orange, penis-shaped stamens.

'What is that?' Lucy asked, pointing to the black basalt figure of a jackal-headed god standing on an ebony plinth.

'It is Anubis, Lord of the Dead, worshipped by the Egyptians,' Chloe murmured reverently, 'and this particular statue is thousands of years old. Milord brought it back with him after going up the river Nile. He's travelled a lot, and likes to collect things wherever he goes.'

There were other figures carved from wood, cruder in execution, depicting masculine beings dwarfed by their overdeveloped testicles and phalli, and totem poles representing the erect organ of generation. But most impressive of all was a life-sized statue set in an alcove opposite the door. Judging by its full bare breasts, supple waist and round hips, the carving depicted a woman, but the face was startling.

'That is the goddess, Balbo,' Benjamin whispered close to her ear. 'She is adored by many and has existed from the dawn of time.'

'But she's so strange,' Lucy breathed, repulsed but fascinated by the creature poised lightly on dancing feet, her arms seeming to writhe and beckon.

'She has her pussy on her face,' Chloe explained. 'Look closer and you'll see.'

Candles in silver holders threw the goddess into relief, but Chloe held another flame high as Lucy crept forward. It was true, Balbo's cloven sexual organs replaced her features, and yet in an uncanny way, they complemented them. Two slanting eyes stared out from amidst the curly black pubic hair, and the large clitoris represented the nose, the vertical slit below taking the place of the groove in the upper lip. And beneath it, the frilled opening of her vulva became her mouth. It was like an exotic flower, and suddenly it occurred to Lucy that a woman's genitalia were something to be admired.

'You understand the power of the earth mother?' Chloe asked her quietly.

'I think I'm beginning to,' Lucy replied, just as softly.

'You are lucky. The master favours you and has ordered us to bring you here to his bedchamber. We are to prepare you for his arrival.'

'Where is he?' Lucy expected him to charge in at any moment, his breeches open, ready to fling her on her back on the bed and have his way with her.

'He has gone to his club,' Benjamin answered. 'Though gambling is as dear to him as fucking, his purpose tonight is to round up his friends, those who will enjoy the revelries due to take place before long.'

Lucy shivered, knowing these 'revelries' would somehow include her. Her eyes were drawn to the massive four-poster bed inlaid with dozens of tiny glittering mirrors and hung with blood-red velvet curtains, and she wondered grimly how many girls had lost their virginity held down on its heavily embroidered coverlet. But she was given no time to ask questions. She was conducted to an anteroom that was small but luxurious, the décor lavishly oriental. A cupola shimmered overhead, a crystal lamp hanging on chains from its centre. Red and purple rays sent out stabbing rainbow shards of colour that fell on an oblong marble bath sunk into the floor, its sides patterned in a heavenly turquoise-blue mosaic. Shelves lined the tiled walls containing cut glass bottles of scented oils and soapstone pots of lotion. There were squat candles of various hues ranged around the bath, and as Chloe took a taper to each one, perfume rose from their crackling wicks.

'But I've already had a bath today,' Lucy protested, folding her arms about her sore body protectively.

'So?' Chloe retorted with a deep-throated chuckle, a kindly amusement flickering in her eyes. 'Now you will have another. Lord Tarquin is fussy. Undress, honey.'

She blushed, hung her head and stood there feeling foolish. Chloe seemed to understand her dilemma, and acting the ladies maid undressed her as if she was a high-ranking princess. First she knelt and undid the ribbons around Lucy's ankles and slipped her shoes off. Then she reached up and her fingers encountered the buckled garters. They gave way beneath her adept touch and she carefully rolled down the fragile stockings. When her young charge was completely naked, she walked over to a table and poured a glass of red wine. She added a dash of white powder to it, stirred it thoroughly, and handed the goblet to Lucy with instructions. 'Drink it all down and get in the bath. We have much to do and little time to do it. We shall be whipped if you're not ready by the time milord returns.'

Lucy obediently drank the wine hoping it would numb some of her intense anxiety, handed Chloe back the goblet, and lowered herself into the water. The tub was so large that she could stretch herself out, her head resting on the edge. The scent of herbs was overpowering, or was it the wine she had drunk? Sweet and heavy, it had left a slightly bitter aftertaste on her tongue.

Lying in the bath, she could pretend for a few moments that she was a great lady, not a country wench sold into servitude. Her eyes were heavy-lidded and her senses were swimming strangely. Her tongue refused to work, cleaving to her palette, and when Chloe brought over another glass of wine, her mouth was so dry that she gulped it down gratefully.

'Sit up, *cher*,' Chloe's voice was a seductive buzz in Lucy's head, 'so I can wash you all over.' And then there were glorious sensations as the Creole's soapy hands drifted across her back, finding every vertebra in her spine and massaging it, and then dipped down between her buttocks to caress her. Meanwhile, Benjamin coiled her wet hair on top of her head, secured it with jewel-headed pins, and then sponged her neck and breasts, circling her nipples without touching them even though Lucy lifted them imploringly. Something was making her lose hold on reality... she could think of nothing but her body's deepening sensual yearnings as pictures formed and reformed behind her closed eyelids, crude images of men and women fornicating in countless positions...

Chloe held out a fluffy white towel and Benjamin helped Lucy rise. She was unsteady on her feet, the room undulating and changing size, its boundaries lost in shadows. She was being patted dry, and then in the next moment she was lying on her back across a high, narrow couch covered by a linen sheet. She stared up at the ceiling feeling as though she was floating up and up… she was hovering over Greyfriars looking down on its maze of turrets and chimneypots, thinking how lovely it would be if she were a bird. London stretched out below her like a map, the Thames snaking though it, lights sparkling here and there, while beyond the city the earth seemed swathed in funereal crêpe. Weighing no more than a feather, she nevertheless felt herself sinking gently and coming to rest on the couch again…

All traces of stiffness from her accident and subsequent chastisements were being massaged away by the two African slaves, and Lucy had never felt more relaxed as her flesh tingled deliciously from the touch of their fingers. They kneaded her muscles and pampered her skin, the oil seeping into her muscles until she felt she would ooze perfume from her every pore. They were flirting with her, brushing her nipples but not lingering, combing their fingers through her bush but not entering her labial niche, even though her hips lifted in supplication. The aphrodisiac ran hot through her veins, adding to her already highly charged state. She closed her eyes and thought of Tarquin, that alarming, devilishly attractive man. She wanted to be taken to him. Filled with the feverish desire to let him thrust his cock to the very hilt in her virgin slot, she groaned.

Benjamin's massaging strokes intensified, and when he pressed the top of her cleft beneath his thumb her clitoris throbbed and her juices flowed. He dipped into them and made little circles round her pleasure-bud as Chloe fondled her breasts, tugging at her nipples and making them stand proud before bending to suck them. Lucy's heart was pounding like a drum and she wondered how much longer she could endure this stimulation without screaming in frustration.

To her intense joy, Benjamin squatted down so his head was on a level with her sex. She parted her legs encouragingly, opening the V of her groove, and offered him the rose-pink folds. Chloe nibbled at her teats, sending waves of desire through her, as Benjamin's fingers rested on each side of her labia while the cool tip of his tongue began lapping at her vulva, moving slowly upwards until he reached the hard nub of her clit, which quivered in response. His fingers and tongue worked together as he licked her as yet untried entrance, and his thumb revolved on her seat of pleasure. Lucy felt the first tremors of a climax spreading from her toes to her thighs to the base of her spine and into her lower belly. It was building rapidly and she was ready for it, oh so ready...

'Benjamin, stop!' Chloe commanded. 'You know what master said, you're not to make sweet with her.'

'Oh please, don't leave me like this,' Lucy implored, propping herself up on her elbows.

'Lord Tarquin wants it,' Chloe said shortly, and pulled her up to stand beside her. 'Now off you go to the privy and empty yourself, bowels as well as bladder. He'll want both your holes ready for him.'

'But...'

Chloe shoved her towards the privy. 'No *buts*. Just do it.'

Lucy wanted to close the door behind her, but the Creole would have none of this, anticipating her movement and forcing it open. 'I need privacy,' Lucy complained.

Chloe laughed. 'You're at Greyfriars now, child, you can forget modesty for good and all.'

The little room was tiled to match the one containing the bath. It was clean and fresh and wholesome, a far cry from the smelly and dingy earth closets Lucy had always known. The seat of the commode was of polished wood, the chamber pot was spotless, and there were even sheets of fine white tissue paper with which to wipe oneself. It was a marvel, and she found herself appreciating all her lordship's little refinements, even if he *was* dominating

110

and cruel.

'Have you had a shit yet?' Chloe asked impatiently, poking her head around the door.

'Yes.'

'Good, now wash your hands. There's soap by the basin and a clean towel. I've already told you that milord is fastidious.'

Lucy emerged smelling of lavender-scented soap and feeling better, although still light-headed.

Chloe was waiting, a robe held in her hands. She dropped it over Lucy's head and arranged the folds. It was a glorious pale-blue silk spangled all over with sequins, so fragile and transparent it resembled a starry mist. The neckline was low, the shoulder straps thin, and ballooning sleeves drifted from them that gathered into points over her hands. Chloe fidgeted with the garment until it draped to her satisfaction, covering Lucy's body discreetly even as the insubstantial weave made her seem all the more naked. She then brought over a pair of flat silver sandals that Lucy slipped on in wonder at how delicate they were; she'd never had anything so fine on her feet before.

Benjamin brushed out her hair and arranged a headdress on her brow, depicting horns holding a crescent moon between them. 'She is the virgin goddess of the moon,' he breathed, staring at Lucy in awe.

'Indeed, our gods will be pleased and will visit us tonight,' Chloe agreed. 'I shall be their mouthpiece and they will speak through me.'

Suddenly a gong sounded, three times, far away in the depths of the house. The Creoles looked towards the sound, their eyes and teeth gleaming as they smiled. 'He's here,' Chloe announced. 'We must go to him.'

Benjamin pressed a knob in the panelling and a secret doorway sprang open.

Lucy found herself standing at the top of a steep staircase leading down into dimness, and a musky, damp smell

111

wafted up towards her. She drew back. 'I can't go down there!' she exclaimed in sudden terror.

'It's all right, sugar,' Chloe murmured, 'trust me. I won't let no one harm you.'

There was nothing Lucy could do but hope against all hope the woman was telling the truth. Slowly, placing one hesitant foot in front of the other, she began descending. The steps were slippery, but Benjamin, descending beside her, supported her with a strong arm. The gong had reverberated into silence, but another sound had taken over, steady, savage and persistent. At first she thought it was the pounding of her heart, and then she realised it was the beat of drums. They passed along a dimly lit passage that was cold, and the damp chilled her toes through the thin soles of her sandals. At first it seemed like a manmade corridor, part of the foundations of the house, but then the walls became uneven, as did the floor, and the stone roof seemed lower and rougher, more like a cave.

A sooty black curtain barred their way, and the throbbing of the drums grew almost deafeningly loud. Benjamin held the drapes aside, and taking her courage in hand, Lucy stepped between them. The cavern was so large its edges were swallowed up by darkness beyond the torches. It was crowded with people, but she had eyes only for one.

Tarquin stood near an altar, a tall figure in a long black robe. The drumming ceased as abruptly as it had begun, and Lucy heard a cockerel crowing somewhere in the shadows. Chloe left her side and walked in the direction of the sound. The watchers were motionless and silent, seemingly spellbound, as Tarquin beckoned Lucy to him. As if hypnotised she obeyed his silent summons, feeling as though she was falling. Fire opals flashed around his neck and in his ears, and he seemed to be towering miles above her in his dark magnificence. He smiled down at her and opened his robe. He was naked beneath it, his body lean and tanned. He took her hand, and placed it on his erect penis.

'Time for you to surrender your virginity, Lucy.'

Chapter Seven

Though frightened out of her wits, Lucy had never felt more alive.

She was aware of the spectators. Tarquin's guests were all male, with the exception of Maggie, who arrived in another man's company. She was wearing a mauve satin bustier very tightly laced, and a full violet skirt slit in several places, her stocking-clad legs, white buttocks and shaven pubis showing through the gauzy material.

To Lucy's everlasting shame and mortification, Tarquin abandoned her to kiss Maggie's hand and caress her nipples where they peeped above the lace of her bodice. 'You've arrived just in time,' he told her.

'So, I've not missed the consummation?' Maggie purred, and dipped her hand into the opening of his robe, encircling his cock with her fingers. He was so hard the foreskin had rolled back and the helm glistened with clear juice. She smiled up into his eyes, and then took her companion's arm. 'This is Barry. He's a groom and mightily well endowed. We fuck everywhere, in the stables, in the garden, even in the coach. I'm thinking of promoting him. I intend to drive a chaise, perhaps even to race it, and he can teach me how. He's an obliging boy, and will do whatever I tell him. Would you care to bugger him, my lord?'

'Not tonight,' Tarquin replied, smiling. 'I'm concentrating on cunt… young, untried and inexperienced cunt.'

Lucy sidled up to Tarquin. 'Can't we be alone?' she whispered.

'Shy, my darling? What a demure little thing you are.'

He slipped his arms around her and cupped the firm globes of her buttocks. His prick pulsed against her belly and dampened her fragile dress. 'You want me to put you over my knee and spank you again? Is that it? I haven't heard you call me master. Have you forgotten my command?'

'No, master.' Her body seemed filled with liquid fire as her nerves and skin remembered the impact of his ruthless palm, the whack of the paddle and the snap of the whip against her skin.

'Milord, are you ready for the ceremony to begin?' asked Chloe, appearing from behind the altar bearing a tray laden with a jug, goblets and a number of black feathers.

'Yes, I'm ready.' He held out his hand. 'Are *you* ready, Lucy?'

She slipped her fingers into his and together they approached a shrine covered with offerings – fruit, money, flowers and bottles of wine – placed before a snake-god with carved, realistic looking scales and emerald eyes. There was also a wooden, wanton looking goddess, an alarming skull-headed deity, and an icon of the Virgin Mary. A crucifix was also mingled in with the pagan paraphernalia, which consisted of axe heads, bead necklaces and white china pots.

'What are those for?' Lucy wondered out loud.

'To hold the souls of the dead,' Chloe replied.

Coals burned in braziers and the dancing flames spread throughout the cave, distilling an unearthly phosphorescent glow over the fearsome paintings and arcane symbols decorating the craggy walls. The guests, lured away from gaming tables by the promise of an orgy, had cast aside their ordinary clothes and donned brown habits with hoods. They were naked beneath them, barefoot and bare-arsed, their testicles hanging low between thin or sturdy legs, their cocks in various stages of tumescence. The

115

company was composed of young men in the main, though there was a sprinkling of middle-aged gentlemen. They waited for the show to begin lolling on couches, served drinks and tasty morsels by male and female slaves chosen exclusively for their beauty, and their submissiveness. The cave echoed with the sharp sound of hands landing on dimpled buttocks. And there were other more sinister noises too, as whips cracked across cringing flesh, leaving scarlet stripes in their wake. Some victims let out piteous cries while others, more experienced and wiser, kept their mouths shut. Some, judging by their expressions of ecstasy, were enjoying the abuse bestowed upon them.

Lucy did not know where to look or what to do, and trembled as Chloe took hold of her, a different Chloe from the gentle woman who had bathed her. This one shook violently and her eyes kept rolling up into her skull, her limbs twitching to the rhythm of the drums as a deep, hollow voice issued from between her snarling lips.

'Give me this virgin's blood,' she intoned.

'We have already given you the black cockerel's blood,' Benjamin said in a formal voice, pouring the warm red liquid into goblets and handing one to Tarquin before distributing the others amongst his most important guests.

Tarquin took a sip, and then passed the cup to Lucy. 'Drink,' he commanded.

The heat of it in her hands, and the acrid odour in her nostrils reminiscent of her father's slaughterhouse, made her stomach heave. 'No,' she cried, 'it's revolting!' She pushed the cup back towards him. 'How *can* you, my lord? It's blood!'

'Only the very best, my dear. It belonged to the finest barnyard rooster whose harem of hens will be devastated by his sudden demise, but the gods demand it.' He held the goblet to her lips, and some of the contents dribbled onto her chin as he tipped it, forcing her to drink.

She tasted the bitter brew and turned her head to one

side, jarring his arm and spilling blood down her sky-blue robe. 'I said I don't want it,' she gasped. 'You can't make me drink it!'

'Naughty, naughty,' he wagged a finger at her, and then gestured to Benjamin. 'The stocks, I think.'

The cave seemed to waver as pink-palmed black hands beat an inexorable rhythm on the tom-toms and a troupe of black dancers whirled and gyrated to the music led by Chloe, who moved as if entranced, tireless and frantic, tearing at their garments and flinging them to the floor. Naked, she knelt across the prone forms of male worshippers one after the other, impaling herself on their enlarged pricks while whipping them with a birch branch and chasing her orgasm, her head thrown back and her face distorted in fierce ecstasy.

Her frenzy was infectious. The guests joined in the wild dancing as Benjamin manhandled Lucy, pulling her over to an object that reminded her of the pillory on the village green where malefactors were placed for punishment. This instrument of correction was slightly different, however. As she stood before it Benjamin swung open the upper half and, his hand at her waist, made her bend over, her legs straight and taut and spread wide apart. Manacles were fastened around her ankles, and then the top section was brought down and padlocked into place. Her face and the upper part of her torso were visible from the front, where her wrists and her head slipped through further holes in the contraption. At the rear only her buttocks were exposed with her legs forced open, her feet planted firmly on the floor. Benjamin added to her embarrassment by folding back her skirt, lifting it up and tucking it into the pillory, out of the way. It was impossible for her to look around, but she guessed how she must appear to those behind her – lewdly exposed, with her bottom crack wide and her labia pouting invitingly. The chill air told her it was wet.

'Lovely *derrière*, Tarquin, old sport,' drawled a well-bred voice, and she felt the touch of soft, moist hands. 'You're a deuced lucky dog. Is it all right if I have a feel?'

'Outside only, Buckley,' Tarquin replied, 'the rest is reserved for me.'

She grimaced as the sweaty palms crawled all over her buttocks, the knuckles brushing her sex, and then others joined them as Tarquin stood before her to meet her outraged eyes.

'You bastard!' she cried. 'Set me free at once!'

Smiling indulgently he jiggled her breasts, which were thrust forward by her stance, and she could not hold back a moan of desire.

'Do that some more, Tarquin, m'lad,' encouraged the foppish rake called Buckley. 'She's wet as a fiddler's doxy, strike me dumb!'

Tarquin pushed aside the folds of her revealing bodice and her breasts were free, the nipples hard and hopeful. He played with them, tweaking and petting them.

It appeared Buckley was no longer the sole beneficiary of the view imparted by Lucy's bare bottom and rosy pussy. She could hear other voices behind her now, raucous, rude and excited, and they were all giving Tarquin advice.

'Poke her, sir.'

'Do it now. Give her a thorough seeing to.'

'Come on. Why are you waiting?'

'Can we have her after you've done?'

Multiple hands were caressing her lower regions, from her waist to her crotch, her thighs, her knees and even her feet. Someone's head was shoved between her legs and his tongue began exploring her vulva and then rimming her anus. Other fingers reached over the stocks to pinch her nipples. Tarquin stood by watching, leaning against a pillar, his arms folded across his chest, his bare feet crossed at the ankles.

Lucy cast him an imploring glance. 'Undo this thing and let me loose,' she begged him.

His lips were the only part of him that moved as his smile deepened.

A hard palm slapped her buttocks, then several more hands followed suit, aggravating her already smarting cheeks.

'Her arse is rosy as the dawn; have you been correcting her?' asked Buckley in a husky, eager voice, and she felt him rubbing his penis up and down the back of her thigh, leaving a sticky trail of pre-cum.

'Earlier this evening,' Tarquin answered matter-of-factly, but his cock was ramrod stiff.

'Can I jerk off over her bum?' Buckley panted.

'No.'

'That's damned miserly of you, sir. What about her mouth, then?' Buckley left her backside and came round to the front of the pillory. He looked just as she had expected him to, a plump man with foppish mannerisms and a paunch that overhung his small appendage; even fully erect it was no longer and thicker than a finger. 'Open up, sweeting,' he said, his hands grabbing her hair and holding her head up mercilessly as his little prick advanced towards her face. 'Give this a sucking.'

Tarquin pushed him aside, and began releasing her from her bondage. Once she was free he stripped off her robe, swept her up in his arms with as much ease as if she weighed no more than thistledown, carried her across to the altar slab, and laid her down across the cold granite surface.

She wanted to scream, but she was paralysed with fear as Chloe loomed over her, apparently no longer in a trance though her eyes were still slightly unfocused. Her bare skin glistened with perspiration, fragrant oil and semen. She raised her arms, her words and gestures directed heavenwards towards her gods, and prayed for a long moment. Then Benjamin handed her a chalice and a black feather.

The candles flared brightly, as if someone had added a pinch of gunpowder, and the shadows formed unearthly shapes on the walls and the roof of the cave. The spectators were now attempting to couple with anyone and everyone. All the slave girls were impaled, and even the young bondsmen had cocks thrust into their hands, mouths and backsides. Lust seemed to shimmer in the air as the drums settled down into a steady, ominous beat.

Lucy suppressed a shriek as Chloe dipped the tip of the feather into the chalice, and drew it out dyed red and dripping.

'Lie still, Lucy,' Tarquin commanded her.

The feather approached, touched her skin, and circled around each of her breasts. The liquid was cool now, leaving a sticky pattern of symbols and enchantments that wove round her navel and formed an arrow pointing directly to her sex lips. The dancers were motionless, grouped around the altar, and as the feather completed its magical designs they sank to their knees and began chanting.

Benjamin removed Tarquin's robe, and Lucy stared up at her master as he positioned himself at the foot of the altar. She tensed as Benjamin ceremoniously applied a few drops of scented oil to her swollen clitoris. Then Tarquin leaned forward, dipped his fingers into the anointing liquid, and slid them around her secret lips, manipulating her pleasure nodule. She was well aware of the indignity of her position, naked for all to see, but her shame was overridden by the passion mounting within her. The drum's measured beat pounded in time with her pulse as Tarquin strummed her bud and skilfully brought her up and up on waves of pure delight, until her climax broke and she was plunged into sensations so acute she seemed to lose consciousness for an instant.

She came to her senses as he knelt over her, took his phallus in his hand, and guided it to her entrance. She felt her vulva slippery with the oil and her own juices as he pushed, and her labia stretched to receive his swollen glans. He had pleasured her so completely, she was happy to sacrifice her maidenhood to him. She lifted her legs and locked them around his waist, drawing him closer, her nails raking his back in response to the agonising pain as he thrust, impaling her on his erection in a single hard stroke.

She screamed as her hymen ruptured. His cock was so large, filling her to capacity, and she was sure she could not bear it. He rested inside her for a moment, letting her feel what it was like to be totally possessed, and it hurt terribly. Every delicate membrane inside her was on fire. Then, as he slid out of her slowly, the torment began to recede. A molten throbbing replaced it, and then an urgent need to have more of that powerful shaft inside her.

The drumbeat quickened and he followed its rhythm, forcing his cock in and out of her faster and harder, and at some point she forgot the discomfort as her hips rose and fell in time with his. She felt hands beneath her, and then Chloe and Benjamin were lifting her, holding her steady to receive Tarquin's tribute. The voodoo followers chanted, the guests applauded and cheered, and Tarquin rammed into her a dozen times more before flinging his head back and roaring his climax. She felt his organ twitching and a sudden gush as he released his semen. He jerked inside her, the last spasm quivering through him, and then pulled out of her.

Lucy flung an arm over her eyes to block out the scene, her sex throbbing, intensely sore and yet strangely eager for more.

'So she was a virgin after all,' Maggie commented.

'Oh yes,' Tarquin sighed, as Benjamin helped him slip his robe back on. 'Now it but remains for her arse to be made as receptive. You and Chloe shall see to that.'

Lucy was aware of hands parting her legs, and looked up sharply to see Chloe pressing a clean white handkerchief to her freshly invaded notch. She tried to pull her thighs together, but the Creole would have none of this until she had finished. Then she suddenly let go of her and held the linen above her head for all to see.

'The blood of the virgin!' she cried, the candlelight flickering over the bright red stains on the white cloth. 'Virgin's blood! Sacred blood!' She dropped the handkerchief into the brazier smouldering near the altar as the crowd shouted in approval.

If this was what being a ruined maiden meant, then there were far worse fates, Lucy mused upon waking next morning in the great bed in Tarquin's chamber.

Sounds from outside the chamber told her it must be mid-morning, or later. A ray of sunlight pierced a gap in the curtains, obliterating the feeble, dying glow of the candles. She lay across Tarquin's belly, her mouth resting so close to his soft cock she was sure she had gone to sleep with it in her mouth. She could not remember much of what had happened last night, or how she came to be in bed.

Every muscle in her body had its own particular ache this morning from the frenzied introduction to all manner of sexual positions Tarquin had put her through. As she lay there, trying to piece together the night's events, still feeling the lingering effects of the aphrodisiac they had given her, she blushed all over.

She raised her head and looked down at her lord and master. In slumber he looked younger, almost innocent, his black lashes lying like fans against his high cheekbones, his wicked eyes hidden. He was so handsome, so aristocratic, as far above her as the stars, and yet she was his chosen one, at least for the moment.

Looking down the length of her no longer virgin body, the bitter taste of bile rose in her throat as she saw the smudged remains of the cockerel's blood still forming diagrams on her skin. Whatever had taken place last night had not included bathing.

A light rap on the door and Tarquin's lids fluttered open. He came awake instantly, glanced at her blankly, and muttered, 'Enter!'

A lean, svelte figure crossed the threshold balancing a silver tray on one hip. Lucy huddled down under the quilt, but the servant ignored her as he glided over the carpet, seeming to walk on the balls of his feet. He reminded Lucy of a crane with his angular body and beaked nose. His thinning brown hair was brushed back into a ponytail, his suit was an impeccable dark-blue, his linen immaculate, and his square-toed shoes with cut-steel buckles shone as if freshly polished.

'Don't hide yourself, Lucy,' Tarquin said with a laugh. 'It's only Powys, my valet.' He tugged the quilt away, exposing her naked body.

Powys remained impassive. 'Your breakfast, my lord,' he announced, in a high-pitched voice that retained the singsong intonation of his native Wales.

'Put it down, put it down,' Tarquin snapped peevishly. 'Jesus Christ, I've a monumental headache this morning. Must have made too free with the port last night.'

'Or with the rooster's blood,' Lucy put in tartly, unable to hold her tongue.

'Is that coffee I smell?' he asked Powys hopefully, ignoring her.

'Yes, my lord.' He placed the tray on the nightstand.

Lucy sat there uneasily trying to cover her breasts with her hands. She may have been on view to all last evening, but to be exposed in the broad light of day was anathema to her. She instinctively sensed the valet despised her; he was staring down his nose at her as he fiddled with the gilt-edged, flower patterned porcelain cup and the silver coffeepot. The aromatic fragrance of coffee reminded her of her very first whiff of this exotic drink in Maggie's establishment. Letitia told her it was drunk extensively among the *demi monde*. Lucy had pretended she knew what this meant, and was later enlightened by Jocelyn. Now, she supposed, she could be numbered amongst them – the kept woman of a gentleman who walked on the shady side of polite society.

She glanced towards the bedside table at the heavenly vision of freshly baked rolls, buttercup-yellow pats of butter and a glass dish of golden honey, and suddenly realised she was ravenously hungry. But Powys poured coffee into the single cup and handed it to his master, and her spirits plummeted and her empty stomach rumbled as she saw that breakfast had been prepared for one person only.

Tarquin accepted the coffee, and sipped it appreciatively. 'More sugar,' he said, and Powys took the cup back. He returned it, and Tarquin tasted it again, presumably to his satisfaction for he kept it. 'Have a message delivered to Lady Cordelia Wareham,' he said. 'Tell her I expect her to be here at three o'clock. I have a task for her. Now get out, but return within the hour to begin my toilette.'

'My lord,' Powys said smoothly, and bowed his way to the door, never once turning his back on Tarquin.

Lucy sat there unhappily, and Tarquin passed her his empty cup with a brusque gesture. 'Fill it up again and pass me a roll, a knife and the butter,' he ordered. 'On second thought, you may butter the roll for me.'

It was torture to obey him and realise he had no intention of sharing his meal with her. He bit into the roll and cocked an amused eyebrow at her, but she refused to beg him for a single crumb. He was rude and selfish and uncharitable and did not deserve her respect.

'I suppose you want me to break my fast in the kitchen,'

she said finally, and made to get out of bed.

'Did I say anything about that? You'll stay where you are until I give you leave to go.'

She sat there silently and sulkily, her breasts exposed, the twin cheeks of her arse like two hot cushions beneath her, her hands linked over her mound.

He leaned back lazily against the frilled pillows, his olive skin swarthy in contrast to the white linen and lace, his chest a mat of springy curls that thinned over his navel, a single line running down to where it thickened out again round his genitals. He ate his fill, and then indicated she should take his plate and cup. 'But leave the butter and wait for me,' he said, throwing back the bedclothes and swinging his legs over the side of the mattress. He rose to his impressive height and headed for the water closet in the adjacent room.

When he returned, his eyes glittered and his lips were curved up in a mocking smile as he bore down on her. He rolled her over on the bed, muttering, 'Show me your arse. I want to see how red it is, how enflamed, like that of female baboons I've seen in the zoo, a sure sign of their readiness to mate.'

'I'm not an animal,' she said defiantly over her shoulder.

'Yes you are, a fiery little hell-cat who needs to be buggered.'

'No,' she cried, struggling. 'I can't. I don't want to! Fuck me in the normal way, please. Show me all there is to know about that. I want you. I can never get enough of you. Oh please, my lord!'

Ignoring her pleas he knelt between her legs, scooped a dollop of butter from the dish, and pushed it deep within her vagina. She cried out and bucked against him, seeking the pleasure. He laughed, and she felt his tongue licking the rapidly melting butter mingled with her copious nectar. Then it was his fancy to add some honey to the sensual brew, careless of the sticky substance staining the sheets.

He slurped at her with evident relish, and she moaned in surprise and pleasure. Again and again he brought her to the point of orgasm, and then made her cry out in frustration as he withdrew his tongue from her clitoris.

She became crafty, controlling herself so he no longer knew how close she was to climaxing. The ruse worked, and an overwhelming spasm wracked her as she reached a triumphant peak, and tumbled down from it in a shuddering cascade of bliss.

He frowned to see she had outwitted him, and heaved her hips up, raising her bottom towards his swollen prick. Her orgasmic moans changed to cries of alarm as he spread the honey mixture higher up her crack, anointing her anus and thrusting his fingers inside her, first one, then two, and then three. The flame of desire still burned brightly inside her, but she was desperately afraid, and she sensed he was in no mood to be merciful. She felt the clubbed head of his prick taking the place of his fingers and entering her, inch by slow inch. His monstrous shaft dilated her with inexorable force, pushing hard. She could not suppress a scream, but he took no notice of her distress, grinding into her until his thick helm had penetrated to the ridge of his foreskin.

Lucy fought to expel it, tortured beyond endurance. This was not pleasure but excruciating torment. He was violating her virginity for a second time and it was a far more agonising experience, unnatural and debased. Tears streamed down her face, which was pressed into the pillow as she was forced to submit to his relentless pursuit of satisfaction. He shoved, but was defeated by his own size and her tight muscles. No matter how hard he pushed to gain entrance to her bottom, her virgin passage refused to give him lodging.

'Damn you!' he swore, trying one last time to rend her passage and plunge into her depths.

'Oh, my God,' she cried, feeling her anus stretched

beyond endurance. 'Get off me, sir!'

'Stupid little tart,' he snarled. 'You *shall* take me, every last inch of me. I'll turn you over to the tender mercies of Chloe and Maggie. By the time they've finished with you, you'll wish you'd been more cooperative with me.' He dragged his tool from her, and she felt his hot semen raining down on her buttocks as he spent himself with a savage groan.

Sobbing, she curled up into a woeful ball, her lower body possessed of pain, both from her punished buttocks and the burning ache in her deepest being.

Tarquin rose, shouting for Chloe, and she appeared as if by magic in answer to his call.

'Master,' she said meekly, her head down, her hands clasped at her waist as she curtsied. 'What is your will?'

'Lucy Browne needs attention. Work on her arsehole. Use whatever you must to render her pliable and receptive. But first, take her to the room designated for her correction. There she will stay, and you'll not let her out of your sight. You know what to do.' He examined his face in the dressing table mirror, passing a hand over his unshaven jaw. 'You will use the butt plugs and dildos tonight, but first of all, Lady Wareham will be arriving to take her to the dressmakers. She needs everything. While she is here, I'll not let her shame me by her lack of fashionable attire. See to it.'

'Yes, sir,' Chloe replied, her black eyes studying the sobbing Lucy. 'Come along, honey,' she cooed. 'You heard what the master said, time for us to get going. You needs to be washed and fed, brushed and combed.'

Lucy felt like a pampered dog, not a lady capable of being the queen of a man's heart, and her misery knew no bounds as she wondered how a man as beautiful and sophisticated as Tarquin could be so cruel.

It was a day like no other. Lucy, recovering from Tarquin's assault on her bottom hole, was given no opportunity to brood on becoming Fate's plaything, and everyone else's, for that matter.

She was allowed to borrow one of Tarquin's dressing gowns. It was far too large for her and she tripped over the hem as the sleeves dangled below her hands, but it was better than walking through the corridors stark naked. She was taken to a large, airy room decorated in azure blue. Wallpaper adorned with little pagodas, quaint figures and tiny bridges over tranquil pools contributed to the serene atmosphere, which was deepened by damask window curtains and velvet upholstery. The furniture was spindle-legged and fluted, the testers draped with lace and gold swags and covered with fluffy pillows.

'Is this my bedroom?' she asked in wonder, not daring to believe it could be so.

'It sure is, sugar,' Chloe answered, moving with her usual lithe grace and speaking more informally now that she was not around her lord and master. 'When you're not sharing the master's, that is. We've got to fit you up with something to wear now. Lady Cordelia's coming to take you out.'

'But I can't buy clothing, I haven't any money.'

Chloe grinned, and it was hard to relate her to the wild priestess of last night's orgiastic rite. 'Don't you worry about that, girl. Milord has accounts at most shops in town. If he says you got to be dressed in style, then that's what will happen. You're going to enjoy this, and so am I.'

Lucy recovered some of her optimism once she stepped into the tub that stood in the dressing room next door. It was not as grand as Tarquin's bathhouse but possessed the same amenities, and when Chloe had soaped away the blood and sweat and love juices staining her body, she started to feel much better and therefore more optimistic.

All she had to wear was the white dress and shawl provided by Maggie, which were hopelessly crumpled even though Chloe had apparently done her best to restore them to freshness.

She was almost ready to go when a footman opened the door and a blonde woman swept into the room. She was exquisitely dressed, her hair piled high on her head and topped by a wide-brimmed hat bedecked with feathers and lace and artificial red roses. She carried a cane decorated with ribbons, a fan and a beaded reticule.

Chloe dropped into a deep curtsey. 'Lady Cordelia,' she said with the utmost deference.

'Get up, woman, and tell me what this is all about,' Cordelia demanded, throwing down her accessories so the Creole had to pick them up. 'I had the briefest of notes from Lord Tarquin. Really, he can be most offhand at times.'

'This is Lucy Browne, his lordship's latest protégée,' Chloe said, as if that explained everything.

'Latest *whore*, you mean,' Cordelia retorted acerbically. Her cornflower-blue eyes rested on Lucy's face for a moment, and then looked her over from hair down to toes. 'A virgin, I suppose.'

'She was, until last night,' Chloe replied.

'He soon put an end to *that*,' she sniffed.

'Yes, indeed, milady.'

'If there's one thing that rouses him beyond belief it's the opportunity to corrupt innocence,' Cordelia observed, and walked across to where Lucy stood.

Meeting the unblinking stare of those worldly-wise eyes, Lucy experienced a chill of trepidation. Then she quivered with unwilling excitement as a kid-gloved hand travelled across her breasts, skimmed her waist and belly and gripped her pussy through the robe's thin muslin. 'Lady Wareham?' she asked shakily, wondering what was expected of her.

'Don't mind me, girl,' Cordelia said, gripping her mound more tightly and worming her middle finger into the damp crease of Lucy's labial lips. 'I know Tarquin very well. He is my master, too. I've seen a string of maidens pass through this house and he wearies of them all. I remain in the background doing as he bids, always there when he decides to call me to his side again. You're an exceptionally pretty jade, but you won't last any longer than the rest of them.' Then, with a mercurial change of mood, she removed her hand and administered a stinging slap on Lucy's backside. 'Enjoy it while you may,' she advised. 'My coach is outside and we are off to the shops. What more can any woman ask?'

Chapter Eight

Covent Garden was its customary busy self. Because the day was sunny and dry, Tarquin decided to leave his carriage at the edge of the piazza and take a stroll, a pleasant enough recreation as he swung his cane nonchalantly and nodded to passing acquaintances.

The Garden had something for everyone – a produce market, the finest shops and taverns and coffeehouses. There was also a theatre, and all the activities and vagabondage that such an establishment attracts, as well as a church and a graveyard. The Garden offered a multitude of diversions. Here a man might find a saucy slut parading her wares, or even a heavily veiled lady bored by her gouty old husband and seeking someone more virile. There were plenty of catamites, too, if one's taste ran to pederasty.

Tarquin responded to the Garden's boisterous atmosphere. It was possible to be wined and dined in one of several first class eating-houses, entertained and sexually satisfied, beaten and robbed, all in the space of an evening. He smiled as he walked, knowing he was very sharp in appearance, wearing the latest mode, his English tailor taking a leaf out of Parisian couturiers' books.

It was here Cordelia had brought Lucy shopping, and his new acquisition smoothly adapted to comporting herself like quality. He had been right in his assessment of her, and was planning, along with Cordelia – who was always ready for a spiteful jest at someone else's expense – to take her along to one of the Duchess of Weyrock's soirées. There he would pass her off as his country cousin. The duchess was a snobbish old harridan who treated him as if he was an upstart, whereas his blood was as blue as hers, probably bluer.

He had engaged a foppish dandy to teach Lucy to dance. He posed no threat, for he was obsessed with himself and unconditionally homosexual; there was no risk he would tamper with Tarquin's latest lover.

As he brooded on Lucy and her satisfactory progress, so his cock awoke in the confinement of his silk breeches and began to enlarge. Chloe and Maggie, with Cordelia's help, had worked on her. Highly skilled as they were, they soon had Lucy accepting a series of dildos, each larger than the last, until her anus had been properly prepared for him. He had left her with the women and made no attempt to see her while she underwent her training, thus arousing her curiosity, desire and need to have him take her again. When the time came she had been pliable, if not exactly willing, to take his phallus into her most secret recess. Now he was seeking a tutor for her. She should learn to read and write and understand sums. Not too much, he did not want her getting above herself; she must stay subservient.

He strolled into the little piazza and saw, seated in the window of a coffeehouse, his physician, Dr Reeves. This eminent man had been the guardian of his health for some years, dosing him with a drug containing mercury if he showed symptoms of the clap, cupping and bleeding him on occasions when he had the ague. Not often, however, for Tarquin had the constitution of an ox, which was surprising given his hedonistic lifestyle.

Reeves numbered the elite among his patients. He would not lower himself to becoming a surgeon. Not for him the daily slog of walking the wards of hospitals devoted to the poor and needy, though he had done his training in them. He left the instruction of medical students in these stinking, unsanitary and overcrowded hospices to others who were more philanthropic. Neither did he dabble in anatomy, or the new-fangled notion of doctors being present during childbirth, considering this should be left to the offices of midwives, as it had been down the ages.

He wagged his head and waved on seeing Tarquin, his broad skull shifting beneath his white, liberally powdered wig, and Tarquin entered the aromatic, dark-panelled interior of this strictly masculine haven. No women were allowed within these hallowed precincts, where gentlemen could discuss politics, or snippets of scandals concerning absent colleagues, or gossip pertaining to the Court. Horseracing came into the conversation as well, along with wrestling, boxing and cockfights, for each and every man there was addicted to gambling.

'Ah, my lord, sit down, sit down,' Reeves said, hauling his bulky form to a standing position and making a leg, indicating Tarquin should join him at table. 'It's some time since I visited you. No recurrence of Cupid's Measles, I take it?'

'Indeed no, sir,' Tarquin replied, sweeping a hand to his heart, placing the heel of his right shoe to the instep of his left, and returning the bow. He straightened, and lowered himself into a chair. 'Nor do I anticipate another dose as my latest conquest was a virgin when I rogered her.'

'Quite so, quite so, my dear sir, but will you be able to resist the charms of other, more experienced ladybirds?' Reeves grunted as the solid wooden bench creaked beneath his weight as he lowered his wide posterior onto it.

'It's unlikely, but haven't you physicians always maintained that a maidenhead cures all venereal ills?'

The doctor harrumphed deep in his barrel chest. 'That may be true,' he agreed. 'What are you drinking, my lord? Coffee or brandy?'

'My thanks, coffee, if it please you.' Tarquin slipped a hand into his pocket and withdrew his snuffbox. He applied a pinch to his nostrils and at the same time extended the box to Reeves.

The doctor balanced a little dune of the powdery substance at the base of his thumb, and sniffed appreciatively. Then an almighty sneeze exploded from him. 'Oh yes… ahem… my word, that's a fine mixture, my lord!' he exclaimed, and wiped his nose and eyes on an already brown-stained handkerchief. Snuff taking was almost as popular as gambling.

'It is in the interests of my young mistress that I'm in the Garden this morning,' Tarquin went on. 'She's a bright lass and I've decided to have her educated. I'm seeking a responsible teacher. Do you know of such a one?'

Reeves pulled a face and pondered, and then inspiration dawned and he brought his massive fist down on the table with such force the china rattled. 'I do indeed, just the very man. My nephew. He's studying law, but could do with some extra work. He lives on an allowance from his father, but you know what students are like, a feckless lot, drinking too much, fucking too much. They've never enough to live on.'

'Where can I find him?' Tarquin asked, resting his chin on the knob of his walking cane ruminatively.

'Look no further, dear sir, he's over there with that gang of ne'er-do-wells. Waiter!' Reeves bellowed at the obsequious individual who had just brought Tarquin coffee. 'Tell that whippersnapper of a nephew of mine that he's wanted over here.'

The waiter went across to where five young men occupied a table well away from their staid elders. They were talking non-stop, gesturing, arguing and discoursing. And the loudest and most verbose of these was a lanky youth with a thin, animated face, clothing that looked as if he had slept in it, and tousled tawny hair that curled over his shoulders, disdaining the restraint of a cue. The waiter spoke to him, and he gave an impudent grin and lifted his cup in salute to Reeves before rising and excusing himself from his fellow students. He was tall and well built and moved with impetuous speed, as if everything that happened to him had to be examined at once, drained dry of knowledge and then tossed aside. He possessed all the arrogance and confidence of the young, and Tarquin felt suddenly old and jaded in his presence.

'This is my sister's son, Charles Prescot,' Reeves introduced him, and they bowed, Tarquin stiffly and Charles with an ironic grace, amusement flickering in his blue-green eyes. 'Charles, let me introduce you to Lord Tarquin Hallagon.'

'Your servant, my lord, and most people call me Charlie.'

'Mr Prescot,' said Tarquin, in a tone intended to put the young man in his place, but Charlie simply smiled, showing off a set of even white teeth.

Formalities over, Reeves grunted, 'Sit down, Charles. By George, you're like a great post looming over me, taller than ever, I vow. Listen here, my lad, Lord Tarquin is looking for a tutor.'

'I'm busy studying, uncle,' Charlie said firmly, easing far down on his spine and stretching his long legs under the table.

'I can see that,' Reeves remarked with heavy sarcasm. 'Far too conscientious to waste time with those rapscallions you call friends. Your father tells me that your lecturers are far from pleased with your work.'

'They demand blood,' Charlie returned briskly. 'Don't put yourself out on my account, uncle. I shall succeed, never fear.'

'I should be mightily obliged if you could see your way clear to assist me,' Tarquin interjected, the cane warm in his palm, seeming to have a life of its own and a personality that demanded it be laid across Charlie's rump.

Charlie cocked an impertinent eyebrow at him. 'It seems

to me that you are educated enough, my lord.'

'It's not for me, but for a lady in whom I have taken an interest, a country girl who will benefit from learning her letters and how to string them together. You could come in daily for an hour. You shall be generously compensated... and she will be entirely in your hands,' he could not resist adding, testing the boy's sexuality. 'She can be a troublesome minx. High-spirited, you know.'

'You may have to give her ten of the best,' roared Reeves, catching on quickly, his face beet-red and his jowls quivering like a turkey's wattles. 'Up with her petticoats and bend her across your lap, your hand smacking her bare bum cheeks, showing no mercy. Ain't that so, my lord?'

'That is for Mr Prescot to decide.' Tarquin gave a non-committal answer. 'He will be her schoolmaster.'

'I haven't yet said I'll take the job,' Charlie reminded them, sitting up straight and subjecting both older men to a sharp glance.

'We must talk terms.' Tarquin added a nip of brandy to his coffee. The figure he was about to propose was a generous one and he hazarded a shrewd guess as to its appeal to a student who lived above his means.

The outcome was that he got his way. Charlie agreed to become Lucy's tutor. 'When do you want me to start?' he asked glumly.

'Today,' Tarquin replied laconically. 'My coach is round the corner.'

'Now?' grumbled Reeves. 'I hoped he'd spruce himself up a little before meeting his pupil. Just you behave yourself, boy, and don't bring disgrace on the Prescot name.'

I am in love, Lucy wrote slowly and painstakingly in the little leather-covered journal she had bought during one of her shopping expeditions. Chloe did not know about it and neither did Cordelia. She was becoming adept at keeping secrets.

It was a month since Charlie Prescot, the tutor assigned to her by her lord and master, had burst into her life like a breath of fresh air. Wanting to please him, and also because she was remarkably quick to learn, she was beginning to put sentences together, and also to read simple phrases. Mathematics continued to elude her, and she thought she might never master the principles of addition and subtraction. But words were something else entirely.

She had prepared her work for Charlie's visit later that morning – letters of the alphabet produced in a beautiful, even script – and now she was concentrating on her diary. She had at least an hour to herself while Chloe looked after her hens and the cockerel that replaced the one sacrificed the night she lost her virginity, and Tarquin was fully occupied with his elaborate toilette under the auspices of Powys. Lucy knew her lord was entertaining tonight and that she would be called upon to take part in heathen rituals and perform sexual acts for the edification of his guests, but for now, she was blessedly alone.

I am in love. Four such simple words, and yet they meant the world. She had imagined in the beginning that she might love Tarquin, but since meeting Charlie she recognised what she felt for her master was passion laced with fear, sensuality divorced from affection, a drug-like sense of submission that served to numb the shame she felt at her wanton, disgraceful sexuality. Every time Tarquin demanded her obedience, chaining her, whipping her and stimulating her as only he knew how to do, her body betrayed her, responding to him and warming up with desire. This combination of pain and lust left her exhausted, and never quite satisfied. Physically, yes, spiritually and emotionally, no.

On the morning Charlie was brought to Greyfriars and introduced as her tutor, a glow had come into her life that had been absent until then. He was no more than twenty-years-old and utterly carefree. He made her laugh, made lessons fun, praised her aptitude, and provided her with the playmate she'd never had. It made her realise how weary she was of being used. Her bottom was sore from the constant pressure of dildos and Tarquin's thrusting cock. Her buttocks were bruised from the application of whip, birch, paddle and his merciless hand, and she felt soiled and degraded because he sometimes allowed her to be fucked by all and sundry.

She began to look forward to her daily lessons, keeping Charlie in her mind's eye during Tarquin's vicious lovemaking, or the sexual sessions led by Chloe and Cordelia, or by Maggie, who was often there keeping a watch on her. These three women took their pleasure of her and of each other, indoctrinating her into the art of Sapphic love. She could not deny she enjoyed it. Women were so curvaceous, so gentle and sensual. They took their time, paying attention to breasts and nipples, the swell of buttocks and thighs, the exploration of those folds and crannies constituting the female genitalia, taking special care with the seat of satisfaction and the jewel in the crown – the clitoris.

Charlie was an unknown quantity. They were never alone, always chaperoned by Chloe or Benjamin. Tarquin obviously did not trust this vigorous young man, and he might well be suspicious if he knew how Lucy felt about her teacher. She sat now mulling over what she had written, tapping the tip of the quill pen against her lips. Charlie was so handsome, so tall and upright. His face lit up with mischief when he smiled, but sometimes there was a serious look in his blue-green eyes that thrilled her to the marrow. Just occasionally, his hand brushed against hers as he passed her a book or checked over her papers, and this brief contact with him was more exciting to her than open-mouthed kissing with anyone else.

She decided on the next sentence and slowly and carefully added, *I want Charlie*.

She had no idea where he lived. He stayed for an hour, and then went away again. She knew nothing about him except that he was studying law. Even so, she took time over her preparations in the morning, selecting her clothing with care from amongst the pretty outfits Tarquin had paid for. The gowns were light and frothy, with short tight stays laced at the back and a flurry of skirts and petticoats springing out from the narrow waists. Her breasts were pushed high, but half-hidden by lacy triangular scarves worn over the shoulders and crossed at the deep V of her cleavage. The colours were fresh, pastels and white, as became a young woman. She had discovered that Tarquin, despite his repeated assaults on her innocence, was fostering her girlish image, the golden blonde, blue-eyed, peaches-and-cream illusion of virginity.

The clock placed precisely in the middle of the marble mantelpiece struck eleven times, flanked by a couple of Dresden china shepherds and shepherdesses engaged in copulation. Lucy hurriedly hid her journal. On the last stroke Chloe entered the room and took her place on the window seat. Almost immediately, there was a light rap on the panelling.

'Come in, Mr Prescot,' Chloe said, almost fondly.

He was there, seeming to fill the lofty room with his presence. He crossed the room in a few long strides and bowed before Lucy, an errant lock of hair falling forward over his forehead as he did so.

'Mrs Browne,' he said, addressing her by the title even unmarried women used, the term 'miss' being associated with very young girls or prostitutes. 'And how are you on this lovely morning?'

She blushed, wanting to reply, 'All the better for seeing you', but she did not dare. Instead, she mumbled something about being well, and was glad when they settled down at the round pedestal table and opened the exercise books, bound volumes Chloe had taken from a cupboard.

'You're doing splendidly, Lucy,' Charlie complimented her. 'I'm astonished at the speed with which you have grasped the principles of letters. I was slow when I first started. I never thought I would understand what "A" had to do with the picture of a rosy apple printed in my rag book primer.'

'I'm sure not!' she exclaimed fervently. 'You must have been brilliant to have achieved your present status of studying law! How impressive. Why, you could end up a judge.' As she waffled on, she was relishing the feel of his thigh touching hers as they leaned over the same book. She could smell his hair, and the faint odour of ale lingering from the night before when he must have made merry in a tavern with his friends. She wondered if women had been present and if he had taken one of them home and slept with her. The thought was hugely unpleasant, and threw her into such turmoil she could not concentrate.

Then she heard him whispering, his breath moving the sparkling paste pendant in her recently pierced ear, 'Come out with me, Lucy,' he implored softly. 'Meet me in Vauxhall across the river or at the Ranelagh Rotunda. These pleasure gardens are so popular and crowded we'd never be noticed.'

'I can't,' she murmured, torn between fear and excitement. She shot a hurried glance over to where Chloe sat, but the priestess was mumbling into her beads, a faraway look in her dark eyes.

'Please, Lucy,' he muttered.

She longed to bury her hands in his hair and draw his lips down over hers. She could feel her pussy getting warm and did not protest as his hand fondled her knee. He explored beneath her skirt and cruised up her leg, and when his knuckles brushed the floss at her mound, each

140

hair seemed to have a direct link with her nubbin, making it swell and poke from its fleshy cowl beneath his light touch. She bit down a moan and moved away from him anxiously. 'It's impossible,' she said very quietly.

'But you would like to? Say "yes", dear Lucy, and I'll arrange it, somehow.'

It was then the door opened with a flourish and Tarquin strode into the room. In contrast to Charlie's scholarly untidiness, he was dressed to perfection in a burgundy suit, his jaw smoothly shaved, his hair immaculately arranged, his frills crisply laundered. Chloe sat up to attention, pretending she had not been absorbed in her spells, and Lucy could feel her own face flaming. Charlie had touched her intimately, and she had enjoyed it.

'Ah, my dear, I see you are hard at work,' Tarquin said in an irritatingly patronising tone. 'How is she progressing, Mr Prescot?'

Charlie opened his mouth to reply, but Lucy shot him a warning glance and answered in his stead, 'I'm not doing well, my lord. I'm such a slowpoke. I fear my mind is not up to the task.'

Charlie looked puzzled, and then smiled. If she appeared to be progressing too fast, then Tarquin might dismiss him thinking she had learned enough, and this would be absolutely unendurable to them both.

Tarquin frowned and his eyes glinted like steel. 'Is this so, Mr Prescot?' he snapped. 'Is she a dullard?'

'She finds it hard, my lord,' Charlie lied.

'Does she, indeed?' Tarquin asked in an ominously quiet voice. 'Then she must be punished. Don't you agree?'

'Ah well… not exactly, sir,' Charlie stammered. 'Sometimes it is wiser to use gentle encouragement.'

'Balderdash. With someone as stubborn as she, I find only harsh treatment works. Take off your coat and sit yourself down on that chair, Mr Prescot, and then put her across your knee.'

Charlie did as he was bidden, but awkwardly, his gestures indicating his embarrassment. Lucy had not seen him in his shirtsleeves before, and marvelled at the width of his shoulders, the broadness of his chest, and at the fair thatch of hair curling at the open neck where he had untied his cravat.

Tarquin, impatient to begin, pulled her over to where her tutor sat, and then placed a hand at her waist, forcing her down until she rested on her stomach across Charlie's lap. Her breasts overlapped his thigh on one side, spilling out of her low-cut bodice, and her bottom was raised high on the other, her straight legs supporting her in a stiff stance. His body was warm, his phallus like a sturdy bough pressing against her. She would have been in a seventh heaven of delight had the circumstances been different.

'I'm sorry, Mrs Browne,' Charlie said, a bit breathlessly.

'Don't apologise to the jade,' Tarquin ordered. 'Lay the blows on rigorously, my man. It is all she understands.'

'I beg to differ, sir. In my opinion, she is a young lady of exceptional talent.'

'Do you want to go on working for me?' Tarquin asked nastily. 'If you do, then I suggest you stop shilly-shallying and get on with it.' He leaned over Lucy and gripped the hem of her skirt, hitching it up and back. Her petticoats came next, first one and then the other. She was now bare bottomed, naked to the waist except for white silk stockings. 'She's very lovely though, isn't she?' he asked languorously, his hand moving over her buttocks and forcing them apart. He dipped a finger between her labial wings and then withdrew it to hold it up in front of Charlie's face. 'Smell her. Have you ever known anything more fragrant? Don't worry on her account. She's enjoying this. Her wet pussy tells me she is.' And he stroked the moist hair between her legs until she could not suppress a sigh.

Lucy could only guess how she must appear to Charlie, like a slut now rather than a lady. She went hot all over as she imagined him looking down at the rounded globes of her bottom cheeks, crisscrossed with a ladder of stripes laid on by Tarquin's whip. He would also see the amber crease between them, and the fluffy fair hair coating the pursed lips of her pudenda. And Tarquin had indeed stirred up her juices so the air was spiced with the oceanic scent that betrayed how receptive she was to the male organ. She turned her head and glanced up at Charlie. His face was intense, his brows knit, and his phallus jerked as it dug into her side.

Tarquin found the tiny nodule of flesh between her tender sex lips and moved it back and forth until she bucked despite herself. Then, as expected, he took his finger away before she could enjoy it too much. 'No, my dear,' he said, shaking his head. 'No one is going to bring you off until you've been thoroughly thrashed. Go to it, Mr Prescot.'

Charlie's face set with sudden resolve. He gripped Lucy's wrists in his left hand and drew her arms up over her head, and then with his right hand he smacked her, hard. She yelled and wriggled on his lap, the heat and wetness of her sex pressing against his leg as she sought friction on her clitoris. He started spanking her more rigorously, getting into the swing of it, belabouring not only her arse but the backs of her thighs, and the edge of his hand even caught her pouting lower lips and made her squeal.

Her cries became louder as her hinds heated up, that strange dichotomy of pain and pleasure sweeping through her loins, her belly, and all the way up her spine. A storm of loud slaps fell in quick succession and she threshed and writhed in torment. Charlie's hand tightened on her wrists as he ignored her protests and spanked her even harder, and with increasing accuracy, until her bottom was a glowing rosy red.

'Well done,' Tarquin said, and shoved her off Charlie's lap onto the floor.

The shock was terrible, and the sense of loss incredible. No promise of Charlie's ardent cock, just Tarquin and his shameful mastery over her.

He dragged her to her knees, holding her head back using her hair as a reign, and made her look up at him. He had opened his breeches and taken out his erection. She looked across at her young teacher. He was still sitting there as if stunned, but there was the blackest scowl on his face she had ever seen on anyone, and just for a second she hated Tarquin. Arrogant and possessive, he was doing this merely to demonstrate his power over her.

He drew her closer until his helm nudged her lips, and then gave a sharp tug on her hair. 'Open up,' he commanded.

Lucy lowered her eyes, accepting his authority over her. Let Charlie look his fill. There was nothing she could do about it. She could only hope that perhaps her performance would inspire him to want some of the same. Tarquin pushed, and she opened her mouth wide and took the whole of his solid length between her lips until it could go no further, blocked by the back of her throat. He held her firmly, rocking slightly back and forth, and she nearly gagged. Then he drew back a little so she could run her tongue over the stem of his cock. He tasted wonderful, and she heard him groan beneath his breath though she guessed he would be standing there with an impassive expression on his aristocratic face. She slid a hand into the front closure of his breeches, and finding his heavy, sap-filled testicles, cupped them gently, almost reverently. Double pleasure for him now, her fingers on his balls and her tongue working on his cock, and she could feel the tension in him as he thrust strongly into her mouth in pursuit of his climax. She held on for dear life, sucking him while playing with his cods, rubbing them and feeling the light coating of hair covering the sac. His excitement was rising, his hips propelling his erection in and out between her lips as if he was pursued by demons, and he groaned with pleasure as every pump of his rock-hard tool brought him closer to his crisis.

Lucy forgot Charlie, forgot Chloe, as she concentrated on massaging Tarquin's tight balls while sucking him fervently, and then on milking him of his seed as he jetted a hot stream of semen into her throat. She swallowed the salty libation and as he withdrew felt more gushing over her cheeks and chin. Then he was once more his reserved self, coolly wiping his cock clean in her hair.

'That is the way to treat an obstinate pupil, Mr Prescot,' he said as blandly as if he was discussing the weather.

'I see, sir,' Charlie answered, rising unsteadily to his feet, red to the ears and with a huge erection tenting his breeches. He looked so distressed that Lucy yearned to comfort him and bring relief to his member, but this, of course, was impossible.

'That's all very well, master,' she complained, rubbing her stinging bottom before lowering her skirts. 'But *I've* not been satisfied. Why do you do this to me, my lord? Am I not to have my pleasure, too?'

'Later, sweeting, later,' he promised, tweaking her nipples as they poked out of her bodice, making them burn and setting her clit throbbing once more. 'I'm not the cruel villain you think me. Indeed, I've a treat for you. St Bartholomew Fair opens in a few days and I've arranged to take you there. You may kiss my hand and say "Thank you, master".'

An outing was a rare occurrence; she was kept virtually a prisoner in the house. St Bartholomew was a famous fair and she was moved he had thought she might enjoy it. She sank down to her knees again and took his extended hand. It was beautiful, with long, aristocratic fingers and strong as steel. She pressed her lips to the back of it.

'Thank you, master,' she murmured.

'That's settled, then,' he said curtly, disengaging his hand. 'Carry on, Mr Prescot.' Straightening his clothes, he made for the door. 'Your hour is not yet up.' He let himself out.

'Oh Charlie, what are we going to do?' Lucy sighed as he took her in his arms.

'Trust me, this is a heaven-sent opportunity,' he murmured, straining her body to his. Their first embrace, and only made possible because Chloe had dozed off in the noonday heat.

As Lucy had written in her journal earlier, *Things have moved on apace. Since he spanked me, Charlie has become bolder. We speak low and make plans. It will happen at the Fair, and then, oh bliss, we shall be together forever!'*

'Tomorrow, dearest,' he promised, and she turned her head so their lips met in their first kiss.

It was as if she had never been kissed before. His lips were warm, dry and firm, and she responded to them passionately, employing all the tricks she had learned from experts. Yet she was shy and trembling. This was such an important moment she feared she might destroy it by being too bold. He was trembling, too, his hands sliding down her silk-covered spine. She moved against him, obeying the dictates of her flesh, lifting her hips and rubbing her pubis against the long bulge in his breeches. Her mouth opened and their tongues met as he clasped her buttocks, pressing his lower body to hers with little rhythmic motions.

Chloe gave a sudden snore and they sprang apart, but the Creole did not wake, simply licked her lips and relapsed into slumber again.

'Charlie, we must be careful,' Lucy warned, gripping the edge of the worktable to steady herself.

'I find it so difficult,' he frowned, keeping his voice

down. 'I can't bear to think of him abusing you, forcing his will upon you and letting his friends make free with you. You are worth so much more, Lucy.'

'It's all right, Charlie,' she said soothingly. 'He has provided for me.'

'He's a monster!' Charlie clenched his fists as if he would smash them into Tarquin's face.

'I pity him,' she countered softly. Yet being Tarquin's slave had not been all bad, she had to admit. 'He refuses to love, or be loved,' she added sadly.

'Unlike us.' His hands clasped her waist and pulled her close. 'Ah Lucy, I can hardly wait. Do you know what you do to me?' He grabbed her hand and placed it on his cock so she could feel how hard it was through his breeches. 'I dream of you every minute of every hour. Every day when I leave here, I'm so aroused that the first thing I do is seek privacy and masturbate. Only then can I begin to function properly. Just think, love, tomorrow night we shall be together! I've given up my present lodgings with two other students, they wouldn't have been suitable for us, and taken a room in the house of Mrs Trott. She is a respectable widow but broadminded and lives above her dead husband's bookshop, which she still runs. That's how I met her.'

'Have you told her about me?' she whispered anxiously. 'And won't Tarquin be able to find us?'

'I doubt it. London is ideal for hiding away. I've confided in Mrs Trott, pretending we're star-crossed lovers escaping parents who refuse to let us wed, and when we've saved enough money, we shall go to Gretna Green and be married there.'

'Oh Charlie, you're so clever.'

He unbuttoned his breeches and she slipped her hand inside them to find his throbbing staff. By now she knew what to expect, but the feel of his hot cock pulsing eagerly in her palm as she stroked it still breathlessly excited her.

147

'That's it... do it harder,' he muttered. 'Oh yes...' he drove his penis through the circle of her fingers, and at that moment, when Lucy knew they were both about to lose control, Chloe stirred, yawning widely. She instantly released Charlie and sat down as he did the same, the table hiding him from view as he struggled to imprison his erection and refasten his breeches.

'*Ahem*... let us try that passage again, Mrs Browne,' he said loudly, his cheeks flushed. 'Now then, take it from the top.'

Lucy struggled to regain control of herself, her nipples peaking, her nubbin thrumming and her fissure so wet she could feel the juice soaking into her petticoats.

He added in an undertone, 'Tomorrow! Meet me as we've arranged. I shall be waiting.'

Chapter Nine

It was one of those bright mornings in August when a full moon hung like a ghostly skull in the benign blue sky and there were no clouds anywhere.

By the time the Hallagon coach arrived and parked near dozens of others in that great area of ground that had been given over to the annual fair for the past seven hundred years, the Lord Mayor of London had already opened it in state and, bowing to tradition, had paused to drink a tankard of wine, nutmeg and sugar at Newgate Gaol on his way. Lucy could hardly contain her excitement.

Tarquin sat beside her, an ironic smile on his face expressing his languid amusement at her childish eagerness. 'My dear girl, haven't you been anywhere or done *anything?*' he drawled, flipping back his lace falls. 'It's only a goddamned fair, after all. Surely such common junketings were practiced even in that backend of the woods you call home?'

She controlled herself, her spine straight, her knees together, her hands linked in her lap. The last thing she wanted to do today was ruffle him. Too much depended on her retaining his favour, for she had arranged to meet Charlie at dusk near the rear exit.

'We had market days, sir,' she said finally, 'and a hiring fair where one could apply for work.' She spoke evenly, feeling herself surrounded by foes, Chloe and Benjamin and even Powys, who was carrying a small trinket case holding objects his master might need during the course of the day and presiding over a picnic hamper. She knew Cordelia and Maggie were also joining Tarquin. They intended to watch the performance given on the open-air stage at nightfall. The audience had been promised an opera about Noah's Flood, with several fountains spouting water and a grand finale when Noah and his family emerged from the Ark with, as promised by the handbill, *All the beasts two by two and a multitude of angels from above*.

Lucy was almost as eager to witness this spectacle as she was to elope with Charlie. Yet she would miss most of it, for it was while everyone's attention was riveted on the drama that she would slip away and join her Romeo. But her love for him was almost eclipsed by the wonders of the fair. Once she had alighted from the carriage she wandered along in a daze, hardly knowing where to look first, her bonnet clutched in one hand, her reticule in the other containing a comb, a small mirror and her precious journal. The sea of booths appeared to stretch for miles, providing food and drink and candy, material by the yard, lace by the ream, and ostrich feathers by the dozen. There were hats and handkerchiefs, shoes and gloves, china and fairings, cheap-jack jewellery, paper flowers, coconut shies and hoopla, songbirds in wicker cages and quacks selling their cure all medicines.

In one quarter of the fair stood a garlanded maypole, and people were dancing round it accompanied by a tabor and pipe. This clashed with other musicians vying for notice – huntsmen with French horns, and a group of harlequins capering and singing and playing guitars. There were trees in tubs and festoons of flowers, both waxen and real, and tents erected to provide tea and wine, gaming tables and dance floors. There were not many beggars in evidence; the crowd consisted mainly of tradesmen and their families, visiting farmers, or members of the upper class accompanied by friends and servants. Even so, Tarquin advised Lucy to keep a firm hold of her purse, as the fair was a hunting ground for pickpockets.

She did as he advised, and though he normally kept her as poor as a church mouse, that morning he had magnanimously provided her with a few coins with which to purchase whatever struck her fancy at the fair. Walking close beside him, she was caught up in a world of colour and smells. Fires flared in braziers, with meat and fish roasting on spits over the flames and thick tendrils of smoke drifting above the booths, where pennants waved in the breeze. The alluring odour of sweetmeats and gingerbread and toffee apples wafted from confectioners' stalls, making her mouth water. Dogs nosed about for scraps, children ran around shrieking with their mothers in hot pursuit, and women of ill fame flaunted their charms, their casual trade behind the tents and in the bushes becoming brisker as the ale flowed and men lost their reservations.

Three dwarfs dressed as clowns were counting money, and a black woman selling silver rings caught Lucy's eye and called to her. Within a rough circle, two men stripped to the waist and dripping with sweat were wrestling before rowdy spectators who had placed bets on the outcome. Overhead, a tinsel-clad girl in an exceedingly short skirt walked a high wire in pointed red slippers, a parasol draped over one shoulder. Then Tarquin stopped by a tent with crimson curtains across the front. They parted, and half-a-dozen handsome young men in gold loincloths ran out throwing small colourful balls into the air. They turned somersaults and climbed poles, graceful and agile, posing for Tarquin's benefit, and Lucy saw her master's eyes narrow lustfully as he considered these seventeen-year-olds. She was disgusted, and thankful she was soon to leave him.

'Come and see the freaks,' he said, a hand under her elbow as he guided her towards a rank of sideshows flaunting gaudy signs with crudely executed paintings of mermaids, bearded ladies and a pygmy calf with five legs.

She hung back. 'I don't want to,' she protested.

'It's rare sport,' he insisted. 'I'll read aloud what it says on that placard... *Here is to be seen a little fairy woman being but two foot two inches high and in no way deformed.* Or what about, *Twin sisters being about thirty years old and joined at the left side from birth. They are both married to different gentlemen and function normally.*'

'No, really,' she said, pity for these unfortunate creatures welling up in her bosom.

'No?' he asked levelly, yet he had never looked more deadly. 'I fancy seeing them mating with these husbands of theirs, or even having a poke at them myself. Do you suppose the proprietor would arrange it, if I offered him a generous sum?'

'I don't know, it seems that anything is possible with money,' she answered tartly, and freeing herself from his grasp crossed over to where Chloe was haggling over a pair of earrings.

The day grew warmer and the crowd wilder as the alcohol flowed and the holiday spirit prevailed. A few fights had broken out, and here and there bare-breasted, tousle-headed harridans shrieked after their men, but these uproars ended in equally noisy reconciliations. Tarquin and his cronies kept to their own side of the pitch, the wealthier side where the stage had been put up. There was a space for the orchestra, and though the seats were merely rough benches without backs, the rich sent their footmen to occupy places for them. When the time came, the rest of the audience would crowd the entrance and fight its way in.

While they waited, the elite sat in the shade of awnings and sampled cold collations prepared by their cooks and served by their valets or butlers. They took snuff and chatted, played cards and gambled and flirted with their various companions. Tarquin fondled Lucy, who was seated beside him, unashamedly lifting her skirt and exposing her pussy while she tried to hide her blushes behind her lace-edged fan.

'Sir, it's broad daylight,' she cautioned. 'Everyone can see what you're about.'

'So?' he replied airily, his free hand tossing the dice on the baize-covered surface of the card table in front of them. He slanted a glance at Cordelia. 'This foolish child is worried because someone might notice I'm about to bring her off. Isn't she silly?'

Cordelia smiled as serenely as the Sphinx and slipped a hand into his lap.

His expert fingers rubbed each side of Lucy's hair-fringed labia, and then pinched the outer lips together, imprisoning her clitoris and making the swelling nodule tingle. She could not hold back a gasp. He smiled tersely and said to his opponent on the other side of the table, 'Double sixes, Buckley. I've bested you.'

'Damn if you haven't!' the plump dandy exclaimed. 'You've the most infernal luck, Tarquin.' 'Tell   you what, I propose another wager,' Tarquin said, whilst continuing to massage Lucy's increasingly wet cleft. 'I'll bet you five guineas that you can't tell me the exact moment when she reaches her crisis. She's completely under my control and will do as I command and keep calm.'

'Done!' Buckley agreed eagerly.

'Now concentrate,' Tarquin ordered, and the others gathered round to watch Lucy intently.

She was offended, silently appalled by his behaviour and near to tears, but his finger on her button was irresistibly seductive. He stroked her as only he knew how to, spreading her labial wings apart and coaxing the sliver of flesh between them to rise up proud, the little head hard as a pea and throbbing with desire. She tried to keep an impassive expression, knowing that if he lost to

153

Buckley she would be punished, but this strain added to the lust pounding inside her, and fight for control as hard as she might, there was no escaping the exquisite sensations carrying her away on them.

She bit her lip, stared out of the tent at the rapidly darkening scene, listened to the hub-hub as the crowd became even more drunk and raucous, listened to the music, the singing, the yells and the bawdy laughter, as the orgasmic waves gathered and swelled inside her, flooding her, impossible to resist. She gripped the arms of the chair and kept her body straight, but suddenly Tarquin pinched the tip of her swollen bud and she climaxed with a violence that shocked her and was impossible to hide.

'Ah, she's peaked!' Buckley shouted gleefully. 'You've lost, Tarquin.'

Tarquin removed his fingers from her juicing cleft. 'Stand up and bend over,' he commanded her angrily.

Miserably, Lucy did so, clasping her ankles with her hands. The bucks and their lady friends watched, so aroused by the spectacle that they began caressing one another intimately, their skirts whipped up and their breeches unfastened. Ripe breasts swelled above daringly fashionable décolleté, the grand ladies no better than the strumpets, who were getting bolder as the sun went down.

Lucy inhaled the trampled grass, the litter, the hot scent of human bodies, and stared at her feet, her little satin shoes peeping out from beneath her skirts. The dreaded moment came all too soon when Tarquin raised her petticoats and her secrets were revealed to all – her white thighs, her plump lower lips, her arse-crack and her buttocks. A sob gathered in her chest, and burst out of her as his makeshift cane swished down, burning into her tender hinds with a vicious stroke.

His fury transmitted itself through his arm and into the fancy walking stick. He was coldly, ruthlessly angry. He had lost money, but above all he had lost face, and any injury to his overweening pride was a capital offence in his book.

Lucy quivered and almost toppled over as he gave her no time to recover from his first blow, the instrument of punishment becoming a lightning bolt in his hand landing mercilessly across her buttocks again and again.

'Enough!' Buckley cried suddenly. 'Keep the damned money!'

'Get up, you baggage!' Tarquin growled, lowering his arm.

She found it hard to straighten up her body was throbbing so with pain. Tears coursed down her cheeks and she leaned against one of the supports of the tent, burying her face in her arms. Tarquin ignored her, once more seating himself at the gaming table with a full glass of wine and a deck of cards. At that moment, in a flurry of silks, waves of perfume and effusive greetings, Maggie made her entrance. Everyone turned towards her, ignoring the distressed Lucy, who took advantage of the distraction to slip outside. A quick look around showed her Benjamin, seated cross-legged on the ground outside a fortune-teller's tent.

'Where is Chloe?' she asked him nervously, not sure she could trust him.

He jerked his head towards the tent. 'Inside having the tarot cards read for her, and her palm, too, and maybe the crystal ball. She can't stay away from gypsies,' he explained, and took another sip from the brandy bottle he had managed to purloin.

'I need to relieve myself,' she told him urgently. 'I shan't go far.' She prayed he would not accompany her. Undoubtedly he and Chloe had been ordered to keep her in sight at all times, but she could see he was already a little drunk and disinclined to move.

He mumbled something and started singing beneath his

breath, rocking to the rhythm. She quickly dodged behind the tent, trying to determine the way to the fair's back entrance. It was getting dark fast. The cooking flames were brighter, the oil-soaked wicks burning in cressets, candles blazed in every booth and stall, and strings of coloured paper lanterns hung on high, short tallow dips, glowing gently. The sun was sinking rapidly, great swathes of orange and crimson fanning out on the western horizon. In the limpid turquoise sky above, stars started twinkling and indigo clouds gathered round it as the moon gained strength over its vanquished rival, dispelling a soft, romantic light over the frenzy below.

Lucy set out in what she prayed was the right direction, hurrying lest her disappearance had been discovered and Tarquin was already dispatching his servants to find her. But the crowd was too great, the confusion too vast, to make this easy for them. Nightfall, the clamour of the fair and her passionate determination were all her allies.

The single concession to sanitation at the fair was a latrine consisting of a ditch dug on one side of the showground. She stopped at the back of a stall, lifted her skirts and squatted, cursing Tarquin roundly. Her bottom was a mass of bruises, and anger hardened her face as she rearranged her clothes and ran off in search of her lover.

It was as well she was no longer a simple farm lass, for strange and lewd sights accosted her from all directions. Everywhere, openly and unashamed, couples were playing the hump-backed beast. Sometimes there were groups of more than two, so that the whole world seemed to be copulating. She saw a man bending a woman backwards over a boarded trestle, his huge bare cock like a spear ready to plunge into her vitals, and others applauded him whilst handling their own tools seeking satisfaction. Lucy kept her eyes down, terrified they might notice her, alarmed by the wildness of their faces. It was like a nightmare…

156

the flare of flames, the creaking of a booth as a man took a whore up against it, the discordant music, the shrill human scream of a crimson cockatoo, the wail of a muddied baby crying for its mother, the chattering of a monkey in a fez and red bolero dragging its chain wretchedly seeking its lost master… then suddenly, unable to believe her good fortune, Lucy turned a corner and saw Charlie leaning on the barrier that formed the fair's boundary. Two massive men with shaven heads and villainous faces guarded it, their job to apprehend anyone hell-bent on causing serious trouble.

'Charlie!' she cried, and flung herself into his arms. She had never been so happy to see anyone in her life.

'Lucy, my darling, you've done it!' He snatched her up against his chest so her feet dangled in the air.

'I'm earlier than arranged, the play hasn't yet begun, but I seized the opportunity,' she explained breathlessly, her heart pounding, her bodily pains forgotten in the desire surging through her whole being for this man.

He set her down but kept his arm around her, clamping her to his side as he hurried her along, leaving the fair a noisy blur behind them. 'Come,' he said urgently. 'We'll take a hackney to my new lodgings. There we'll go to bed, Lucy. It's almost our wedding night.'

'Oh Charlie,' she sighed, transported with happiness.

Charlie's room was in a tall, narrow house near St Paul's churchyard. It was a district traditionally dedicated to booksellers, and Mrs Trott's establishment was no different. Her home was behind and above a shop crammed full of musty volumes and new works. It smelled of leather and printers' ink and dust mingled with the odour of fish, cabbage and tomcats spraying their territory. Mrs Trott was inordinately fond of cats and the proud owner of six.

As she explained to Lucy when Charlie paid the cabman

and conducted her inside, 'I never had no children, you see, Mrs Browne. The good Lord saw fit to deny me this joy, but my darling pussies make up for it. They are my babies, aren't you, sweethearts? Even more so now my dear husband has passed on.' She cuddled a large, ferocious-looking tabby that glared at Lucy with a baleful yellow eye, the other having been lost in a fight. Meanwhile, an off-white, longhaired feline wound itself around Mrs Trott's skirt, mewing plaintively. 'I hope you'll be comfortable in my humble abode, Mrs Brown, but I don't cook for my guests. There are plenty of pie shops near at hand.

'As I've already discussed with you,' she addressed Charlie now, 'I expect exemplary behaviour from those who inhabit my house, no drunkenness or depravity. I was moved by your story, Mr Prescot, and that is why I have bent my rules and am permitting you to share your room with this young lady. I can see she is a person of refinement, and I trust you will make an honest woman of her as soon as possible.'

'Of course, dear lady,' he vowed, bowing and kissing her hand. 'And I can't thank you enough for being so understanding.'

'The pleasure is mine. I always do what I can for the students who grace my shop. Such a fine body of young men, I always think, and my husband was of the same opinion. He was never happier than when surrounded by earnest students and giving them of his wisdom and knowledge. I have tried to carry on this practice.'

'Indeed, and you do,' Charlie said with a perfectly straight face, but once Lucy and he were alone in his tiny attic room, he laughed uproariously. 'She likes the boys, all right, and so did her husband, from what I hear, a regular sodomite.'

Then there was no time or inclination to think of anyone else. The light was dim and the atmosphere hot even though the dormer windows were open to a moonlit view of tumbled rooftops. There was a creaky single bedstead, a couple of battered chairs, a table heaped with books, papers and quill pens, and there were nails on which to hang clothes hammered into the sloping whitewashed walls. Everything was seedy and makeshift and none too clean, but to Lucy it was heaven.

They stood in the middle of the room, his head almost touching the beamed ceiling as he held her tenderly. She could feel his heart thumping madly as he pressed her body against it. He bent his head and captured her mouth, his lips softly seeking, his tongue tentatively exploring hers as it greeted him. He sucked, licked and tasted her, and she savoured the moment, anticipation warming her pussy, making her moist and overloading her clitoris with longing.

He released her and knelt at her feet, his head up, his wheat-gold hair falling down his back. 'I'm going to undress you, Lucy.' His arms came around her hips, straining her towards him. Then he rose, lifted her in his arms, spread her out across the bed, and proceeded to carry out his promise.

She did not flinch at his touch, in fact, she felt as if her body and soul were expanding, reaching out to him fervently. She spread her hand over the smooth fabric of his breeches, feeling the hint of steel in his strong thighs, and then let her fingers graze the long line of hidden flesh swelling in his crotch.

He hiked up her skirt, unbuckled her garters and rolled down her stockings. Then he lifted her feet one by one and licked each of her toes as well as the delicate arches of her feet. It was as though he wanted to worship every inch of her before he spread her legs and examined her warm, wet intimacies, his fingers fluttering over her labial wings and stroking the head of her bud.

'I did this without seeing it the other day,' he murmured,

hoarse with emotion. 'Now you are permitting me to stroll in your private garden, to wonder at the perfection of your foliage and to inhale the scent that is sweeter than roses.'

'I'm only just learning about poetry,' she gasped, lifting her hips towards the exquisite touch of his fingers. 'But you speak like a poet, surely?'

'I am inspired by you.' He urged her to half sit up so he could unlace the back of her dress and the stays beneath it.

'You're so skilful at this it makes me wonder if you've had a lot of practice undressing females,' she could not help but remark, the serpent of suspicion suddenly marring her Eden.

He chuckled, but answered neither yea nor nay as he opened her bodice. It fell away from her breasts, leaving nothing but the silk chemise. Her nipples crimped, and he slipped his hands across her ribs from behind to cup each perfect sphere. She leaned back against him, closing her eyes in sheer bliss as his thumbs rolled over her teats until they were double their size, ripe berries offering a feast.

She felt his lips on the back of her neck, brushing aside her tangled curls, and when he kissed her just where her spine and the base of her skull connected, the sensation was so acute that she found herself on the brink of climaxing. And while his lips lingered there, leaving a trail of magic, he never stopped massaging her breasts.

Unable to wait any longer, she stripped off the chemise and loosened the belt of her skirt along with her petticoat strings. She heard his sharp intake of breath, and was shocked by the anger in his voice as he cried, 'My God, did he do this to you?'

Her welts ached as he touched them, and filled her with that sick desire taught her by her master. She let Charlie draw her towards the lighted candle on the bedside so he might see her marks more clearly.

'Yes,' she admitted, 'it is Tarquin's work. I displeased him this afternoon and he chose to punish me in front of his friends.'

'The man is a fiend,' Charlie raged quietly, kissing every mark on her skin. 'I'd like to call him out!'

'You can't do that. Duelling is against the law. Besides, he's an expert and would probably kill you.' She desperately attempted to cool his dangerous wrath. 'I don't want anything to happen to you, Charlie. I should die without you!'

'Oh, Lucy, precious girl,' he answered with so much warmth and ardour that she stripped off her remaining garments and then quickly helped him out of his, loosening his cravat, opening the buttons of his balloon-sleeved shirt and unfastening his breeches.

He was as well built as she had expected him to be, his torso brown from exposure to the sun. It invited kisses, and she ran her lips over his chest, tweaking his nipples with her teeth and breathing deeply of the masculine musk at his hairy armpits. He kicked off his shoes and hose, freed himself of his breeches and stood before her, his hands on his hips, making her even more aware of the insolent thrust of his shaft and the purple plum of his glans.

Lying on her side on the bed, she took her fill of his nudity, and this seemed to embarrass him, for he suddenly leapt down beside her and pulled the feather quilt over both of them. He held her tightly, and she found his stiff, throbbing appendage with her hand. Then she slid beneath the covers and licked it from root to helm with long, sweeping strokes of her tongue. He lay still beneath her ministrations while she cradled his sap-filled balls and tickled his anus with her little finger. She did not intend for him to come that way; she was too greedy to feel him inside her. She sidled back up his body until they were face-to-face again, and he pressed her back against the mattress with her thighs outspread and her labial lips parted.

'I can see right into the heart of you,' he whispered, and his breath caressing her pussy made her moan. 'Your pink cleft glistens, and at its crest lies your beautiful little button. You want me to rub and lick it, don't you? Just like you rub and suck my cock.'

'Oh yes,' she breathed, ignoring the pain of her welts, wanting to forget everything in glorious union with her beloved. 'Charlie, take me,' she moaned as he teased her sex, playing with her, the blood coursing through her clitoris as he pinched it gently. She was so thoroughly aroused that she climaxed almost instantly. Finally, he thrust a knee between her legs, and leaning over her guided his cock to her slippery entrance. He held it there for a second, rubbing the glans against her hot orifice. Lucy was beside herself, lifting her hips higher and opening her legs wider so he could thrust his penis inside her and give her the thorough ploughing she craved.

His control snapped and he took her without further preamble. She wanted to scream with the sheer joy of being penetrated by his sturdy member, which filled her completely, butting against what felt like the core of her flesh. When he withdrew, it was as if he took part of her with him, and when he plunged again she felt complete and deliciously replete. Then his cock swelled even more and his movements became frantic, all his pent-up longing for her gathering in a great explosion of feeling, and she felt his seed spurting in hot jets, filling her with his tribute.

'I love you!' he shouted. 'I love you!' as the spasms ceased and he slumped down over her, his face buried in her hair.

I have never been more content, Lucy confided in her diary. *Charlie and I are so happy in our love nest. We have been here a week and no one has come for me. I do not venture forth from our room and study while Charlie attends lectures. Sometimes, in the evening, we go to a tavern and spend time with some of the other students.*

She was alone and it was afternoon. She had fallen into the habit of going back to sleep once Charlie left. He usually brought food on his return, but she knew he had little cash to spare. His father kept him short, and Charlie was apprehensive as to what would happen when he found out about her.

'He can't stop me marrying,' he declared defiantly. 'But he can cut me off without a shilling, and I'm not yet qualified enough to enter Chambers and be taken on as a junior partner.'

'Don't worry, Charlie, dear,' she would say as he lay across the rickety old couch, his head in her lap as she brooded over him with an almost maternal tenderness. 'I can get work.'

'No,' he answered sharply. 'You'll do no such thing. Stay here where you're safe. I don't want you falling into Tarquin's hands again.'

She could forget the difficulties when he was there, but during the long, lonely hours without him, it was hard not to worry. She had arrived with nothing save the clothes she was wearing, and the few coins her master had given her to buy something at the fair. Charlie could not afford to buy her clothing and she realised that, had she been more circumspect, she might have left Greyfriars with at least a change of garments. As it was, all she could do was take her chemise and stockings down to the yard at the rear of the house, draw water from the well, and make an effort to wash them. To save money on the laundry bill, she also attempted to clean Charlie's shirts and cravats in the same fashion, hanging them out of the attic window to dry. It was hard work and not very rewarding, as the articles never truly looked clean.

Apart from these minor irritations, she was wonderfully

happy and buoyed up by love. Her reading and writing skills were progressing quickly, surrounded as she was by primers and subject to Charlie's tuition. He expressed pride in her progress and boasted about it when they went drinking with his friends.

She had never met young men such as these. They were well connected, but unlike the members of the upper crust she had come across when living with Tarquin, they were keen on learning, always questioning and questing. In general, they were a lively bunch of forward thinkers who condemned the government more often than not, and wanted to do something for the good of mankind. She listened to them, entranced, absorbing their ideas and forming opinions of her own. Her education was advancing rapidly, but not in the way Tarquin had intended. She even began to ask why was it that women were not allowed to go to university or become doctors of medicine. This question, however, was answered only by blank stares and an awkward silence.

Lucy and Charlie were summer lovers, blessed by the golden warmth of the sun, saving on candles because the nights were short; saving on fuel because the attic was under the eaves and the tiles retained the heat; saving on food because one did not get so hungry when it was warm. Charlie did not look ahead, but Lucy, although full of laughter when he was nearby, was not so confident about the future when he was absent. Through her deepest being, like the fog that hung over the river at dawn, there drifted a vague premonition of disaster.

'Ah, there you are, brother-in-law,' drawled Rodney Prescot as Dr Reeves was ushered into his sanctum. He was an imposing, broad-shouldered, thick-necked man who carried his years well. He was standing in breeches, top-boots and shirtsleeves, his wig cast aside, his bald head glistening with a light patina of sweat brought about by his exertions.

'Good day to you,' Reeves replied, more than a trifle apprehensive, as he had a pretty good idea why he had been summoned to this fine house in Mayfair.

Rodney was engaged in whipping one of the maidservants. The girl was naked apart from black woollen stockings, and strung by her wrists from a metal ring fixed over a hook set in a beam. This position forced her to stretch high, scrabbling for a purchase with her toes. She was of generous proportions, with big breasts and wide fleshy hips, and both areas were painted a fiery red by the vicious lash of Rodney's whip. Her ankles were also secured, her legs wide open and giving no protection to the dark pelt of matted curls growing over her mound or to the brown-red lips of her sex. That Rodney had been exciting himself by beating her for some time was evident by the large erection distorting the front of his breeches. His eyes shone with an unnatural light, his coarse features twisted in an expression of raw lust. Reeves had never been able to understand what his wife, Georgina, saw in him, and had concluded it was his station and wealth that had persuaded her to marry him.

Reeves was a straightforward man. No saint, to be sure, and frequently unfaithful to his wife, but he had never found it necessary to enter the realms of bondage and flagellation in order to fire his cannon. A kindly, well-upholstered and discreet prostitute was all he needed, and he looked askance at Rodney and his ilk, who insisted on punishing their paramours, though he had to admit to becoming randy at the idea of a playful spanking.

'Where's my son?' Rodney swung round to glare at him, and then turned back and lunged at the hapless maid, plunging his podgy fingers into her pussy and penetrating deep into her female cavity.

The girl shrieked and bucked, and Reeves, distressed for her, wiped his face with a handkerchief. 'I have no idea of Charles's whereabouts,' he replied stiffly, wishing to leave this wine cellar that Rodney had transformed into a torture chamber.

Rodney gave the maid a few more swipes with his whip, and rounded on him again angrily. 'You must know, you see him about town, don't you? Wasn't it you who found him this confounded job as a tutor?'

'Yes, it was, and I bitterly regret it. I thought to help him, but it seems he has run off with his pupil. This is deuced awkward for me, as Lord Tarquin is a valued client and sorely offended by Charles's actions. He is blaming me for it!'

'So he should. Blast my son to hell!' Rodney lifted his arm and brought it down again with such vigour that his feet almost left the floor. The leather bit into his victim's flesh, the whip coiling round her ribs and catching the underside of her breasts as her screams rang in the rafters.

'Why take it out on the poor lass?' Reeves remonstrated, resisting the urge to fell his sister's odious husband with a single blow from his powerful fist.

'She likes it. Don't you, sweetheart?' Rodney leered into the girl's tear-streaked face. 'Her quim is very wet. Look…' He palpated her, and then held his glistening fingers up to the doctor's face. 'She's a dirty trollop, waggling her tail at every man in the vicinity. I have to keep order amongst my servants. It is my bounden duty.'

'What tosh,' Reeves muttered, and made to leave, but Rodney had not finished with him.

'Stay!' he said so imperiously that Reeves halted in his tracks.

Rodney directed the whip at the maid's crotch. It winged between her legs and struck the sensitive lips of her sex. She screamed again, and sagged in her bonds. Rodney laughed, then reached down and opened his breeches, displaying his long, thick member. He stroked it until it attained even larger proportions, and stood where the girl could see him as he masturbated, his cock-head slippery with pre-cum.

'You're a monster, sir, with monstrous lusts,' Reeves expostulated. 'Were you a patient of mine, I might well suggest you suffer from priapism.'

'What the devil is that? Speak English, man, for God's sake.' Rodney's voice was shaky as his hand moved swiftly over his cock, milky droplets flying from the tip.

Reeves cast him a disparaging look. 'It means licentiousness,' he answered caustically, 'and lewdness, a preoccupation with virility and sexuality. You fit the case without a flaw.'

'By God, at least I'm a man, not some doddery old busybody who can't keep his nose out of my affairs,' Rodney snarled, slowing his pace and pressing his tool in order to delay orgasm. 'I repeat, where is my son?'

'And I say again that I don't know.' Reeves was rapidly losing patience with this overbearing bully.

'He's left his lodgings. I got this information out of one of his friends. He didn't want to talk but I made him.' Rodney's eyes half-closed as he rubbed his dick in the girl's hair and then pushed it into her mouth. 'He's now living with his slut, but no one knows where. I won't tolerate it, Reeves. He'll have to come and see me soon for next month's allowance, and then I'll make bloody sure he never goes back to her.'

'What are you going to do?' Reeves was anxious for his nephew. He had never much liked him, but he was Georgina's son, after all.

Rodney's face took on a sly look as he rocked his hips, moving his cock in and out between the maid's lips. 'Leave that to me. I haven't quite decided, but rest assured he'll never return to his filthy little whore of a mistress...' He looked down, seeming to lose the thread of his thought as he dragged his penis from the girl's mouth. The fingers of his right hand curled round his shaft and he worked it with rapid strokes, blind to everything but his need to reach climax.

Reeves was disgusted, yet he could feel his own member swelling involuntarily. He backed towards the door as Rodney grunted and jets of creamy spunk shot from his helm, spattering the girl's face and hair and trickling round her neck, where it lay like a string of pearls. Sickened, he wondered if he should find his sister and tell her Rodney had unpleasant plans for her son. He could also say her husband was a debauched rake and philanderer. Yet he hesitated to collapse her house of cards, for on the surface she seemed content with her lot, busy with her afternoon tea parties, her gambling games and her charity work amongst the poor. And Lord Tarquin had been threatening to ruin his good name and thus put a stop to his flourishing career among the well to do, and Charlie was not worth as much as that.

It was on an evening at the end of their second week together that Charlie did not return to the attic. He had told Lucy he might be late, as he had to go and see his father for his monthly handout. At first she did not worry, but as it began to grow dark and still he had not returned, her anxiety intensified. She sat at the old table, her hands clenched into balls on its knife-scarred surface. She heard the church clock strike nine, and then ten, and terror grew like a thick miasma inside her. Finally, huddled inside her cape, she ran down the uneven stairs and let herself out the front door.

She made it through the cobbled streets to the tavern frequented by students. Charlie was not there and no one had seen him. She left quickly, alarmed at being surrounded by men, missing Charlie's protection. Rushing home, she prayed all the way that he would have returned during her absence.

The house was dark, the hallway steeped in gloom. She

entered the attic wherein she had known true love and happiness. It was as deserted as when she left it. She was alone, without Charlie. He had vanished as if he had never existed, a figment of her imagination.

Chapter Ten

'I think I may be able to assist you,' Mrs Trott said, poking her head round the door of the subterranean area of the house she inhabited. A ginger cat brushed by her, tail in the air, the puckered eyelet of his arse winking at Lucy as he jauntily took himself off down the passage.

'Yes, Mrs Trott?' she asked politely, though she had been avoiding the woman for days. Now, faint with hunger, she was forced to leave the attic and hunt for food anywhere she could, begging if she had to.

'I've not seen that young man of yours lately,' Mrs Trott continued, leaning against the doorjamb, her arms folded over her sparse bosom. 'Could it be he has abandoned you? I hope to goodness you're not in the family way.'

'He's gone off on business, he won't be long,' Lucy answered, keeping her voice level and giving no hint of the panic that overwhelmed her. 'And no, I'm not with child.'

Mrs Trott's eyes were like shards of ice as she looked Lucy up and down. 'Then aren't you the lucky one,' she remarked with a disparaging sniff. 'Many a lass is not only abandoned when her lover has had his fill, but finds herself carrying his by-blow, too. Business, you say? That's not what I've heard.'

'And what, pray tell, is that?' Lucy asked, unable to hide her frantic eagerness for news. There had been no word, no sign, and she was half mad with worry. She was even contemplating going back to Maggie, or throwing herself on Tarquin's mercy, though this would amount to the same thing, those two being as thick as thieves. She was reluctant to do so, however. Besides which, she hated the thought of leaving the attic in case Charlie returned and found her gone. Hunger was making her light-headed, however, and she had no money and no way of supporting herself, apart from the obvious one she wanted to avoid at all cost.

Mrs Trott was obviously enjoying herself immensely. She moved closer, bringing with her the smell of strong spirits. 'Some of Charlie's friends have been in trying to sell their used study books.' She grabbed Lucy by the arm, her fingers like claws with half-moons of dirt under the long nails. 'I quizzed them, and there's a rumour going around that his father weren't too pleased he was living over the brush with you,' she hissed, her spittle showering Lucy's face. 'Seems like Mr Prescot senior sent your Charlie packing to Holland, so they say, to finish his schooling in Amsterdam.'

'Charlie would never have agreed to leave me behind,' Lucy cried, her heart like an open wound inside her as she remembered his generosity, his love, and his passionate possession of her body.

'He had no choice. His father had him bundled into a coach and driven to Dover in charge of a bunch of tough servants. You'll not see your fine young bucko again, so what about the rent? You owe me for two weeks.'

'I know,' Lucy replied, trembling. She was aghast by what she had just heard. Charlie had been sent abroad. Holland might as well be Africa or even the moon for all the chance they stood of being reunited. 'I don't know what to do,' she admitted miserably. 'I've nothing to sell.'

Mrs Trott gave her a toothy grin. It was not a pleasant sight as her front teeth were rotting away and the rest were already blackened stumps. 'Yes, you have, deary.'

'What, Charlie's possessions? He had precious little.'

Mrs Trott's red wig shook so vigorously as she laughed that it seemed about to slide off. 'No, no, you're sitting on a fortune. Sell your quim, my girl.'

'I'm not walking the streets!' Lucy shouted indignantly, having the presence of mind not to mention Tarquin or Maggie and the fact that she could probably go back to them.

Mrs Trott assumed a coaxing air, sidling up to her and saying, 'No one is suggesting you should. No, dear, I've a gentleman in mind for you. He stays here sometimes when he's up from the country. Oh yes, he's a landowner, a squire, no less. He's seen you and expressed his admiration and desire to meet you.'

Lucy drew away, wanting to rush back to the safety of her room, although it was safe no longer. It was not even hers as she could not afford to pay for it. 'I'm not to be bought,' she insisted coldly.

'You're so touchy,' Mrs Trott chided her. 'Has anyone even mentioned money? Here is a gentleman who I'm sure would be only too willing to assist you.'

'I don't recall meeting him. When did he see me?'

'He was looking from an upper window and saw you doing your washing at the well. He told me then that he was smitten by your beauty and wanted to make your acquaintance. What d'you say? He's supping here tonight. Why don't you join us?'

The idea of free food was desperately appealing to Lucy, free food and maybe even a glass of wine, too. Perhaps the squire was a man of culture and bearing. She was sick and tired of staring at the four walls of the attic missing Charlie dreadfully, her body throbbing with longing. 'Very well,' she said at last, 'and thank you, Mrs Trott, but I'm not making any promises. Um, I don't suppose you have a slice of bread to spare? I'm famished and want to look my best tonight.'

'Come into the kitchen, dear.' Mrs Trott slipped her arm around her waist. 'I knew you'd come round to my way of thinking. Squire Rutland will be over the moon.'

It was fine to eat again, but Lucy felt the price was high as she sat at table in the shabby parlour that evening with Mrs Trott and her guest. A coal fire smouldered sullenly in the corner fireplace, throwing out only a modicum of heat. The food had been fetched from the nearest cook shop by the pale wisp of a girl who was the maid-of-all-work for Mrs Trott, who relied on her to prepare meals in the ordinary way, but this was a special occasion.

'Would you care for some more mutton, squire?' she simpered, and piled his plate with further mounds of meat, potatoes and carrots. 'I do like to see a man enjoying his victuals.' She picked up the wine bottle. 'Can I tempt you to another glass of claret?'

'You may, dear lady.' He wiped his greasy mouth on the back of his hand. 'Capital bit of mutton this, never tasted better, not even from my own flocks. What say you, Mrs Browne?'

Lucy could not tell him it was like manna from heaven after her fast. Instead she smiled, gave him a demure glance and said, 'Indeed, it is excellent, sir.'

'You come from the country, don't you?' he asked, talking with his mouth full; no man of refinement this, but a rough-and-ready son of the soil.

'Yes, sir,' she replied, wondering if she could bear to become his mistress, this square-cut man of medium height with a ruddy, weather-beaten face, a large hooked nose and hazel eyes set in deep pouches of flesh. He was forty-five if a day, and looked as if he had indulged his appetites from the cradle. His untidy, sandy hair was liberally streaked with grey and drawn back into a cue. Introduced to her as Squire Percival Rutland, he had put in a bid for Lucy with as much finesse as if he was attending a cattle market. His clothing was serviceable – a cloth jacket and wrinkled buckskin breeches, a once yellow waistcoat now daubed with gravy stains, a grubby cravat tied askew, and muddy riding boots. She had recognised his type at first sight, having seen similar fellows striding around her village, local landowners and gentleman farmers born into property, roughcast gentry to whom the peasants doffed their caps.

'Can't fault country lasses,' he went on, leaning back in his char and belching heartily. 'Best in the world. All that fresh air brings roses to their cheeks and gives 'em a down-to-earth understanding of what's what when it comes to mating. You've no airy-fairy notions about it, have you, Mrs Browne? Oh, damnation, I'm going to call you Lucy. Does that suit you?'

'Yes, sir.'

He grinned and reached for her knee beneath the table. 'My name's Percy, by the by. We don't have to stand on ceremony, do we? Mrs Trott told you I'm mightily taken with you, didn't she?'

'Yes, sir,' Lucy repeated, her expression impassive, though her first instinct was to shove his invasive hand aside. She did not, however, controlling her natural aversion and allowing his fingers to cruise higher beneath her skirt until they brushed her bush. She suppressed her thoughts of Charlie, concentrating on self-preservation.

Percy's ruddy face advanced closer to hers. She could smell wine on his breath and there was nothing remotely attractive about him, yet his fingers tugging at her pubic hair sent little arrows of pleasure winging to her nubbin.

'Are you going to come with me, lass?' he asked bluntly. 'I want you to live in my manor house. I'll treat you like a queen. What do you say, eh?'

She knew she had no choice, but was determined to drive a hard bargain, so she thrust his hand away, smoothed down her skirt and closed her knees tightly together. 'There are a few things we need to get straight first,' she said crisply, ignoring Mrs Trott's frantic warning signals. 'First, I need some garments.'

'Agreed,' he said promptly, and drained his glass, which

Mrs Trott promptly refilled. 'I'll take you to the second-hand clothes dealer first thing in the morning. Soon have you kitted out.'

'That won't do,' Lucy said with a haughty tilt to her chin. 'I won't be fobbed off with any old flea-ridden clobber. I want new, or nothing.'

He glowered, his bushy brows drawn down, but she out-stared him. 'Oh have it your way,' he conceded. 'But not one of these top-priced shops where all the fashionable ladies go. One thing you'll need is a riding habit. We chase foxes and deer at Oldmead, and I'm Master of the Hunt and will expect you to entertain other members at Sharpfell Manor. Now how about a kiss to seal the bargain?'

'Sir, please don't,' she protested as he reached for her.

'Well, what is it you want?' He smiled, ready to be indulgent for the time being. 'I was planning on consummation tonight. My old fellow's ready for it,' he declared, and unfastened his breeches, displaying a large cock that, though only partially erect, was enough to make Lucy's eyes widen.

'I need your assurance that my account with Mrs Trott will be settled,' she told him. 'I won't permit intimacies until you've carried this out and fulfilled your promise to buy me clothing.' Once she would never have dared speak thus to a gentleman, but experience was shaping her into a mercenary maid who knew that any show of weakness would be used to her disadvantage.

'Oh, very well, I see you're a greedy vixen like all the rest of 'em. But if I'm not going to fuck you tonight, then I'll get drunk.' He turned to Mrs Trott. 'Have your servant fetch the chamber pot from the sideboard. I'm fair bursting with piss.'

The whey-faced maid did as she was bid. Rather unsteadily, Percy rose and crossed to where she stood. Lucy heard him urinating loudly into the china receptacle and shuddered inwardly. It seemed Fate had been toying with her and was now about to return her to the barnyard from whence she came.

After they had been shopping the next day, Percy booked seats on the mail-coach. He tried to get beneath Lucy's skirts before they finally left Mrs Trott's establishment, but she would have none of it.

'Damn it, I've just spent a considerable amount on you, wench,' he protested when she rebuffed him. 'And paid off that old biddy, Mrs Trott. Bookseller, my arse, she's nothing but a bawd.'

'I want to get on our way, Percy,' Lucy told him firmly, packing her diary in her reticule, and also slipping in a few of the primers from which Charlie had taught her to read. She was forced to leave the rest of his things as Mrs Trott had demanded them in part payment of her fees, and the miserly squire agreed. Lucy had already deduced he was tight-fisted, another characteristic of his breed. He had almost wept when the dress shop presented him with the bill.

Percy was given no chance to molest her in the coach on the way to Oldmead. It was too full for him to do more than grope her thigh and subject her to lecherous glances. His estate lay in Buckinghamshire, and they passed through the golden countryside of late summer where haymaking was in progress. The journey was broken by several stops to change horses, and Lucy was reminded of her first venture into the world, when she had been chaperoned by the Reverend Jollian.

At last the coach clattered over a stone bridge spanning a narrow river and entered a village, where it pulled up at an inn near the Market Cross. Coming awake, yawning and stretching, Lucy's fellow travellers began piling out. Percy, who had not slept the entire journey he was so intent on eyeing her and feeding his lustful fantasies, was one of the first to disembark.

'Come on, girl, don't hang around,' he said brusquely, and began supervising the offloading of her luggage.

Lucy watched, worried about her new clothing. It had been a real pleasure to be measured up and accommodated by the dressmaker. It had made her aware of how much she missed being pampered at Greyfriars. She was also starting to miss Tarquin, and this alarmed her. Percy was a very poor substitute, indeed, for her beautiful sadistic master.

'Afternoon, squire,' said a man in a smock and gaiters, doffing his battered hat. 'Good to see you again.'

'Fetch my gig, Jeremiah, it's round the back of the inn. The landlord will show you where and harness my horse to it. Then bring it here and load up,' Percy ordered briskly, and Lucy noticed how several more people were greeting him humbly, with the respect due to their betters. She was also aware of them staring at her, no doubt wondering about this fancy piece the squire had brought back with him from London. She stiffened her spine and returned their glances without flinching, glad she had donned a new dress with a matching cloak in a deep shade of green. Her hat was wide-brimmed and flaunted feathers, and her gloves and pumps were of the softest leather. She looked like a lady, not a village drab, and she had also lost her country drawl under the tutelage of an elocution master provided by Tarquin who, she knew, had had plans to pass her off in society. This might have been fun, and she felt a pang of regret it was unlikely to happen now.

Soon she was seated next to Percy on the front seat of the gig, her baggage behind her. He shook the reins, clicked his tongue and applied the whip. Harnesses jingled, there was the crisp sound of iron shod hooves, and the gig bowled over the cobbles. Lucy's nostrils responded to the familiar smells of the country – the scent of bonfires and flowers, wild garlic and pines. Through gates she glimpsed brown cows chewing the cud in the lush

177

meadows, the rich odour of their manure mingling with the others. It brought her childhood back in an emotional rush, and she felt tears welling up in her eyes as she thought of her dead family. Then she was aware they had left the lane and entered a bridle path winding between the trees just wide enough for the gig's wheels. Percy drove down it confidently.

'All the land hereabouts belongs to me,' he grunted.

'And the people, too?' she could not help asking acerbically.

'The majority,' he answered, with a sidelong glance at her face. 'The feudal system still applies here, though we live in modern times. On the whole, folk know which side their bread is buttered.'

'Are you married, or have you ever been?' She was curious about this individual who would now shape her future.

'I was, years ago, but my wife died in childbirth. I've not bothered to take on the snaffle again, though I *should* wed, if only to keep the Rutland line going. I've plenty of bastards but no legitimate heirs. Wives, though, they want to rule a man's life. Do this, do that, wipe your feet before you come into the parlour, attend church on Sunday. I can't be bothered with it. Why d'you ask? Fancy marrying me, do you? Maybe I'll offer, if you please me, but I've got to see if you fuck well first.' He drew in the reins and the gig slowed to a stop. He promptly hauled Lucy out to stand on the forest floor, and guessing what he wanted, she marvelled at her own strong feelings. He was vulgar and uncouth yet he was all man, as his swelling penis proved where it pressed against her belly through their censorious clothing.

'Mm… you're a fine filly, Lucy.' He wrapped his arms around her, his hands hot on her back beneath her cloak. 'Can't wait to bury myself between those thighs.' Then he turned away and tethered the horse before urging her into a secluded glade by slapping her bottom teasingly with his whip. Warning bells set up a clamour in her brain as she suddenly realised he would like his sex earthy, with an element of horseplay and brutality, and the way he flourished the whip was a key to his requirements. Her buttocks already stung, but it was an ache she recognised and which dampened her maidenhair.

'Over there,' he said, pointing to where a fallen trunk lay across the grass.

Holding up her long skirt, she walked towards the dead tree. It was old and large and lichen-encrusted.

'Now then, take off your lower garments and bend over it,' he commanded, replacing the whip in his hand with a riding crop.

'But it's rough,' she protested.

'Do it,' he insisted, and his crop bit into the backs of her thighs through her skirt.

She hurriedly loosened the band of her skirt, and stepped out of it. Her petticoats followed, and she carefully laid them down on her cloak, choosing a dry patch of grass where neither would be marred. The cool breeze played around her naked buttocks and fondled her warm pussy. Her chemise rode up, exposing her to the waist, and her breasts spilled out of her bodice as she lay across the gnarled oak. Her hair had come loose, freed from her hat, and tumbled down over the log.

Percy seized her wrists and tied them together with a piece of hemp baling twine taken from one of his pockets.

'Ouch,' she complained as the rope chafed her skin. 'There's no need for this, sir.'

'There's every need. I'm master here and you'll do what I tell you.' He thrust a knee between her legs and spread them. This position brought her clitoris into contact with a protruding knot of wood where a small branch had once been. The rough bark scratched her, but her eager bud responded to the pressure and she could not repress a moan of pleasure. Percy was behind her, and as his hands gripped her hips she felt his bare penis warm against her bottom cheeks. He pushed, and she felt her vagina expanding as his formidable organ slid deep inside her. He began riding her, and raising his arm brought the riding crop down again and again as he thrust. Her buttocks stung and burned from the blow, and her mons pushed against the knot in the wood, aching to bloom in an orgasm.

'Go it, lass!' he yelled, his cock plunging violently in and out of her. 'Tally-ho!' His arm was in ceaseless motion, the crop landing relentlessly on her thighs, her bare shoulders and the small of her back.

She felt the fires of a climax rising to consume her, her inner muscles clenching around Percy's convulsing penis as he came in savage jerks, pumping her full of semen.

I hate it here, Lucy wrote, her journal open across her knees as she huddled close to the fire. The flames roared halfway up the wide chimney, but dragged every draught in the library with them. The windows did not fit properly, rattling in the gusts of wind that flattened the rain against the panes, and the door hung lopsided on one hinge. It creaked constantly unless a piece of furniture was jammed against it. It was the same everywhere at Sharpfell Manor; tumbledown walls, roofs that leaked, draft-filled fireplaces and clogged gutters.

Lucy's spirits sank when she saw it. A Tudor-style, black-and-white timbered house that must once have been gracious, it had suffered through a succession of careless owners who refused to spend money on its maintenance. Percy, it seemed, was the worst offender yet. He filled the place with his hounds and his frequently inebriated friends, oblivious to everything save hunting and drinking, fornicating and collecting rent from his tenants. At first, Lucy had thought to clean it up and turn it into a home, but she ran foul not only of Percy but of the slatternly maid, Doris, who objected to moving her posterior from the rocking chair by the fire in the servants' quarters.

Percy was out hunting despite the frigid October weather. She had declined to join him, but she could hear servants in the great hall getting the bottles and tankards ready for his return with a gaggle of likeminded companions. She would be expected to entertain foul-mouthed gentlemen and horse-faced ladies who considered themselves superior to her.

I want to escape but don't know how to set about it, she wrote, her chilled fingers clasped round the quill as it scratched over the paper. *I can't endure a winter here. I shall perish with the cold. Percy is the unmannerly oaf I thought him at the first going off. He likes to beat me, to treat me as if I'm an animal. Often I crawl around on my hands and knees naked while he abuses me, and when he is in his cups, he encourages his companions to use my body any way they want. It is far worse than when I was with Tarquin. At least I lived in luxury there. One thing is for certain, I'll not leave here empty-handed as I did when I fled Greyfriars.*

She had not forgotten Charlie, far from it, but she had discovered a steely core inside her that helped her survive. She wanted to go back to London, but travel was not easy, and it would be nigh impossible once the snows set in. Somehow, she had to find a way to leave soon. She had an ally in a personable stable lad who found it impossible to hide his admiration every time their paths crossed. They met often, as Lucy rode daily, glad to get out of the house with its rank smells and the constant irritation brought about by the hounds barking and copulating and scratching at their fleas.

Her journal was her only consolation. Having somewhere to jot down her emotions, opinions and comments offered her a freedom of expression otherwise denied her. Charles had taught her well, and the simple reading primers she had brought with her helped, too.

The commotion in the courtyard outside the window announced the hunters had returned, noisy and triumphant and already tipsy from swigging frequently at holster-held brandy flasks. With a grimace of distaste, Lucy screwed the silver lid back on the inkbottle and put it in the desk along with the quill and sander. Her diary she slipped behind a line of books in a glass-fronted cabinet, confident no one in that uncultured household would disturb it. Percy used the library more as a room in which to display his sporting trophies than as a place of quiet study and contemplation. She could hear him clumping into the hall and shouting as he went.

'Lucy! Hey, Lucy! Damn and blast it, where is that jade? Lucy?'

There were other voices now, shrill female shrieks of mirth accompanied by the deeper, heartier notes of their male companions and the happy barking of the dogs. It was not long before someone knocked on the sagging door.

'Who is it?' she snapped.

'Blaketon, Mrs Browne,' the male servant quavered in his high-pitched old man's voice. 'The master wants you.'

'Tell him I'll be with him in a while,' she answered. 'I'm going to the bedchamber to change into something more suitable.'

'Very well,' Blaketon croaked, and shuffled away.

Lucy had no intention of making herself beautiful for Percy, but she slipped up the backstairs and dallied as long as possible, until she knew she could delay no longer.

The great hall glowed with light from the roaring fire and the candles in great iron circles hanging from the rafters. Lucy made her way down the main staircase slowly and quietly. No one noticed her; they were all too intent on feasting and drinking and hallooing as they cheered their host, who was intent on taking his pleasure.

The long refectory table had been cleared of platters, bottles and glasses at one end, and the blowzy Doris sprawled there on the greasy, wine-soaked boards. The sight of her turned Lucy's stomach.

A great white blob of a woman, Doris's dirty petticoats were hiked up around her thick waist, her massive breasts flopping out of an unlaced bodice as Percy sucked her nipples, which were the size of organ stops. His guests were in varied states of unbridled lust as well. The skirts of riding habits were hooked up out of the way and bare arses displayed. The women stuck their buttocks out provocatively while men in calfskin breeches with the flaps down over hairy bellies, their upright pricks at the ready, walloped them with pliable crops, the triangular tips made of red flattened leather. The older females, in powdered wigs kept in place with snoods and low-crowned toppers, bared their opulent breasts and rubbed their clefts or those of their nearest companion, screeching like banshees as they reached their crisis.

Lucy, frigid outside but on fire within, walked steadily towards the table. Percy was oblivious to her presence, and she had an uninterrupted view of Doris's rotund belly and the wedge of thick black fuzz covering her mound. Her legs were wide open and her pussy showed swollen and shiny wet, her clitoris rising aggressively from its hood. Percy hovered between her knees, his cock sheathed in his fist. He worked it hard through the circle of his fingers and it seemed to glow red with desire, a single crystal drop appearing in its slit tip.

Doris gave vent to a moan, offering her sex to him, her legs dangling over the edge of the table. Percy lowered himself between them and sank his face into her moist delta, his tongue diving into her love-channel, and then finding her bud and feasting on it. The buxom maid groaned loudly and lifted her hips from the table, chasing the pleasure promised by his tongue, but Percy left her abruptly and rolled her over onto her stomach.

Her buttocks were impressive, round as hillocks with a deep crevasse between them. Lucy was not surprised to see a latticework of stripes, some old, some new, embroidering the dimpled, snow-white flesh. The hard smacks Percy bestowed on them echoed through the hall as his audience cheered him on. Doris's huge posterior quivered, flushing blood-red, and then his rampant penis disappeared between her enflamed cheeks. She yelped, and he spanked her again viciously.

'Up the arse!' he shouted. 'That's where I'm going, slut.' He pushed against the dark moue of her anus. She grunted like a stuck pig, and then set up a howling sound that rose to a crescendo as Percy thrust into her fundament. He pumped away inside her, forcing his phallus in and out of her tight orifice, his expression that of a man tortured beyond endurance.

Lucy turned on her heels and walked out of the hall.

Her shawl wrapped round her, chilled to the bone by what she had just witnessed, Lucy made for the stables, determined to bring matters to a head. She passed through the kitchen, where flames danced in the fireplace and the air was filled with the succulent smells of a meat stew. Skivvies were pretending to be busy while the overweight cook dozed by the hearth, his beefy hands folded over the dirty apron spanning his generous paunch.

Lucy spotted Fergal, the stable lad she was about to seduce. She had intended to go outside and find him, but destiny had decreed otherwise. He was eating bread and cheese at the long pine table. She strolled up to him casually, and put a possessive hand on his shoulder. 'Come with me,' she said.

'Yes, Mrs Browne.' He stared up at her, flushing to the roots of his dark hair. 'Certainly, Mrs Browne.' He was not much taller than she, but broad-shouldered in his livery.

She led him out of the kitchen, up the servants' stairs and along the corridors to the master bedchamber. She was careful to leave the door unlocked behind them. Let Percy discover them in the act, and be damned to him.

'Young man, oh beautiful young man,' she whispered, untying his cravat and divesting him of his jacket and waistcoat.

'It's you who are beautiful, ma'am,' he answered unsteadily, proud and yet also ashamed of his burgeoning erection.

They stood on the threadbare rug by the fitfully smouldering fire. 'It's cold,' she said. 'Let us go to bed.'

Soon they were lying naked beneath the down quilt and she was encouraging him to feel her all over, taking delight in showing him how to pleasure her. His body was slim, his legs well formed, his cock large and his balls deliciously tight.

'No, not yet,' she said, pulling her mouth away from his eager tongue and stopping him when he wanted to open her knees and insert his stiff tool inside her. 'This is the way to please a lady. Look…' She let her thighs go slack, and then spread her labial wings with her hands to display her clitoris. 'This little button of flesh is the seat of all joy. It's not just a case of cock in cunt and everyone is happy. I need you to rub it so… to wet it with my juices or your spittle, like this… I need you to coax it from its hood and make it swell and shine like a pink pearl, and then continue rubbing it or sucking it until I reach my zenith and come for you.'

'You mean you want me to kiss you there?' he asked, smiling in astonished delight, for all the world as if she had just offered him the moon and stars.

'Yes, that's what I want.' Such naivety was touching and she fondled his cock affectionately, holding it in her palm, enjoying the feel of his satin-soft skin and the smoothness of his helm. 'Haven't you had a sweetheart

185

before?'

'I've walked out with one or two, but they never let me… you know, touch them in any way. Not their breasts or their private parts.'

She lifted her pelvis towards him, took his hand in hers and guided his fingers to her nub. 'You're a virgin?' The idea was intriguing.

'Yes, ma'am,' he breathed huskily, rubbing her tentatively but eagerly.

'My breasts, Fergal,' she moaned as her pleasure mounted. 'Suck my nipples.'

He leaned over her, and his lips fastened on her teats with the avidity of a hungry infant. He was a natural, nibbling and gnawing, licking and kissing, and the sensations formed a direct link with her agitated clitoris.

'Is that right, ma'am?' he paused to ask.

'Oh yes, don't stop!' she begged.

He grinned and went back to work, increasing the slippery friction on her bud and lapping at her nipples. She could feel the coil tightening in her depths and the waves of ecstasy cresting higher.

'Did I do it?' Fergal asked, delighted to see her squirming and crying out breathlessly as she climaxed.

'Oh yes, you did it,' she sighed, and pulling him down on top of her impaled herself on his shaft. He gasped and pumped and suffered an orgasm after only a few swift strokes, and as he did so the door was flung open and Percy strode into the room, his face twitching with fury.

'What the hell's going on here?' he demanded, and brought his crop down across Fergal's uplifted rump. 'You, boy, get off her at once!'

'Sorry, squire,' Fergal muttered, his cock dripping with semen as he pulled out of Lucy and stood awkwardly beside the bed, trying to hide his genitals with his hands.

'You damn well *will* be sorry!' Percy bellowed.

'Oh stop it, do,' Lucy snapped. She sat up, drawing

the quilt about her body. 'What's eating you, Percy? Can't you endure the sight of a handsome stripling taking his fill of me? He's well endowed. Better than you with all your whips and crops. I saw you fucking Doris. You stick your cock where you will, so why should I be faithful to you and only take other lovers of your choosing?'

'Get up and get out!' Percy yelled even more loudly. 'You're nothing but a whore! Get you gone from my house!'

'Can I come with you?' Fergal piped up eagerly, grabbing his breeches and holding them in front of him.

'No,' she said cruelly and decisively. 'I shall travel alone.'

Lucy reached London two days later. She had packed everything she considered belonged to her, cajoled Blaketon into driving her to the inn, spent the night there, and took the mail-coach to London in the morning.

It was like coming home as she stepped out onto the street. She considered taking a cab to Mrs Trott's in the hope a letter might have arrived from Charlie addressed to her. She was not without money, having helped herself to some of Percy's hidden hoard thinking it her just dues, but she knew she had to get established somewhere before it ran out.

London, dirty, smelly and crowded. She stood on the street in her second-best outfit, her luggage beside her. The rain seemed to have settled in for a long visit, but it failed to dampen her spirits. She breathed deeply of the abundant smells, vowing never to return to country life.

'Lucy Browne!' shrilled a female voice behind her, and she swung round to find herself facing a familiar figure, a vivacious, well dressed, brown-haired woman who rushed up to greet her with outstretched arms.

'Jocelyn!' she cried, astonished and alarmed.

'You look prosperous,' Jocelyn observed, taking in

Lucy's clothing and leather bags with keen grey eyes. 'Where have you been?'

'I've been staying in Buckinghamshire.'

'You gave Tarquin the slip. They said you had run away with your tutor, but I'm out of touch. I left Maggie's establishment and struck out on my own.' She looked exceedingly smart herself in a plush cape and gown, a feathered hat perched on her high bouffant hair. Gems sparkled at her wrists and ears and against the creamy skin of her cleavage, exposed by a low neckline.

'So you won't tell them you've seen me?' Lucy asked anxiously.

'Of course not, my dear, we did not part the best of friends. I'm in partnership with another, more genteel, lady. She makes hats and employs several of us skilled in that direction.'

'You're no longer a harlot?' Lucy blurted.

'I didn't say that.' Jocelyn's rouged lips curved up in a secret smile. 'Madame Colette Pascal doesn't confine her business solely to millinery. Why do you ask?'

'I shall need to find employment soon,' Lucy confessed, the rain finally starting to dampen her enthusiasm. Her feathers were waterlogged and her skirt was wet to the knees.

'Not returning to the country?'

'No, nor to Tarquin.'

'And the tutor?'

'Has gone abroad.'

'Right then, I'll introduce you to Madame Pascal,' Jocelyn said briskly. 'Ah, here comes my escort.' She rounded on a portly gentleman wearing a triple-capped overcoat and polished boots. 'There you are, darling. I've met up with a long lost friend. Take us to madame's shop, please. Lucy, this is Lord Cecil, my latest lover, and may I say, the most virile.'

Within a short time, Lucy was ensconced in Lord Cecil's

188

fine maroon coach, which boasted his family shield on the doors. Jocelyn flirted with him the whole way. Apparently, they had spent the night at the tavern, and Lucy wondered what lay before her when they reached Madame Pascal's shop. By now she was wise enough to guess that making hats was a front for something else entirely.

She was pleasantly surprised. Colette Pascal welcomed her warmly, a chic, beautifully dressed lady with every hair in place. While not an aristocrat, she carried herself like one, and listened in silence until Lucy had poured out her history, omitting nothing.

The upshot was that Colette offered her a home, and Lucy learned to trust this lively, thirty year old businesswoman who besides owning a successful millinery shop was also the madam of a flourishing house, which far from being bawdy was exquisitely and tastefully run. The young ladies who were such an asset in her showroom were provided with bed and board and encouraged to entertain gentlemen who frequented the store to purchase bonnets as gifts for their wives, mistresses and daughters. It was a most discreet establishment, and everyone seemed more than happy with the arrangements, including Lucy, who had not yet been called upon to act the whore.

Gaining in confidence, and earning praise for her knowledge of sewing, she began going out, at first accompanied by Jocelyn, and then alone. She sometimes delivered orders, borne along in the Pascal chaise with several big round hatboxes beside her, and sometimes visited the haunts where she and Charlie had once met his friends. Despite Colette's warnings, this was accomplished on foot.

The days stretched into weeks and it seemed Tarquin had forgotten her. She viewed this fact with mixed feelings, which included anger, fear and desire.

Chapter Eleven

'You didn't really believe you could escape me, did you?' someone whispered in Lucy's ear.

Hearing was one of the senses left to her. She was blindfolded, but the whiff of damp and incense, and his own unique body odour coupled with the sound of his voice, told her it was Tarquin who had waylaid her while she was out walking, bundled her into his coach, and transported her back to Greyfriars's caverns. She was furious, yet highly aroused feeling his hands on her, his masterful air filling her with the desperate need to be possessed by him again.

'How did you know where I was?' she gasped, disoriented.

He chuckled wickedly. 'Lady Cordelia entered *Chez Pascal* in search of the latest headgear. Madame Colette's establishment has a reputation for the most elaborate and fashionable bonnets, although those in the know are acquainted with other facts about her. She sells more than frothy hats, it seems. Her milliners are as beautiful as their creations. But you are aware of this, being one of them.'

'Let me go, master,' she begged, finding his forearm and clinging to it. 'I want to earn an honest living, and Madame Colette says I have a rare skill for making silk flowers and designing hats. I could go far there. Give me the opportunity, *please*.'

'I have no intention of stopping you, if that's what you really want, but you are obligated to me, as you well know,' he answered harshly, diving a hand between her legs and gripping her mound through her skirt. 'As my slave, you will never be free of your bonds. You see, Lucy, you'll never be an honest woman for you have the instincts of a harlot. You'll return to me again and again.' His grip tightened. 'Tell me, what happened to that treacherous tutor, Charles Prescot? Did he love you and leave you?'

'His father sent him abroad,' she panted, unable to resist grinding herself against his tantalising frottage. 'I was returning from Covent Garden when your bullies apprehended me. I went there hoping to bump into his student friends, who may have had word from him.'

'A forlorn hope,' Tarquin said sardonically. 'And you, my girl, need punishing for the shabby way in which you treated your master. Naughty, disobedient chit! Chloe, string her up.'

Lucy struggled, but in vain. She was stripped naked and carried and dragged across the flagstones, which felt icy against her bare feet. Then her arms were raised above her head carefully, so as not to disturb the blindfold, and manacles snapped around her wrists attached to a pulley dangling from the rafters. She could see nothing, but her mind's eye vividly filled in details of the cave's equipment.

They were not alone, and she recalled Tarquin's penchant for spectators. The snap of leather on flesh resounded beneath the arched roof. She imagined wild scenes taking place all around her, and twisted in a fruitless attempt to break free. Her flesh crawled with anticipation. She had no idea from which direction her chastisement would come, or what form it would take. One thing was certain, however, she had insulted Tarquin by running away, and this would not be forgiven.

Tears dampened the scarf blinding her and she gritted her teeth, her breasts rising and falling as she sucked in shallow, anxious breaths. Then she shrieked when, without warning, clamps were fastened to her nipples, the metal teeth biting cruelly into her teats. Then another pair cut into her tender labia, but her cry of agony at their application was cut off as a ball-gag was thrust into her mouth.

Then hands began touching her all over. They caressed, stroked, slapped and teased, and she knew there were women as well as men around her. Then lips and tongues glided over her body and her arousal mounted as a mouth sucked at her clit while another parted her crack from behind and worked an expert tongue into her anus. The cave was silent now, save the occasional rustle of clothing and her own strangled voice groaning behind the gag as her need to climax became unendurable.

At first she longed for the cock she could feel pressing between her legs to be Tarquin's, and then it no longer mattered who brought on her crisis as long as she achieved it. The orgasm was swelling in her loins as her body responded to the relentless stimulation, swaying where she hung. But suddenly, all the hands, mouths and cocks vanished, and she could not believe such cruelty as she bucked her hips wildly against empty air. Then, coming from nowhere, she heard the snap of a whip and searing heat scorched her skin. She wanted to scream, but only a muffled moan escaped her gagged mouth. She bit down on the soggy leather ball, heaving at the foul taste of it. She knew who wielded the whip; she recognised Tarquin's expertise, the way he flicked his wrist and aimed the blow as though the weapon was a part of him. He attacked her from every side on her buttocks, her shoulders, her back, and even her belly and her breasts.

'Oh!' she cried, writhing beneath the attack. 'Have mercy, master, please! I'm sorry! I'm sorry!' The agony was so appalling she wilted in her chains, the torment in her manacled wrists as nothing compared to the pain in her nipples, the grim torture in her labia, and the hot, devastating desire roused in her lustful sex by the merciless sting of the whip.

She braced herself for another blow, but it did not come.

Instead, she felt fingers at her crotch, and the relief she experienced as the clamps were removed from her nether lips was beyond belief. Then the blood coursed back into her labial wings with a vengeance, and the sensation was so excruciatingly intense that she nearly came.

'Tarquin,' she whimpered. 'Oh my lord, my master… my love!' she gasped as he thrust his cock deep into her belly, and she climaxed, her pussy clenching around his beautiful erection.

'You are quiet, *ma petite* – is there something wrong?' Colette asked Lucy.

'No… well, yes,' she confessed. She was back in *Chez Pascal*, seated on a high stool at the long trestle table where she was working, its surface strewn with silks and feathers, sewing cottons, sequins and beads.

'Do you wish to tell me?' Colette enquired kindly. 'We are quite alone at the moment.'

Lucy relented, needing someone to confide in. Colette made no comment, her busy fingers snipping silk petals and handing them to Lucy, who did not pause in wiring them together and fashioning lifelike roses as she talked.

'I know milord Tarquin,' Colette said. 'He is arrogant. But you have feelings for him, I can tell. You love him.'

'Not like I love Charlie, but he's lost to me.' Tears spilled down her cheeks. 'I wish I was in the position to be independent of Tarquin. As things stand, he has but to snap his fingers and I come running. If only I had a fortune of my own, then I could take him or leave him, maybe even make him dance to *my* tune.'

'This I would like to see,' Colette admitted with a rueful smile. 'And I think I may be able to arrange matters. Leave it to me. I have a little plan unfolding in my mind.'

A week has passed since I was abducted by Tarquin's bullies. Lucy made this entry sitting up in bed, her diary open on her lap, her writing equipment balanced precariously on a tray beside her. She shared a bedroom with Jocelyn, but the latter spent much time with her lover, Bella, when she was not engaged with Lord Cecil or others like him. She had invited Lucy to join in her frolics with Bella, but she refused. She seemed to have entered a quiet, industrious period, during which she applied herself to work and waited for Colette to make the next move on her behalf.

Madame is going around with a mysterious look in her eyes, she continued writing. *She has been so kind, never forcing me to take part in any activities of an amatory nature. She seems sincere when she says I am talented with my needle. But what with paying for board and lodgings, which she takes out of my wages, I find it impossible to save any money at all. It makes me sad to think I shall never rid myself of Tarquin or find my dear Charlie. I have not ventured forth since Tarquin captured me, keeping to the house. Madame Colette tells me to apply balm to my stripes. She wants them to heal quickly, but refuses to tell me why.*

Finally, Lucy was called to Colette's office where she sat making entries in a large ledger. Though she might exploit her employees somewhat, she was always scrupulously fair and looked after them like a mother hen, making sure they received a portion of the money paid to her each time they opened their legs for a gentleman caller.

'Lucy,' she said, sanding the pages and closing the book. 'I am about to give you the opportunity to better your circumstances. Sit down and hear me out.'

Lucy settled on a stool close to the fire, and Colette swung round in her chair as she spoke. 'There is a gentleman who calls here sometimes, not frequently, for he is elderly and has difficulty in keeping his member erect. I am given to understand by several of my girls who have tried that he is impotent.'

'And what has this to do with me?' Lucy asked, clasping her arms around her body, suddenly chilled even though the fire leapt brightly between the glittering brass andirons.

'I think you have the qualities he seeks, Lucy. Despite his wealth, he is a lonely man and dreams of having a beautiful virgin to call his own.'

'But I'm not a virgin,' she protested.

Colette smiled. 'I know, but you have retained a fresh, girlish approach to life despite your setbacks. You look virginal, and there is a way you can trick him into believing he has taken your maidenhead on your first night with him. A linen cloth smeared with chicken's blood secreted under the pillow, and then tucked between your legs after intercourse, is a device that has been used by many a woman to convince a man he has ruptured her hymen.'

'But... but...' Lucy stammered, unwilling to participate in such a deception.

'Think of the advantages. Sir John Beaconfield has an estate in the country, a house in town and a fortune in the bank. He has made his money through shipping and insurance. He has no family, no wife and no children. He needs someone on whom to lavish his love and attention. I have an instinct for matters of the heart, Lucy, and I am certain he will like you. Don't you want to be spoilt and pampered by a doting old man who won't bother you too much in bed? Think how angry Tarquin will be when he finds out you've slipped the net and are no longer his slave unless you choose to be.'

This, above all else, swung the scales in Lord Beaconfield's favour, and it was arranged that Lucy should be introduced to him that evening.

She sat, nervous as a kitten in the luxury of Colette's best parlour, looking very much the innocent maiden in a simple white dress with a single rose pinned over her bosom.

Her hair was brushed out loosely and fell to her waist, her hands were covered in lace mittens, and her feet peeped out from beneath her skirt clad in pink pumps. Looking at her no one could possibly guess at the number of men who had penetrated both her pussy and her bottom.

As she spoke with Lord Beaconfield, Lucy was touched by his shyness and by his longing for a companion.

'She is every bit as delightful as you told me, madam,' he said to Collette, who was chaperoning the meeting. 'May I talk with her a while in private?'

'Certainly, sir,' Colette conceded graciously, rising with a rustle of taffeta. 'I shall return in ten minutes,' she added primly, and left the room.

It was an odd courtship. The old gentleman did not touch Lucy, but simply sat in a hard-backed chair scrutinising her. He seemed as pleased as a child with a new toy. 'Tell me, Mrs Browne,' he crossed his thin legs in their white silk stockings, 'are you a virgin as Madame Pascal avows?'

'If she has said so, and you think her true to her word, then it must be so, sir,' she replied with feigned shyness.

Her confusion seemed to delight him, as if it somehow proved her innocence. 'I do believe her, my dear.' He leaned forward earnestly, his hands folded over the inlaid handle of his walking stick. 'You are the sweetest young lady I have seen in ages. Could it be you might consider accepting my adoration and visiting me tonight? We could drive there in my coach.'

Lucy's panic was not entirely false. She leapt up, her hands clasped to her breasts, her appearance that of a wild bird about to be caged. 'Oh sir, I don't know… you do me too much honour. How could you adore someone as lowly as myself?'

He struggled to his feet, left his stick leaning against the chair, and lurched towards her, his arms outstretched. 'You're as virtuous as you are beautiful,' he declared, and she found herself clasped in arms that were no stronger than they looked, her face pressed to his lacy jabot. 'Oh Lucy, if I may? Lucy, dearest child, can it be you'll consider my invitation? You make me feel like a boy again, a boy wooing his first love!'

'Oh sir, I'm overwhelmed,' she sighed.

'I'm aroused, dearest!' he said triumphantly. 'My male member is coming erect for you, only for you, Lucy.'

She ventured a hand downwards and closed her palm over the weapon struggling to attain an upright stance. Sir John groaned and seesawed his hips, rubbing his cock against her fingers through his brocaded breeches. 'Spare my blushes, sir,' she implored, despising herself for her hypocrisy.

'I beg your pardon, my princess,' he said, pulling away but clasping his tool in one hand as if to convince himself it was truly alert and ready. 'If you agree to accompany me, we shall consummate our union in style. The master bedchamber of my house in Hampstead is at your command. Come with me. Please say you will.' He lowered himself to his knees with great difficulty, and Lucy felt pity for him as he took her hands in his and looked up at her with an expression of dogged devotion.

At that moment, Colette returned and took the scene in at a glance. 'Well, sir, I see Lucy has inspired you,' she remarked with a trace of irony.

'She has, madam.' He attempted to get up, but was unable to do so until his manservant, who had followed Colette back into the drawing room, assisted him. 'I have asked her to come home with me tonight, and am awaiting her decision with bated breath.'

'What do you say, Lucy?' Colette asked gravely. 'Will you go with him?'

Lucy had already made up her mind. 'I will,' she said meekly, 'but I would like to return here in the morning. I enjoy flower making.'

'Whatever you want, sweetheart,' he said, almost skipping with excitement, his arthritis momentarily forgotten.

'Go and fetch your cloak, Lucy,' Colette advised. 'Sir John and I need to speak further on this.'

'Madam,' he said, 'you have done me a great service.' He handed her a leather bag that clinked invitingly. 'There will be more, of course, if our encounter is successful. I feel confident that I shall shoot my cannon tonight.'

'You must take good care of her,' Colette warned sternly. 'She is indeed a sweet creature, and I don't want any adverse reports of your treatment.'

'I promise, dear lady, that I shall treat her like a princess.'

It was dark when Lucy arrived at Heath House, and therefore she was unable to fully appreciate its grandeur. She was aware only that it was huge and turreted, and that the front windows shone brightly with many candles. Her spirits soared and she was content to have Sir John lead her inside, introduce her to his servants, and then conduct her to the master bedchamber.

Darkly panelled and dating from the reign of Henry VIII, there was evidence of wealth and luxury everywhere. Lucy found a bath in the adjoining dressing room, the hot and cold water provided brought up by a fleet of footmen, and the commodes even had upholstered seats. Sir John promptly dispatched a maid to help her undress.

'Thank you,' she said to the girl. 'I can manage myself, apart from those little pearl buttons at the back.'

The maid hung her clothes up in the armoire and Lucy retained her chemise. Instinct told her John would want her to, the short garment giving a teasing glimpse of the golden floss covering her private parts. She dismissed the servant and curled up in a wingchair by the fire, wondering if he would give her an expensive present, one she could take to a pawnbroker. She intended to open an account in a bank in Threadneedle Street, the same establishment Colette patronised.

She was beginning to nod off, lulled by the warmth, her mind wandering in that curious space between sleeping and waking, when there was a commotion at the door, and she opened her eyes to see John entering followed by his attendant carrying a warming-pan by its long handle. It contained heated bricks. The man went to the bed, whisked back the quilt, smoothed the pan over the sheets, covered them again, and departed.

'Not abed yet, my love?' John crooned. 'How thoughtful of you to wait up for me.' He was speaking to her as if they had been a married couple of many years. He was even less desirable now in a flannel nightshirt that only partially covered his bony calves, and a sleeping cap with a long point tapering down to a pom-pom had replaced his grand periwig.

'I didn't want to fall asleep and miss the fun,' she remarked, with a sharpness he appeared not to notice.

'You look so sweet in your tiny undergarment,' he told her, and she could see that his nightshirt was lifted at the front. 'I'd like to see you bending over, your bottom in the air and that chemise sliding upwards showing me your perfumed garden, your perfect pussy and your bare buttocks, my dear. I want to whip them and watch them turning red. I want to make you cry, and then to ravish you.'

'You would be so cruel to me?' Lucy asked, her eyes wide.

'Just a very little, just a pinch of pain to add to our pleasure, my love.'

'Oh, very well,' she sighed, and approaching the bed, knelt so her torso rested across it.

'Lovely, lovely, what a good girl you are!' he exclaimed, and then she felt his bony fingers dipping into the valley dividing her bottom cheeks. She hated to admit that his touch excited her, old lecher that he was, but it seemed her wayward clit would respond to just about anyone.

She thrust her backside up against his questing fingers. They were slippery, coated with her juices. He muttered endearments, and then spanked her. Her chemise dulled the sting, but the blow was still surprisingly hard and it was no act when she cried out.

'Hush, my dear… there, there,' he said soothingly, and spanked her again, then again.

'I'm sorry if I've offended you, sir!' she sobbed dramatically. 'Please forgive me!'

'Nay, child, you are the pinnacle of perfection. Your dear little rump is as pink as a rosebud.'

Thus began my curious friendship with this remarkable nobleman, Lucy wrote in her faithful journal. *I let him believe he had conquered me with his mighty weapon. I jest, of course, for it is one of the smallest I have seen. But I made the appropriate noises of a girl being robbed of her maidenhead and produced the linen smeared with chicken's blood and he seemed convinced. Methinks he is prepared to deceive himself and turn a blind eye, needing desperately to fulfil his dreams. Who am I to say him nay? He is good to me, and that is enough.*

She divided her time between *Chez Pascal* and Hampstead House, and for the first time ever she felt protected and cared for. Tarquin no longer constituted a threat, and she was even consoled for the loss of Charlie. She had only to mention the smallest desire, and Sir John saw that it was satisfied. Her wardrobe was now the envy of Jocelyn and the other girls, and her bank balance was building nicely. Colette was more than pleased as well, for she had earned John's eternal gratitude, and he was generous to those who served him well.

Lucy spent most every night with him. She read aloud

to him and he taught her to play chess. They talked for hours, and John, proud as a peacock, made her his hostess when he entertained his erudite friends, who enjoyed discussing painting, sculpture and poetry, books and antiquities. Yet when in their cups, these scholarly gentlemen were not slow to appreciate the lovely girls she introduced to them, her colleagues from *Chez Pascal*.

It was at one of these parties that she met Tarquin, and was rocked on her heels by the sight of him.

'Slut,' he hissed, while maintaining a bland smile as he kissed her hand in greeting.

'I was not aware you knew Sir John.' She succeeded in speaking calmly even though she was trembling all over, his sexuality striking her between the legs with the speed and force of an arrow.

'There is much you do not know about me,' he pointed out, with a lift of his dark brow. 'But you should be aware that, no matter what you do and however much you think yourself the great lady, you still belong to me.'

He managed to inveigle her behind a marble pillar, hidden from view of the guests milling about the reception room drinking wine, laughing and flirting. His hand came up between her thighs, lifting aside the lavish silk skirt and petticoats. She could not help spreading her legs to give him easier access, and his manicured fingers grazed teasingly through the moist softness of her labia, tracing the deep groove and fondling her swelling clitoris. She could also not help sighing, and he chuckled as he inserted a finger into her wet delta, penetrating her innermost sanctuary. She was barely aware of the crowd behind them and her duties as hostess as he rubbed her bud and she swayed, her hips chasing the tantalising pleasure.

'You're still a little slut,' he whispered. 'Aren't you? Look out there. Can you see your protector?' He spun her round and directed her gaze to where John was deep in conversation with his cronies. 'I wonder what he would say if he could see us?'

He spread her legs and guided his rearing cock towards her opening with one hand, the other massaging her clit. Then he stabbed deeply into her from behind as she bit back the cry that rose to her lips.

Someone was calling her name, 'Mrs Browne, are you there? Sir John has need of you,' said a deferential footman, all crimson plush and silver epaulettes.

She slipped off Tarquin's erection, smoothed down her skirt, and walked out from behind the pillar, her head held high.

Tarquin grabbed her arm, arresting her progress for a moment. 'Don't think this is over,' he warned. 'We shall meet again very shortly. You won't be able to stay away.'

Lucy avoided contact with Tarquin, stopped badgering the students for news of Charlie, and concentrated her energies on helping Colette in her business and keeping her trysts with John. Then one evening when she arrived at Heath House she was met by the grave-faced butler, with the news that Sir John had suffered a stroke, and died.

Chapter Twelve

Lucy was in the depths of despair. Once again she had lost someone dear to her, and did not realise until he was gone just how important he had been in her life. Sir John's lawyer, Gregory Wilson of the firm of *Wilson, Sykes and Pollard*, had taken immediate charge of the late man's property.

'Nothing is to be touched,' he ordered, hustling everyone from the master chamber where the body lay. He was a tall, commanding figure with a cultured baritone voice. His profession insured that he was held in high esteem, and he was accustomed to being obeyed.

Lucy glanced at him through tear-filled eyes, disliking his hectoring tone. He was not handsome, but his hawk-like profile possessed a certain grim nobility.

He went among the servants, instructing them. The funeral would be in five days, and until the contents of the will were disclosed, the house was to be run as usual. They were not to panic. He could give them no guarantees, but it was likely their jobs would be secure, whoever inherited. Then he homed in on Lucy. 'You need another kerchief,' he said sympathetically, handing her his own. 'You were fond of the old fellow?'

'Of course, what do you take me for, a hardhearted Jezebel?'

'No, I've attended several of the gatherings you helped host, and I could see how Sir John shed years in your company. I admired you for that. You made him laugh and made him feel loved.'

'He was a loveable man and I shall miss him greatly,' she declared, dabbing at her eyes with a handkerchief. 'I want to go home.' She was cold, chilled to the bone.

'Permit me to drive you there.' A new expression flickered in Gregory's eyes. 'My coach is outside.' He was genial, helpful and almost avuncular, but she was suddenly aware of him as a man.

A footman brought him his greatcoat and three-cornered hat while another servant fetched Lucy's cloak and bonnet. Gregory held out his arm and she placed her hand timidly on his sleeve. The servants, following the butler's directions, lined up to see them off. She glanced back at the house. The windows were already being shrouded in black, and a sombre crêpe wreath had been positioned in the centre of the front door. It was all so final she felt as though her heart would break.

She huddled into a corner of Gregory's carriage as he rapped on the roof with his cane. The driver pulled on the reins, and the four-horse team set off at a brisk trot. He moved over to sit beside her, a big, comforting presence, and she made no objection when he slipped an arm around her and drew her towards him until her head rested on his shoulder. She inhaled snuff and cologne and his musky body scent, responding to his maleness as he kissed her brow, her tear-stained cheeks, and then her quivering lips.

'There, there,' he crooned, one of his hands finding its way beneath her cloak and cupping her breast. 'Don't upset yourself. You can rely on me for help.'

'Have you no respect?' she demanded weakly. 'Sir John is not yet cold and you seek to seduce his mistress. I'm no whore, you know.'

'I know. You're a courtesan, my dear, not a low-priced harlot. You are one of those clever, beautiful ladies who are kept by notable men. They act as his hostess, entertain his guests, and become renowned for their wit and intelligence. They are often the power behind the throne. I'll advise you, Lucy. You can rely on me. Now, how about forgetting gloom and despondency and giving my prick a suck?'

Mesmerised by his words, she lowered her head towards his groin, her golden hair falling to cover him as she unbuttoned his trousers and her mouth went about its task.

Lucy spent the time till the funeral working, as usual. She realised that having lost her protector, she must now fend for herself once more. She thanked heaven for Colette, who advised her on mourning wear and accompanied her to the church, walking beside her as they followed the hearse drawn by black horses with tossing ostrich plumes. Pale sunshine warmed the solemn scene, and the number of people who came to see John to his last resting place pleasantly surprised her. But there was one person who she had not expected to see – Tarquin.

He stood by the graveside like a dark angel, and she recognised Cordelia beside him, her alabaster complexion complemented by her black gown. They were staring at her across the yawning cavity that was waiting to receive the coffin. She ignored them, clinging to Colette's arm on one side and Gregory's on the other. As far as she could tell, no relatives attended John's interment. He had spoken the truth when he told her he was the last of his line and had no kin.

She longed for the ordeal to be over, but could not avoid the wake held at Heath House. John's faithful servants had prepared the funeral meats, and Lucy found it strange and unnerving to pass beneath the portals and not find him there. Guests thronged the reception room, talking in the subdued tones reserved for such solemn occasions. Soft-footed lackeys bore salvers of delicacies and trays holding bumpers of wine. The butler performed his duties impeccably, and the wake went smoothly. Then finally Gregory took his place at a table, spread papers across its inlaid surface, and addressed the gathering.

'Ladies and gentleman,' he began, his confident voice ringing out under the ornate ceiling. 'I am about to read The Last Will and Testament of John Amos Beaconfield, Knight, as witnessed by me a few weeks before his untimely demise.'

His rich voice rolled on and Lucy listened with half her attention only, more interested in why Tarquin had that sharp look on his face. Firstly, Gregory read the small bequests. Each member of the staff received a purse, and a larger amount was left to the butler and housekeeper. A generous sum went to the personal manservant who had accompanied John everywhere, acting as valet, bodyguard and nurse. Antiques and books from his collection were bequeathed to some of his erudite cronies, with enough revenue to start and support a public library.

The guests shifted restively and cleared their throats, everyone eager to know who would get the lion's share, for John was reputed to have been fabulously wealthy.

'And now I come to the disposition of the major part of Sir John's effects. He wrote here, and I quote, "*I leave my properties, monies, investments and everything I possess, apart from the items already here bestowed, to my friend, companion and love, Mrs Lucy Browne*".'

A gasp rose from over two-dozen throats, and every face turned towards Lucy, who was rooted to her chair in astonishment. She felt someone grip her hand. It was Colette. Waves of heat laved her and the room started spinning. She bowed her head and closed her eyes, and when she next raised her lids, it was to see Tarquin fixing her with a piercing stare.

The next weeks were busy ones. Lucy's life changed dramatically. She spent much time in Gregory's office or at Heath House going through papers and sorting John's possessions. She retained the staff, who now regarded her as their new employer and transferred their loyalty from their late master to her without question.

Gregory proved to be a staunch ally. He had known about the Will, of course, when she pleasured him in the carriage, but had been unable to tell her. Now he offered sound advice and led her through a bewildering labyrinth of financial procedures, teaching her how to avoid the pitfalls. She was aware he desired her, but she kept him at arm's length. She had enough to contend with and did not need further complications. There was an added worry, too.

She confided in her diary, *It is a fine thing to be a woman of substance, but whenever a gentleman approaches me, I wonder if he is after my fortune*.

All was suspiciously quiet on the Tarquin front. Like a sly fox he had gone to earth, but she had the gut feeling she had not heard the last of him.

When she could lay hands on some of her cash, she helped Colette buy the house next door to *Chez Pascal*. The millinery business would expand into it, and they planned to extend further into the world of fashion, making gowns and gentleman's clothing as well as hats. Colette now had the opportunity to take on more young ladies, doing a brisk trade in flesh, as usual, but with added space and luxury.

Lucy was free to sit back and review her situation. She was young, healthy and wealthy. There was much to do, and Gregory advised her to retain her role of famous hostess, opening her saloon to men of letters, artists, musicians and politicians. She was also toying with an idea that had taken root in her mind when she heard of her good fortune. It had occurred to her that she might turn one of John's properties into an orphanage for girls. She dreamed of being its patron and insuring that every form of help was provided – a loving atmosphere, a decent education, and prospects for when the girls grew up.

Surprised and somewhat piqued by his silence, she was

plagued by thoughts of Tarquin. It was months since she had been rogered by a virile male. The idea of passionate encounters obsessed her, and her own fingers no longer satisfied. She was about to journey to her country estate when she made up her mind to visit Tarquin first, on her own terms.

Wearing her most flamboyant and expensive gown and cloak, she set off in her carriage. It was getting dark and the moon had not yet risen. Greyfriars was a formidable place, but she was not afraid any more. When a manservant opened the door at her peremptory knock, she brushed past him asking, 'Where is your master?'

The man stood his ground, staring down his nose at her, though obviously confused by her regal manner and fine clothing. 'Is he expecting you, madam?'

Lucy tapped the bulge at his crotch with her closed fan. 'Just tell me where I can find him.'

He started, and stepped back. 'He is in his apartment…'

'I know the way,' she said loftily, and swept up the main staircase.

When she reached Tarquin's room, she walked straight in without knocking. A woman was singing, slightly off-key, accompanied by a lute.

Benjamin stopped playing and Chloe paused in mid-note.

'I was expecting you,' said Tarquin, from his magnificent mausoleum of a bed.

Lucy did not reply, simply strolled towards him with a soft rustling of skirts. She pulled off her gloves and unfastened her cloak, which she let slither to the floor. 'You are very confident in yourself, Tarquin,' she remarked.

'Not so much in myself as in your weakness. Or is it your strength?' He gazed at her quizzically. 'Who is the master and who the submissive here? Is it possible you have gained a certain power over me? Did you and Charlie indulge in painful pleasures?' He stretched his long limbs languidly beneath an exotic, sable-trimmed robe.

'No, ours was a simple, uncomplicated love.'

He stifled a yawn behind his hand. 'How very boring,' he opined, and then his eyes flashed as he added, 'But you enjoyed it when I told him to spank you.' This was a statement, not a question.

'Only because it gave me the chance to get close to him,' she retorted.

'You're a very poor liar, my dear.' He moved so his robe opened over his phallus. It was not erect, but it was so large it did not need to be to arouse her. 'And you may think you hate me, but you need someone to hate and blame. You enjoy being a victim, Lucy. You love belonging to a real bastard who'll make you feel like royalty at one moment and like the lowest slave the next. The uncertainty is exciting. It keeps your blood running hot. Tell me, who do you think about when you're playing with yourself?'

She wanted to lie and say Charlie, but of late he was fading from her secret fantasies. She trembled as she looked down at him, convinced he could read her like a book. 'I… I don't have to answer that. It's nothing to do with you. I'm here on a social visit.'

'You did not give my footman your calling card,' he said silkily. 'Surely the most famous, or should I say, *infamous*, courtesan in town would have known this was the polite thing to do. But I forget, you're a country wench at heart, picking up airs and graces along the way, a doxy who struck lucky. Tell me, my dear, exactly how much did Sir John leave you?'

'I have only a vague idea. My lawyer deals with my finances. In any case, even if I did, you'd be the last to know.'

His face hardened and he snapped his fingers at Benjamin and Chloe, who immediately jumped to their feet. 'You're insolent, Lucy,' he snarled, rising. 'How dare you address your master thus? You've earned a severe beating.'

Lucy turned to run, but Benjamin caught and held her while Chloe stripped off her clothes. She stood there shaking, nothing more than an ignorant chit again. Her inheritance was of no use to her now. Of course, her coachman and grooms knew where she was, but she guessed they were seated in the kitchen, quaffing ale and meat pies and minding their own business, as good servants should.

'On your knees,' Tarquin commanded, and she knelt. Then she felt Benjamin's hand at the nape of her neck, forcing her lower.

With her head to one side, her cheek rested on the floor and her breasts swung forward, her nipples chafed into points by the pile of the oriental carpet. Her bottom was lifted high, her legs parted so the tiny hole of her anus, her wet vulva and the pink lips of her labia were all exposed. She felt Tarquin step behind her, but did not dare move.

'I shall not restrain you,' he said quietly but menacingly. 'You will remain like that of your own volition or the punishment will be increased.'

She heard the slight rustle of his robe as he moved, like the stirring of dry leaves. Then the flexible thongs of a calfskin flogger tickled the flesh of her bottom. They explored her, licking the side of her thighs, darting round her arse and stroking lightly over her shoulders.

'Get on with it,' she begged, her nerves taut as bowstrings.

'Did I say you could speak?' he hissed, bending over her, his warmth pressed to her back, his cock leaving a trail of silvery dew along her spine.

She shook her head, her curls cascading like a golden waterfall around her face. 'No,' she whispered.

'No *what?*' he demanded, pinching one of her nipples.

'No, *master!*'

'That's better.' He straightened up. 'Put all others from your mind. You have no master but me. I am your reason

210

for existing. You belong to me, body, soul, mind and spirit.'

'Yes, master,' she whispered, knowing it was true. She shuddered as he touched her crotch with the flogger. Energy pulsed through her and she held her posterior higher, chasing the sensation. He snapped the thongs harder, and a burst of searing pain shot through her pussy that made her cry out.

'Be silent!' he shouted, and she was momentarily hopeful as the flogger was removed. Then she realised he had merely exchanged it for something more severe.

She recognised the feel of a bamboo cane as it landed like a line of fire across her flesh. He used it with superb control, knowing it could cut into her skin if he was not careful. She shrieked beneath the second blow, and was robbed of breath by the next. No longer able to remain still, she writhed on the floor, the sound and feel of each whack nearly robbing her of reason. He punished her more intensely because she was moving and screaming, but she no longer cared, helpless beneath his domination. Then the pathway to surrender opened and she entered that strange area of peace like the eye of a storm in which she and Tarquin became one, immersed in each other.

When he stopped beating her she collapsed across the carpet, but was promptly lifted in his strong arms and taken to the bed. Someone made certain she was lying facedown. Lotion was applied to her stripes while she sobbed and winced and yet, paradoxically, bemoaned the loss of the bamboo's brutal caresses, which had been bearing her towards a fierce climax.

'Kiss it,' she heard Tarquin say, and she felt her lips on the lightly furred back of his hand.

The bed became a raft floating on a sea of passion as he fed on her, warming her mouth with his, fondling every inch of her, careful not to add to her soreness. He turned her round and raised her with a pillow beneath her hips so no pressure was brought to bear on her bottom, and then parted her thighs and licked her clitoris until she was consumed in the fiery furnace of an orgasm. As the bliss intensified he slid his cock into her, setting a rhythm she followed passionately.

On that extraordinary night, she experienced not only Tarquin's cock, but also Benjamin's pierced and ringed tool, his dark skin contrasting with hers as their bodies merged. On that night, she fully accepted in her soul that Tarquin was right. He knew her better than anyone. She loved it that he punished her until she wept, and then made her feel as invincible and sexy as the goddess Balbo, like the most desirable woman on earth.

Before leaving for the country, Lucy held a ball at Heath House still clad in mourning black, but organising an event that would have delighted John. She did not invite Tarquin, but with Colette's help provided racy entertainments, catering for all tastes. It was pronounced the event of the year. Then, leaving Gregory in charge of her London affairs, she had her new ladies maid, Nita, pack several bags and ordered her best coach to be prepared. She was on her way to Bunbury Towers, to view yet another part of her inheritance.

Travelling had not yet lost its excitement for her, especially since she now had several smart vehicles to choose from. The one she selected for the journey was slung on leather straps to aid suspension, and the interior seats were sprung and upholstered in crimson plush. It was fitted with little cupboards with sliding doors and candles in special lanterns, everything for the comfort of the passenger. There was even a porcelain chamber pot with a silver lid under one of the seats.

Nita, her companion, was a plain-featured, staunchly loyal, no-nonsense young woman. She was utterly reliable and Lucy had every confidence in her. She settled back to enjoy the trip, so vastly different from the time she shared a coach with Percy, or endured the insults of people like Mrs Clough and her objectionable offspring. Independence was a grand thing, and she put her feelings for Tarquin in abeyance for the time being. Time enough to think about him when she returned to London.

It was a pleasantly warm day and the countryside was burgeoning – buds bursting, birds nesting and newborn lambs skipping behind their solid dams. The roads were not too muddy, and there was little likelihood of getting stuck in a rut or having to repair a wheel. They kept up speed, and though they stopped twice at posting inns to change horses, they made good time to the place where they would be spending the night. Lucy, glancing out the window as the sun went down, suffered a feeling of *déjà vu*.

'Nita,' she said, sitting up, her eyes alert, 'where are we? I've been here before.'

'Don't rightly know, madam,' Nita replied. 'But the road we've been travelling on goes west and somewhere in the valley lies Bunbury village and Bunbury Towers.'

'West, you say? My own home was in the West Country, a place called Cheselton.' She slid the window down and leaned out. They were driving along a cobbled street that was instantly recognisable to her, and sure enough, when they reached the market square, the coach bowled under an archway and halted in the yard at the back of an inn. Lucy spotted the sign creaking above the main door and recognised the tavern where she had stayed once before under very different circumstance, *The White Boar* in Westmarsh.

One of her grooms appeared at the door and opened it for her. 'Are we spending the night here?' she asked crisply, resting her hand in his.

'Yes, madam, this is where Sir John always stayed. Bunbury is thirty miles away. We shall reach it tomorrow.'

Sure enough, the very same landlord came out to greet

her, bowing to the ground and obviously having no idea this extremely beautiful and elegant lady was the poor chit he had helped all those months before.

'Don't you recognise me?' Lucy asked with a smile, genuinely delighted as he ushered her into the parlour.

He stared at her more closely. 'There's something familiar about you,' he confessed, his hands clasped over the front of his striped apron.

She flung back her hood. 'I'm Lucy Browne!' she exclaimed, her hair shining in the lamplight.

His face registered amazement. 'By all that's holy, so you are! Good gracious me! Who'd have thought it? You've come up in the world, if you don't mind me saying so.'

Lucy glanced around the parlour, the place where she had slept and been attacked by Rufus and Simon Clough. It seemed smaller and more unprepossessing than she remembered it. 'You'd be astonished if I were to recount my adventures,' she said warmly. 'But I made a vow that I'd come back and visit you one day and repay your kindness. Can I see your wife, Annie?'

'Of course, my lady,' he said, tugging at his forelock and bowing, thoroughly disconcerted. 'I'll fetch her.'

She placed a detaining hand on his arm. 'No,' she said, 'I would like to go to the kitchen myself.'

Annie knew her at once, and was not in the least thrown by her fine clothing and cultured speech. Lucy sat at the table amidst pots and pans and half-prepared food and they talked like long lost friends. Because John had stayed there many times before and they recognised his carriage, she pretended she was a distant cousin who had come into his money, there being no one else for him to leave it to. She did not tell Annie what had really happened to her. Somehow, she was ashamed, and she did not want to risk that honest, hardworking woman's condemnation.

She supped in the parlour, treated as an honoured guest,

and was then shown up to the best room. It was all oak panelling and Jacobean chairs with leather seats trimmed with fringes and copper nails. A log fire cast a welcoming glow from the stone-carved hearth, its mantelpiece upheld by mythological figures. Rugs were dotted like islands on a floor shiny with beeswax. There was a washstand with a prettily patterned china bowl and a jug containing hot water.

'Don't bother to unpack,' Lucy said to Nita. 'Simply get out a fresh gown and underwear for the morning. Good night, and sleep well.'

The maid had a room further down the corridor, and when she had gone, Lucy sat on the dressing table stool and gazed at her reflection in the mirror as she unhooked her earrings and removed her necklace before taking the pins and combs from her hair. She ran her hands through the freed mass of curls, shaking her head and relishing the lack of restraint. Nita had already helped her out of her gown and the short stays she wore beneath it, and now she took off her chemise and lifted her breasts in both hands, rubbing her thumbs over her nipples. They immediately hardened, and answering pleasure echoed in her clitoris.

When she had removed her spool-heeled shoes, she rolled down her silk stockings and stood up. Viewing her body critically, she twisted round from the waist so she could look at her buttocks. The marks of Tarquin's cane remained, though much faded, and she touched them gingerly, a sensual thrill racing through her as she remembered the pain and humiliation that was always followed by extreme pleasure.

The inn had fallen into sleep and silence; not even a dog barked. She settled down in the sweet-smelling linen of the large four-poster bed, a feather mattress beneath her and another on top of her covered by a patchwork quilt sewn by clever fingers, probably Annie's.

She was sleepy yet aroused, and in a half-dreaming state, she lay on her back with her legs spread, caressing her nipples and then letting her hand wander down over her belly. She fondled the crisp hair of her mound and dipped into her moist sex. The folds parted and she wetted a finger in the abundant moisture seeping from her pussy, spreading it up to her hardening bud. The feeling was so exquisite that a small cry escaped her lips. She did not hurry; she had the whole night before her during which she could delay orgasm, or come over and over again. In many ways, her hand was her most satisfactory bedfellow, and at times like these she wondered why she bothered with men, or even other women.

Her bare skin felt like satin, her nipples were crimped like flower buds, and her clitoris had swollen to its full size. She pressed her left hand to her mound and stretched it gently towards her belly, making the clit stand out. The sensation was so intense she held off for a moment, rubbing all around it and avoiding the tender head that, if touched, would precipitate her climax, and she wanted to make the pleasure last.

Her wet labial folds had thickened and she toyed with them before running a finger to the stem of her clitoris, tracing it back to where it joined her pelvis below the surface. The need to orgasm increased. At last, unable to hold back, she gave in to her little tyrant's demands, making it slippery and rubbing it frantically, the feeling gathering in her loins, tingling from the tips of her toes up her legs and spine until it suddenly burst in a spectacular firework display that shook her whole body.

'Ah… ah!' she murmured, all feelings, all sensations, enveloping her.

She kept her finger in place until the spasms receded, then sleep claimed her and she sank into a dreamless slumber.

Lucy did not know how long she slept before she was

216

awakened by a sound outside the inn. The candle on the nightstand had burned down only a little. Her hand still clasped her mound, her fingers sticky with her juices. She removed it and sat up, straining her ears. The sound came again... a horse's hooves striking the cobbles. She got up and crept to the window overlooking the courtyard. The full moon had risen and the scene was clearly illuminated by its silver light. As she watched, a man swung down from the saddle, made for the door, and hammered on it with the butt of his whip.

Lucy gulped, unable to believe her eyes. She knew him, would have recognised him anywhere. It *had* to be him, though how, or why, she could not guess. In an instant she was racing from the room, down the stairs and through the parlour to the front door. She forgot she was naked; all she cared about was reaching he who stood outside.

She struggled with the hefty bolts, and finally managed to draw them back and lift the latch. The door swung wide and in a second she was in his arms, gazing up into his astonished face, breathing in the fresh air of the moonlit night, and Charlie.

'Come in, come in!' she gasped, pulling him across the threshold.

'Lucy?' he breathed. 'I don't believe it!'

'Upstairs, I'll explain later.' She dragged him by the hand and led him back the way she had come.

The landlord appeared when they were halfway up the stairs. He was in his nightshirt carrying a candle in one hand and a blunderbuss in the other, and he was amazed to see a completely naked Lucy accompanied by a young man. 'Is everything all right, madam?'

'Yes, yes,' she answered briskly. 'This is a friend of mine, Mr Charles Prescot.'

'Very well, madam. Um... will that mean an extra place for breakfast?'

'Yes,' she nodded and brushed past him, obsessed by

the need to get Charlie to her bedroom.

Once inside it, she closed the door firmly behind them. He had changed a little, only his shoulders were broader and his face had lost some of its boyish softness. He pulled off his hat and she saw his hair was as wheat-brown and curly as ever. He was staring at her as if she was an apparition.

'Lucy, how is it that you're here?' he asked shakily, and his hands moved to clasp her arms and draw her bare body against his buckskin breeches and wool jacket.

'I could ask the same of you,' she replied, her head tilted back to look up at him, her arms gripping him as if she would never let him go.

'I've just come back from Holland,' he explained, and the warmth increased between them as their bodies, if not their minds, demanded no more talk, intent only on being reunited. 'I've finished my schooling. My father is dead and I was hell-bent on finding you again.'

'Oh, Charlie,' she sighed, and burrowed into him. It was as if they had never been apart. 'No more talk, not now.' He kissed her and she felt like a virgin untouched by man. She untied his cravat and eased him out of his jacket and waistcoat. Then, unable to wait any longer, she pulled him down on the bed, her fingers busy with the fastening of his breeches. They fell into each other's rhythm, and she opened herself completely, her soul as well as her body. His kisses were perfect, moving from her mouth to her breasts and then down to circle her navel and arrive at their destination – her aching clitoris. She was transported, her orgasm wild and prolonged, and then she dug her nails into his bare buttocks as he knelt over her, his cock thick and ready. She admired it down the length of her own body, then took it in her hand and guided it into her niche.

Now she was complete, flesh-to-flesh, their secretions mingling. He filled her, stretched her, his glans kissing her innermost flesh with every thrust. She embraced him with her legs as well as her arms, hitching her heels on his shoulders to give him greater access, raising her hips and hugging him as if she would never be parted from him again.

'I can't hold back,' he grunted, driving his cock into her faster and harder. 'Oh, my beautiful Lucy!'

He was so strong, so young and so full of passion, and she gloried in it, feeling him pounding away, seeing the look of ecstasy on his face as hot spurts of his semen flooded her. She cradled his head against her breasts as he slumped down beside her, his cock leaving a silver pathway across her thigh.

'Who has been whipping you?' he wanted to know as they lay peacefully together afterwards.

'Tarquin,' she replied at once, having made up her mind that there would be no secrets between them.

'You still see him?' He did not sound pleased.

She propped herself up on one elbow and looked down at him. He was so handsome and dear to her that she could hardly speak for the emotion choking her throat. But she was determined to tell him everything. 'I couldn't afford to stay at Mrs Trott's after you disappeared. I wanted to wait for you, or at least until you sent a message, but I had no money.'

'I know. I went to see her. She said my letters to you never arrived.'

'Did she also tell you that she as good as sold me to a friend of hers, Squire Rutland?' she asked angrily, hating the memory of that mean-spirited woman.

'No,' he replied, and taking her hand, lifted it to his lips.

She poured out every detail of her life since he left her, the squire's brutal treatment, Colette's kindness and Sir John's generosity. She confessed she was still Tarquin's sexual slave, and when his face darkened as he heard about her encounters with other men, she asked him frankly if he had remained celibate in Holland.

He flushed. 'I visited the prostitutes in Amsterdam,' he admitted, 'but it was just for physical relief. I never stopped loving you, Lucy, and I vowed to return to England and search for you. This is what I've done. With father dead and mama ready to do anything I want, I shall introduce you to her. I have my own income now, besides money left me by my father. I have joined a firm of solicitors as junior partner.'

'But why are you here, in this part of the country?'

'I tried looking for you everywhere in London, then I remembered you once telling me you came from Cheselton in Somerset,' he murmured, teasing her nipples into rosy peaks as he spoke. 'It was a long shot, but I thought if I visited your village someone might have heard from you.'

'It was fate, surely, that arranged for us to meet like this. I'm on my way to Bunbury Towers, my countryseat. Just think, Charlie, we can do whatever we please now. We are rich beyond any dreams of avarice.'

'Will you marry me?' he whispered, touching her as if she was made of spun glass, fragile and precious to him.

'We'll talk about it in the morning,' she said, wanting to lose herself in him again and let the future take care of itself.

When dawn light stole between the drapes, it found Lucy perched on the window seat scribbling in her diary. She had a shawl wrapped around her shoulders, and every so often she glanced across at the bed where Charlie lay sleeping like a baby.

He wants me to marry him, she added to the entry recounting his sudden return. *Do I want to be Mrs Prescot? The name has a fine ring, but if I commit myself he will have to understand that I shan't become a meek little goodwife. I want to do as Gregory suggests and keep open the saloon at Heath House. I want to start an orphanage, and heaven only knows what other plans may present themselves once I've clapped eyes on Bunbury Towers. As for Tarquin? Ah, me, there's another kettle of fish entirely. He offers me excitement like no one else. I love Charlie. He has my heart and soul, but Tarquin? Ah, that devil of a master of mine. He's wicked, and I never could resist a little touch of badness.*

Her writing was interrupted by Charlie's sleepy voice calling, 'Lucy, come back to bed. I've something for you. It's bigger than ever and just waiting to pleasure you.'

She smiled and sanded the wet ink, then slipped her journal and pen into her reticule. This was her secret narrative and no one should read it yet. One day, perhaps, she would find an amanuensis to help record her adventures, but just for now she wanted nothing more than to snuggle under the quilt and make love with Charlie.

More exciting titles available from Chimera

For a copy of our free catalogue please write to:

Chimera Publishing Ltd
Readers' Services
PO Box 152
Waterlooville
Hants
PO8 9FS

or email us at:
sales@chimerabooks.co.uk

or purchase from our range of superb titles at:
www.chimerabooks.co.uk

Sales and Distribution in the USA and Canada

Client Distribution Services, Inc
193 Edwards Drive
Jackson
TN 38301
USA
(800) 343 4499

Sales and Distribution in Australia

Dennis Jones & Associates Pty Ltd
19a Michellan Ct
Bayswater
Victoria
Australia 3153